Anne of the Isles
and Other Legends of Brittany

Anne of the Isles and Other Legends of Brittany

by
Paul Féval

translated, annotated and introduced by
Brian Stableford

A Black Coat Press Book

Acknowledgements: We are indebted to David McDonnell for proofreading the typescript.

English adaptation, introduction and afterword Copyright © 2007 by Brian Stableford.
Cover illustration Copyright © 2007 by Anne-Claire Payet.
http://www.crysantis.net

Visit our website at www.blackcoatpress.com

Table of Contents

Introduction

This collection assembles four of Paul Féval's *nouvelles*, all of which pretend to be based in Breton folklore. The first three were among his earliest published works, and were all reprinted in one of his most successful collections, *Contes de Bretagne* [*Tales of Brittany*] (1844), along with a preliminary character-sketch of an itinerant storyteller (which I have not reproduced). The fourth was written much later, for a collection of *Les romans enfantins* [*Children's Novels*] (1862); it is actually a drastic redaction of one of his early historical novels, *Les Belles de Nuit* (1850), but its adaptation for children has the effect of magnifying its relationship to its pseudo-folkloristic component, which links it to the three earlier stories in its literary method.

Although the ostensible nature of these stories implies a certain triviality, and they have usually been regarded, not inappropriately, as *jeux d'esprit*, they also set some interesting literary precedents, and might be reckoned more significant than they seem at first glance. The essential deceptiveness of their method has served to obscure their originality; some readers, at least, must have taken at face value the claim—shored up by introductory material and annotations as well as the preface added to *Contes de Bretagne*—that their folkloristic elements really were recycled stories whose author was merely passing them on. In fact, all four were wholly invented; although the third cites several pre-existent folkloristic motifs *en passant* and the legend featured in the fourth is grafted on to an actual item of Breton folklore, the third considers its borrowings merely as instances of superstition and the fourth uses the legend of Ys, rather arbitrarily, as a platform for further, and more crucial, inventions.

7

Most of his contemporary readers were, of course, fully aware of Féval's pretenses, and perfectly willing to share the joke whenever he allowed their falsity to become obvious. By the 1840s, when Féval launched his career, there was a long tradition in French literature whose contributors imitated folktales for various literary purposes. Important new ground had been broken in the late 17th century, when the production of *contes de fées* had become highly fashionable following precedents set by Madame d'Aulnoy, and again in the 18th century when Voltaire demonstrated the ingenious refinement of the *conte philosophique*. In the early 19th century, the writers associated with the French Romantic Movement, especially Charles Nodier, produced French equivalents of German *Kunstmärchen* ["art folktales"]. Féval must have had all these precedents in mind when he set out to make his own use of ideas drawn from or misrepresented as items of Breton folklore, but he was operating in a new fictional medium and the nature of his impostures was markedly different from any of these august predecessors.

The circumstances of Féval's decision to make a career as a writer are of considerable relevance to his decision to mine Breton folklore for inspiration, and to the methods of development he employed in its usage. He had been born in Rennes, one of the most important towns in Brittany, but his father, Jean-Nicolas Féval, was not a Breton, having held appointments in several regions in the course of a legal career whose culmination was his appointment as a judge in the Cour Royale de Rennes. Almost as soon as he had settled in Rennes in 1800, however, Jean-Nicolas Féval–who was then 31 years old–had married a local girl, the 19-year-old Jeanne-Joséphine Le Baron de Létang. Whereas the Féval family was solidly bourgeois, Jeanne-Josephine's surname signified greater pretensions. The noble families of Brittany had, however, fallen on hard times long before the Revolution of 1789, and little remained of their former greatness but nostalgic affectations.

Although Jean-Nicolas Féval died in 1827, before Paul's 11th birthday, Paul was carefully prepared to follow in his father's footsteps. He was ensconced in the Collège Royal de Rennes on a scholarship, with the long-term aim of entering the Faculté de Droit to qualify as a lawyer. He did, in fact, eventually do that, but his progress was not without interruption, by far the most significant hiatus being the Revolution of July 1830. Féval, as a vociferous supporter of the deposed Bourbon King, was in a tiny minority at the Collège, and it was thought politic to remove him from the premises for his own safety (he was not yet 14). He went to live with his maternal uncle, Comte Foucher du Carreil, at the Château de Cournon, near Redon, where he had previously spent vacations. The depth of the impression left upon him by that old house, whose ruination had been almost completed by its siege in the aftermath of the 1789 Revolution, is obvious in many of his Breton tales and novels, many of which are set in the vicinity of Redon.

Féval qualified as a lawyer in 1836, but gave up that profession with remarkable abruptness after a single disappointing appearance in court. How soon afterwards he went to Paris is unclear, but when he did go, determined to make a living from his pen, it must have seemed to him that he was casting off half of his heritage rather than any mere *métier*. He was, in effect, renouncing his father's ancestry in favor of his mother's; it was probably inevitable that he would make a great deal of literary use in his literary work of Breton settings and Breton history, and that his representations would be loyally affiliated to the ideals that seemed to him to be central to Breton aristocratic identity. Those ideals were primarily those of Roman Catholicism, supplemented by an overweening nostalgic fondness for the Age of Chivalry, when Brittany had been effectively a realm in its own right, distinguishable from the other baronial conglomerates of feudal France.

Féval had to go to Paris to be a writer, because Paris was the only significant marketplace for writing, but that did not mean that he had to absorb Parisian values. There was also a sense in which he went to Paris to do battle against its citizens–to inform or remind them of the cost of their past conquests, and to protest against that cost. He was well aware of the manner in which writers like Honoré de Balzac and Prosper Mérimée had used Brittany as a kind of imaginary reservoir of barbarism, and he wanted to depict it in a different light, as an arena of tragic heroism. In the context of that struggle, though, Breton folklore always seemed a double-edged sword, representative of exactly the kind of intellectual barbarism of which Balzac and Mérimée made fun, as well as a rich source of literary inspiration and valuable narrative color.

For this reason, Féval's use of folkloristic material–at least in the material that he chose to reprint in book form–was always ambivalent, very rarely permitting any authentic intrusions of the supernatural. Even when he transfigured folklore into religious propaganda, he was very reluctant to sanction miracles, and that reluctance sometimes diverted his plots into bathetic anticlimaxes. On the other hand, such anticlimaxes were not entirely inappropriate to their subject-matter, given that Brittany's Age of Chivalry really had faded away into enduring ignominy, without any hint of miraculous redemption.

Although Féval chose to place "*La femme blanche des marais*" [*The White Lady of the Marshes*] ahead of "*Anne des Îles*" [*Anne of the Isles*] in *Contes de Bretagne*, presumably because it is a better story, I have reverted to a chronological order of presentation, because it permits a better appreciation the way that Féval's work in this vein developed. "*Anne des Îles*" was not the first story of this stripe that he published– Jean-Pierre Galvan's *Paul Féval: parcours d'une oeuvre* (2000) gives a brief description of a story entitled "*Le souper de Guerbehel*" [*The Supper of Guerbehel*] (1839), subtitled "légende bretonne"–but it was the first he elected to preserve in book form; he left the earlier ones unreprinted even though he cannot have lacked opportunities to make more use of them.

"*Anne des Îles*" was originally serialized in *L'Union catholique* on September 15-17, 1842. It was Féval's second serial in that periodical, and his third all told, although none of the three qualifies as a novel and none was much longer than two *nouvelles* that had appeared in single issues of the *Revue de Paris* in April 1841–notably "*Le club des phoques*" [*The Seals' Club*], which had provided Féval with his first significant literary breakthrough.

Although *feuilleton* serials were already commonplace in French periodicals, the Golden Age of the *roman feuilleton* was yet to begin in 1842. It was not until 1843 that the awesome pulling power of Alexandre Dumas' *Les trois mousquetaires* [*The Three Musketeers*] and Eugène Sue's *Les mystères de Paris* [*The Mysteries of Paris*] became key factors in a burgeoning circulation war, and forced every editor in Paris to give top priority to his *feuilletons*. In 1842, therefore, most *feuilleton* serials were relatively short novelettes and novellas rather than full-length novels, and they had not yet begun to pander to the vagaries of popular taste in the way that the majority were compelled to do from 1844 onwards. Féval did not become embroiled in the more desperate kind of crowd-pleasing until he was commissioned to write *Les mystères de Londres* [*The Mysteries of London*] [1] in frank imitation of Eugène Sue; that novel began serialization in the December 20, 1843 issue of *Le Courrier français* under the pseudonym "Sir Francis Trolopp." "*Anne des Îles*" is, therefore, fairly typical of the sort of work that was in demand at the time of its publication, not merely in its brevity but in the relatively selectivity of its audience.

This is not to say that "*Anne des Îles*" was not intended to be a crowd-pleaser; it most certainly was–but the crowd in question was well-defined and select, and the story makes no concessions at all to the sentiments and prejudices of potential

---

[1] (See Notes p. 235.)

readers outside its primary audience–quite the reverse, in fact. It is, quite overtly, an item of religious propaganda, intended to flatter and support the faith of the readers of *L'Union catholique*.

The policy of employing stories based in local folklore for propagandistic purpose was much older than the French literary tradition of philosophical and Romantic *contes des fées* [fairy tales], having long been a key element in the strategy of Christian conversion. Pagan rituals had routinely reconfigured as Christian feasts by the Church, and pagan folktales were frequently imitated or transfigured in the legends of the saints contained in such texts as Jacobus de Voragine's 13th-century *Legenda aurea* [*The Golden Legend*]. Féval set himself to continue this tradition as well as the other in his work for *L'Union catholique* and its kindred periodicals, which gave him his first publishing opportunities when he moved to Paris with the determination to become a writer.

The footnote that Féval appended to the subtitle of "*Anne des Îles*" virtually gives the game away in acknowledging that the tale is quite unknown in the region to which it refers, but it attempts to redeem that absence with a fanciful account of the manner in which it might have been transplanted to the region of Morbihan with which Féval was familiar, and where he had perforce to claim that it had been told to him. In fact, the only item in "*Anne des Îles*" that can qualify as honest folklore is its use of a tradition alleging that the island of Sen (or Sein) had been the last refuge of druidism in France. The rest of its subject-matter owes something to previous literary accounts of wreckers but the story's immediate inspiration probably lay in newspaper accounts of the heroic exploits of Grace Darling, the English lighthouse-keeper's daughter who became one of the first celebrities manufactured by popular reportage.

Grace Darling had made her famous rescue in 1838, not long before Féval's story was written, and that probable inspiration helps to explain why the story is so glaringly anachronistic in its juxtaposition of heroic monks involved in the conversion of Breton pagans–which tacitly places the story's action somewhere around the 6th century A.D.–with modern sailing ships that belong to an era at least 900 years later. Féval tries to explain the anachronistic aspects of the story by suggesting that tellers through the ages must have embellished it, but if one took out the sailing ships, little or nothing would remain; it simply would not make sense were it relocated to an era into which relics of druidism might actually have survived to clash with nascent Christian ideals. The resultant mishmash does have a eccentric charm of its own–because rather than despite the jerkiness of the narrative and the abject failure of the principal characters to accomplish their declared aims or fulfill their repressed desires–but for modern readers, the greatest interest the story retains may be the manner in which it is mischievously echoed in another mid-19th-century work, Eugène Sue's *Les mystères du peuple* [*The Mysteries of the People*].

Sue was probably not entirely pleased when Féval produced *Les mystères de Londres* in frank imitation of his most successful novel, even though imitation is the sincerest form of flattery. There was a stark ideological contrast between his work and that of his imitator; whereas Sue was a fervently anti-clerical socialist, Féval was a devoutly Catholic royalist. Sue surely would not have minded another writer following in his footsteps had he stuck to them more closely, but to have someone copy his literary methods while flatly opposing his political principles must have been annoying. It is not entirely surprising therefore, that he harbored enough of a grudge against Féval to take an opportunity to turn the tables.

Les mystères du peuple was written in exile following Louis-Napoléon's *coup d'état* of 1851, when Sue had been banished along with other supporters of the 1848 Revolution. Sue intended it to be his masterpiece; although billed as the history of a proletarian family through the ages, it also poses as a history of the Gallic race, which allegedly preserves something of its essential identity in the French peasantry despite perennial repression by Royalty and the Church. Writing in the aftermath of the Romantic Movement during the pri-

13

mary phase of anthropological pseudoscience, it is not surprising that Sue's idea of the essence of the French people recalled German notions of *volksgeist*, nor that he elected to root that essence in the supposed beliefs and practices of druids. When he had to come up with his own account of the origins of a sense of Gallic identity–allegedly forged by the necessity of uniting in resistance against Julius Caesar's invasion–he evidently remembered Féval's account, in *"Anne des Îles"* of the suppression of that identity by the Church he abhorred. The first of the 19 novellas making up *Les mystères du peuple* is, in consequence, entitled *"La faucille d'or, ou Héna, la vierge de l'Île de Sen"* (tr. as *The Gold Sickle; or, Hena, the Virgin of the Isle of Sen*).

In Sue's fake legend, as in Féval's, the virginal heroine's father is named Joël. Héna is no Grace Darling, nor is she a Christian convert (the story is set in 57 B.C.), but she does play a similarly pivotal role in the ideological history of the region. Instead of risking her life for Christ, however, she offers it freely in a human sacrifice to the druid deities. Féval's story is correct in observing that we do not know the names of the gods of the druid religion–because its practitioners wrote nothing down, everything we know about it is hearsay, mostly taken from Julius Caesar's account of the Gallic wars–but where Féval is content to maintain a discreet silence, Sue invents with typical boldness. Sue names the chief druid deity Hesus, in order to pretend that not only is his legend the "true" version of the story on which *"Anne des Îles"* had supposedly been based, but also that the Christ she represents is merely a distorted carbon copy of a much better original–a god whose worshippers would do far more than rescue shipwrecked sailor, but would actually offer themselves to be burned in wicker cages to facilitate the workings of his will.

What Féval thought of Sue's decision to echo one of his early stories in an intended masterpiece we can only guess, but he was probably more amused than annoyed. He never attempted to write anything on the same panoramic scale as *Les mystères du peuple*, but when he wrote his own transfiguration of the legend that Sue had co-opted into his other vast enterprise, *Le juif errant* [*The Wandering Jew*], he indulged his taste for ludicrous mockery to the full, while carefully reiterating his own Catholic ideals.[2]

"*La femme blanche des marais*" was serialized in *L'Union catholique* on December 17-29, 1842. It was carefully planned to fit the season; the chapters actually set on Christmas Day presumably appeared in the issues published immediately before and after the Christmas holiday. It is worth noting that this was 12 months before Charles Dickens issued the first and most famous of his "Christmas books" in England, as *A Christmas Carol in Prose*, which popularized the tradition of publishing such seasonal *nouvelles*, so Féval is entitled to be recognized as something of a pioneer in this respect.

"*La femme blanche des marais*" is the most carefully-constructed of the four novellas reprinted here, and the most convincing as an item of "fakelore"–to the extent that references to the White Lady of the Marshes can now be found in tourist-guides to the area. It is the most energetic and upbeat of the stories, largely because it has the best hero in Chantepie–a character who established a model for other engaging Féval heroes, such as Pistolet in *La rue de Jérusalem*.[3] The relative modesty of Chantepie's achievements is entirely appropriate to the story's historical background, which had to be constructed in the knowledge that the Château de Malestroit could not be saved from the ravages of the wars of religion.

The story also illustrates the manner of deploying folkloristic material with which Féval was most comfortable: producing fictitious historical echoes of allegedly archetypal patterns. Although no supernatural event is featured in the story, the whole narrative acquires a marked supernatural quality by virtue of the main characters' acute awareness of, and psychological responses to, the knowledge that they are repeating a much older story. They think and act as if they are being inexorably steered by an invisible hand–as, indeed, they are.

The destruction of so many of the old châteaux of Brittany during the nation-wide outburst of violence that followed *La Saint-Barthélemy*–the St Bartholomew's Eve massacre of the Huguenots of Paris on August 23, 1572–was a key element of the process of gradual ruination that is Féval's primary subject-matter, and he takes more trouble than usual in "*La femme blanche des marais*" to place an elaborate historical backcloth behind his invented apparition. The name Ermengarde is presumably borrowed from Ermengarde d'Anjou, whose married Alain IV, Duc de Bretagne, in 1093 and became the effective ruler of Brittany when Alain went to fight in the First Crusade, remaining the principal power in the land until her death in Redon in 1147.

Seen as a Christmas story, "*La femme blanche des marais*" makes a sharp contrast with *A Christmas Carol*, relying for the poetic justice of its ending on a revenge completed rather than anything echoing the Christmas spirit of generosity and good will. It is, however, more in tune with some of Dickens' subsequent Christmas books, especially *The Battle of Life*, a harrowing tale whose allegorical component and narrative method are not dissimilar to Féval's. It would have been interesting to see what Féval might have done in subsequent ventures had the tradition of Christmas stories caught on in France to the same extent that it did in England.

"*Le joli château*" [*The Lovely Château*], which first appeared in *L'Univers* between March 23 and April 12, 1844, shapes up for some of its length to be an even better story than "*La femme blanche des marais*," but gradually loses its impetus and dissolves into a mess of uncertainties and self-contradictions before suffering an unexpectedly abrupt and direly disappointing termination that the author cannot possibly have intended when he began it. It is possible that the abrupt ending resulted from an unexpected editorial instruction to cut the story short received while the serialization was in progress, but this is unlikely; it seems more probable that the author simply could not make up his mind which of the two explanations casually offered in the final chapter he actually favored, and realized that in hesitating between them, he had failed to lay proper foundations for either.

The fact that the story was published while Féval was working flat out on *Les mystères de Londres* might well indicate that it was something he had begun earlier and abandoned half-way through, then fixed up hurriedly in order to obtain quick sale, or it might indicate that he bravely set out to produce a second serial alongside his sprawling epic–*Les mystères de Londres* eventually ran to 300,000 words–but could not stand the pressure of simultaneous production.

If Féval did try to write the installments of "*Le joli château*" alongside those of *Les mystères de Londres*, he had presumably done the same with "*Les aventures d'un émigré*"–a similarly extended novella that ran in *Le Quotidien* on March 5-13, 1844–and that may have convinced him that he could do it. If he failed in this instance, the practice presumably did him good; in later years, he often had two serials running simultaneously. Whatever the reason was for cursory abortion of "*Le joli château*," Féval made no attempt to provide the story with a more consistent build-up or a better ending when he reprinted it in *Contes de Bretagne*, nor when he produced a "revised and corrected" edition of the collection for reprinting in the wake of his "conversion."

The disappointment created by the omission of the ending to which "*Le joli château*" should have been aiming, in which Arthur and Yaumi–whether alive or dead–would have turned the tables on Luc Morfil, hoisting him with his own petard by confronting him with their own set of contrived diabolic manifestations, is further compounded by the total abandonment of the story's most interesting subplot. Presumably, Anne Parker would eventually have revealed some telling details of what had happened 80 years before, and how Simon Troarec was eventually frustrated in *his* schemes; the improvised ending does take the trouble to pick up her story, but only to dispose of her in an absurd fashion that renders her presence within the novella quite irrelevant. Féval, like all make-it-up-as-you-go *feuilletonistes*, was always likely to leave a few subplot-threads dangling untidily, but rarely as limply as this one.

What makes "*Le joli château*" interesting despite its failings, though, is that, as in "*La femme blanche des marais*," Féval introduced several narrative devices and moves here of which he was to make much more use in future. Some of its elements are echoed with greater sureness in "*Les Belles de nuit*" and some others with equal hesitancy in *Le livre des mystères* (1852).[4] Most importantly, perhaps, it is in this story, more than any of the author's other early works, that the reader finds a clear precursor of the distinctive macabre humor that marked so many of Féval's later works. That element of irreverent sarcasm helps considerably to excuse the awkwardness of the climax, even though it makes one wonder how the comedy element might have been extrapolated had the dénouement come to proper fruition.

The novel on which "*Les Belles de nuit*" is based was published as *Les Belles de nuit ou Les Anges de la famille* in *L'Assemblée nationale* between September 21, 1849 and April 27, 1850. Although the novel version similarly features a contest between two sons of Penhoël and the Marquis de Pontalès, the circumstances of the struggle are quite different, being located in the aftermath of the 1789 Revolution. The novella version, issued in *Les romans enfantins* (E. Ducrocq 1862), is set in the late 1840s and thus has an entirely different historical background. Although both versions are named for equivalent characters, the *belles-de-nuit* of the novel (who are named Diane and Cyprienne) are less significant to the plot than those of the novella, and the particular item of "fakelore" defining them is part of a more elaborate pattern. The novella is, therefore, no mere abridgement but a distinct work that echoes and overlaps the earlier one much as folkloristic themes are echoed and transfigured in so many of Féval's Breton novels and novellas.

Although the legend of Ys, on to which Féval grafts his account of the *Belles-de-Nuit*, is now quite familiar as an item of folklore, most of its literary versions–the best of which are Robert W. Chambers' *"The Demoiselle d'Ys"* (1895) and Norman Douglas' *They Went* (1920)–owe their inspiration to the successful opera *Le roi d'Ys* (1888), whose libretto was by Edouard Lalo. Whether Lalo had read any of Féval's versions of the story is unclear, but it seems equally probable that he obtained the story from the same proximal source that Féval did: a collection of Old Breton ballads issued in 1839 by T. Hersart de Villemarqué, *Barzaz Breiz*. Hersart's volume included French translations of the ballads and elaborate historical commentaries of a rather fanciful stripe, which seem to have been an important source of inspiration for Féval's deployment of Breton folklore.

The authenticity of Hersart's ballads was challenged at the time of their publication–some commentators suspected Hersart of following the example of James Macpherson, the inventor of the Gaelic poet Ossian and the true author of his works–and the matter has remained controversial. Although Hersart surely drew on authentic ballads, he probably subjected them to some reconfiguration, as all writers did in subjecting items of oral tradition to literary discipline; the fact that Old Breton was a long-dead language that had left very little writing behind undoubtedly encouraged such improvisation. The legend of Ys had, however, received brief mention before in French chivalric romances, including Marie de France's well-known *lais* (c.1170).

The earliest records we have of Cornish and Welsh analogues of Ys are similarly located in chivalric romances; in the prose version of *Tristan*, composed at about the same time as Marie de France's lays, the hero is said to come from Liones, a land connecting Cornwall to the Scilly Isles. In Welsh adaptations of Arthurian elements of the *Matière de Bretagne* [*Matter of Britain*]. Liones was more usually rendered as Lyonesse, and was sometimes displaced into Cardigan Bay; it was that version of the legend that first obtained a significant

19

echo in modern English fiction, in Thomas Love Peacock's *The Misfortunes of Elphin* (1829). Peacock transfigured and embellished the legend to a considerable extent, in much the same fashion–if not quite the same spirit–as Féval's improvisations, but it is unlikely that Féval had actually read *The Misfortunes of Elphin*. Even if he had, Féval's version of the story of Ys remains a significant literary precedent, and not merely by virtue of his elaboration of the story with the *Belles-de-Nuit*.

The "legend" of the *Belles-de-Nuit* as formulated by Féval is, of course, based in the fact that the phrase was used in 19th-century French in three different ways, referring to night-blooming plants, stars–especially stars that appear to be shining alone in the sky as dawn approaches (usually, but not necessarily, the planet Venus)–and tiny clouds of vapor produced in association with morning mist, which sometimes wander in the breeze. The notion that the uses of the term reflect a pattern of quasi-elemental spirits is ingenious as well as original, and its adaptation to the context of the Roman Catholic faith is deftly achieved, arguably making a neater fit than "*La femme blanches des marais*" does as a Christmas story.

Contes de Bretagne was the first volume that Féval reissued in the series of revised and collected editions of his works that he began publishing in the late 1870s, presumably because it had first been produced before his perceived backslide from Catholic ideals had begun, and needed very little in the way of ideological reconstruction. I have not compared the two versions, but I suspect that there is very little difference between them. The texts of "*Anne des Îles*," "*La femme blanche des marais*" and "*Le joli château*" that I have translated are, however, the original book versions, taken from the Michel Lévy edition of 1862 (which was retitled *Les dernières fées*). The version of "*Les belles de nuit*" that I have translated is from the revised and corrected edition of *Les romans enfantins* issued by Victor Palmé in 1878. Again, I have not compared the two versions, but I doubt that the modifications were extensive; the main difference between the two editions seems to have been the omission from the second of one entire novella, "*Les mémoires du diable*" [*The Devil's Memoirs*], of whose production Féval seems to have repented—much as he repented the tacit trafficking with the Enemy in which he dabbled in novels in the *Habits Noirs* series which identify Colonel Bozzo a little too closely the Devil.[5]

I have not made any substantial alterations to the texts of the first three novellas, but I have abridged the text of "*The Belles-de-Nuit*" very slightly by deleting several specific references to the story's supposed addressee, a girl named Georgette who was a friend of Féval's daughter Joséphine. Although Joséphine is the dedicatee of *Les romans enfantins*, none of the stories in it is addressed to her, although one is addressed to her brother Paul. This is slightly puzzling, especially when one observes that the dedication describes two stories that Féval actually told to Joséphine, neither of which was ever published—and both of which sound far more colorful, and perhaps more exciting, than the collection's actual contents.

(This discrepancy emphasizes the fact that all of Féval's published *romans enfantins* are purely literary products, not written versions of stories he actually improvised for his children; their invocation of specific addressees is an artifice. As the dedication makes clear, the stories Féval actually told his children were wholehearted fantasies in which the supernatural was given free and flamboyant rein—but he was always very reluctant to do that in his published works; those I have translated as *Vampire City* [6] and *The Wandering Jew's Daughter* are exceptional.)

I ought perhaps to note, in addition, that in translating the dialogue in all the stories I have followed Féval's own policy of making no attempt at archaism. No matter when his stories are notionally set, Féval always has his characters speak in a fashion that his contemporary readers would readily understand. In doing likewise, I have carried the modernization process a little further, in recognition of the fact that we are now living in the 21st century rather than the mid-19th, while maintaining a reasonably faithful adherence to the wording of the original texts.

Brian Stableford

Anne of the Isles

A Breton Tradition [7]

A long time ago in Finistère, near to the place where the town of Audierne was built, there was a village whose name is no longer known. Its outermost houses were on the edge of the sands, and washed the shingle of their walls in the waves during the high equinoctial tides. To one side of the village was the sea, to the other, a heath–a heath as arid as the sea, and as vast. Bread was often lacking in the hovels.

Now the people of the region either did not know, or had forgotten, the good God who comes to the help of those who suffer. They whispered; they blasphemed And when, in the distance, the warning cannon boomed in the Baie des Tré-passés,[8] they fell to their knees and gave thanks to the Devil, then went down to the shore in crowds. The more furious the tempest was, the more joy they felt in their hearts. It was for them that the tempest worked.

"The sea has its crops," they said, "as does the land; the tempest is the day of harvest."

That was what they called the ships in distress which the torment threw on to the coast. When the crop–which is to say, the broken vessels–ripened, they ran to fall upon the shipwrecks.

"Equal shares!" they also said. "To us, the goods and the brandy; to the sea, the corpses!" And on the sands themselves, a hideous feast began. They drank, they slept, and then they drank again. Sometimes, a villager, overcome by drunkenness, might fall down a second time, and then awake, pale and dying, and drink again–and when he fell down again, it was never to rise again. When there was no longer anything to drink, they went back to their huts. Inertia followed intoxication. Those who did not die in the orgy died of starvation. Such was the way in which the people of the coast lived, before the town of Audierne was built.

People talk about the islands of America, which are full of tobacco and gold–people talk about them, but where are they? Who has seen them, save for sailors–and sailors are all liars. They lie dreaming in their string hammocks, and it is with their dreams that they entertain us on their return. The truth is that there are no islands in the world as beautiful as the isles of Brittany, and Ouessant is the most beautiful of those isles.

One day, the King said to Milord Jean: [9] "Ask me for one thing that is in my gift, my man, and you shall have it." Milord Jean did not ask for Nantes, nor Rennes, nor Saint-Malo, nor even Douardenez. He said: "My King, I would like Ouessant, the beautiful isle." The King smiled, but he did not know Ouessant. He had never seen it proudly raising its head in the middle of the Ocean. He had never seen the white diadem of mist crowning its forehead on summer mornings. The King did not know Ouessant.

In the days before Audierne was built, Ouessant had only one village, whose inhabitants were scarcely any better off than the people of the coast. They lived by pillage. When shipwrecks were lacking, they set their boats on the water and extorted ransom from the pious monks of the Île de Sen. The latter prayed to the Lord night and day for the conversion of their pagan neighbors, but the people of Ouessant–and especially those of the coast–had no wish to believe in a religion that commanded them to help shipwrecked sailors instead of finishing them off.

This is what happened on one autumn evening, in mid-September, when the tide was high.

The bell of the little monastery of Sen had just sounded the Angelus. All the doors had already been closed, so great in the convent was the fear of the pirates of the Yroise.[10] Occasional lights appeared here and there at barred windows; the candles were being lit in the chapel. Just as the first lines of the prayer became audible outside, a side-door of the convent opened and closed noiselessly and an old man, leaning on a long white staff, began to descend the sandy slope that led from the holy house to the sea.

He seemed to be very old, and walked with difficulty. From time to time, he paused to catch his breath; he lifted his head then and studied the sky anxiously.

The Moon, running behind the clouds like a white ship surrounded by vapor, occasionally emerged all of a sudden, and cast its light boldly upon the old man's forehead. He was a man who had reached the utmost limit of life. His face was calm and gentle. His bald head was surrounded by a crown of white hair, so fine that it resembled the wisps of spring fog that play upon the crosses of calvaries at first light, describing silvery diadems about the divine forehead of Mary's son.

The night was calm, but for an inhabitant of that region there were several manifest signs in the air of the approaching storm. The subsiding clouds were darkening in color on the horizon; the mist was breaking up, allowing expanses of sea to be glimpsed here and there; a few mute flickers of light split the sky in the distance.

The monk continued on his way; the poor old fellow was making haste; rivulets of sweat formed on his wrinkled cheeks. As his face was struck by the first gust of the sea breeze, which suddenly sprang up, he released a dull groan.

"Holy Mother of God, pray for us," he murmured.

He tried to increased his pace, stumbling over the shingle, often being forced to stop to wait for a glimmer of light to show him his path.

Suddenly, several lanterns appeared on the Breton coast, which began to vacillate like the lanterns of ships bobbing on the waves.[11] Sometimes moving in a straight line, sometimes changing direction abruptly, they imitated the motion of a tacking ship.

The monk stopped as if overwhelmed.

"Lord God!" he cried, falling to his knees. "Will you not permit that the Devil should be vanquished in the hearts of these miserable savages?"

Anne was the daughter of Joël Bras, more commonly known as the priest of the isles. Joël, during his lifetime, had been the last relic of a once-powerful community whose name was familiar to the old.[12] He could conjure storms with the aid of the ninth string of his harp, and ride on the shaft of a lance to pay visits to the evil spirits. He was a powerful and redoubtable man; the people of Ouessant and the coast feared him. It was said that his dwelling-place contained incalculable treasures. When the servants of the true God had come to establish themselves on Sen, they had wrought several conversions at first–but Joël had become irritated. He had threatened to compose a song so fearsome that the sea would quit its bed and whiten the highest roofs of the village with its foam. Joël was believed, and the holy monks were persecuted.

Joël, however, had passed from this life, and his daughter, the beautiful Anne of the Isles, had inherited all his influence. Anne was a pagan, like her father, but she was gentle and compassionate; more than one unfortunate shipwrecked sailor owed his life to her. If the deceptive lanterns of the coast sometimes suddenly ceased shining, no longer drawing sailors in peril to certain death, it was because Anne had a bow and arrows, and her arrow never missed its mark.

Like all the priestesses of that time, she was sworn to celibacy, but the false religion she professed now had only the feeblest empire over the hearts of the men of Ouessant and the coast. The last priest was dead; Anne was beautiful. The young men of the region, who knew no other god than their passions, looked at her with desire.

The boldest of them, Niel Roz de Kermor, leapt into his boat one evening and disembarked on the shore of Sen, beneath the cliff where Joël's daughter made her home. Niel tied up his boat and climbed the cliff. The following day, the boat's debris was strewn upon the sands of Ouessant, and no one ever saw Niel Roz de Kermor again. After that, everyone trembled at the mere mention of the name of Anne of the Isles. The blood of Joël ran in her veins. She was a priestess and a magician. Woe betide any man whose path crossed hers!

In the evening, when fog enveloped the bay, her boat was sometimes seen, playing like a light wisp of spray upon the highest summits of the waves, then descending precipitously into the troughs between the billows, before climbing up the turbulent slopes to fall and rise again. The fishing-boats turned aside from her course. Not for all the gold in the world could a man have been found between Douardenez and the isles of Ouessant to cut across the wake of her skiff. Even if it necessitated a long detour, they would take to the open sea rather than cross that magic barrier—where, it was said, Death hid just beneath the surface, lying in wait for his prey.

Anne seemed to encourage this custom herself, and avoided the gazes of men. It only took a minute for her to lose herself in the mist or behind a rock. Neither reefs nor submerged rocks could inhibit her progress. The slightest draught of water seemed sufficient for her skiff. Perhaps she even knew how to leap like the flying fish of which ocean-going mariners tell—fish that have wings and fly just like birds, or so the sailors say.

During storms, she lowered her sail and quit the rudder. One might see her then sitting in the stern of her boat, immobile, with her arms folded, in an attitude of intrepid indifference. Then, where the fishing-boats foundered, Anne's boat would pass by, stroking the water with its keel, scarcely moistening the timbers of its hull in the foaming waves. Storms respected Anne, who was Joël's blood.

No one could say that this powerful virgin was a malevolent creature. If Niel Roz de Kermor had been punished, it was because he had been reckless.

A time came, however, when Anne of the Isles began to board her skiff more frequently, and to come much closer to the coast. When the weather remained calm, she kept her distance, as she had before, but when the sea wind surged into the bay she came running. Her boat, ever swift and sure of its route, ploughed the sea–in more than one sense of the word. Anne searched for unfortunates in need of her help.

Superstitious fishermen often grew fearful in seeing Anne's skiff pounce upon their distressed ship, as a sparrow-hawk falls upon it prey. They trembled and invoked the impotent gods of their forefathers. As Anne approached, the fishermen, paralyzed by fear, would cover their faces with their hands and let themselves fall into the bottom of their boat. When they got up again, they found themselves safe and sound on the shore; Anne and her skiff had disappeared.

Some of them finally became bold enough to dare, in these moments of supreme peril, to keep one eye open and watch this woman surrounded in mystery. They saw her put her hand to her forehead and then to her breast, then to each shoulder in turn, murmuring unknown words, as the monks of Sen did. They saw her throw a little grappling-hook on to their boats, hoist her sail, and thus take them in tow. They went quickly then, so quickly that they lost their breath. To these, the daughter of Joël said as she left: "Remember! And do for others as I have done for you!" Then her skiff would set forth on the waves again, and lose itself behind the billows.

This conduct had changed the course of the superstition. Anne was regarded as a favorable divinity; she was still feared, but she was loved, and if she had demanded anything but pity for shipwrecked sailors, they would undoubtedly have obeyed her.

When the monk arrived at the goal of his nocturnal excursion, the sky was completely covered by thick clouds. The swell was mounting, and the sinister racket that is the precursor of the tempest was audible in the distance over the waves.

The old man had stopped on a bare and arid cliff standing sheer above the Ocean. He released a profound sigh of relief, like that of a man who has just completed an onerous task. Rapping the rock with his iron-tipped staff, he sat down.

Nothing in that wild and remote place seemed to motivate the monk's joy; there was no cross to which he might have come in pilgrimage, and no roof for half a league around to which he might have come for a rendezvous. Even so, the old man waited patiently. He held his head in his hands, reflectively.

A voice, which was exquisitely soft, but also strong and vibrant, pronounced these words close at hand: "In the name of the Father, the Son and the Holy Spirit, Dom Geoffroy, I greet you. Be welcome." And, as large drops of rain driven by a furious wind lashed the monk's bare forehead, a small and gentle hand seized his in the shadows.

A moment later, he was sitting on a wooden seat in a kind of hall illuminated by a resinous torch. Kneeling beside him was a young woman of 18 years, whose charming face almost disappeared beneath a profusion of blonde hair cascading over her shoulders. She inclined her head and spoke; the monk listened. When she fell silent, the monk began to speak in his turn, and in the name of the Lord he forgave the sins that she had just confessed in the secret tribunal.

Anne of the Isles–it was her–got up and pushed back her beautiful curls. "Father," she said, "I thank God for having sent you to me at this hour, for the storm promises to be terrible, and my duty is calling me."

Dom Geoffroy did not reply. He studied the young girl in a contemplative manner, seemingly plunged in a profound reverie. He was doubtless thinking of that divine clemency which, causing a salutary herb to grow beside the poisonous one, had placed an angel of devotion and charity in the vicinity of the ferocious people of the coast.

The very place where he presently found himself encouraged his reverie. It was a kind of semi-subterranean hall constructed in a large anfractuosity in the rock.[13] A massive granite table in the middle–on which were engraved certain symbols, customarily employed by sorcerers and priests of the sinister religion followed by the people of the coast before

Audierne was built—told of the ceremonies that had previously been conducted in this refuge.

The gilded sickle that had served Anne in the days when her father had initiated her into the secret knowledge was suspended on the wall next to old Joël Bras' harp and sacred knife—but the harp, the blade and the sickle were covered in dust, while the image of Christ hanging above the young woman's bed shone, testifying to the respectful care lavished upon it every day.

From outside, on the heights of the cliff, none of this was visible. The roof of the subterranean dwelling, almost as old as the ground, was covered along its entire length by a bed of moss and sea-wrack similar in every respect to the surrounding vegetation.

"My daughter," the monk said, eventually, "you are strong and you are courageous, but you will not be sufficient to your task tonight."

"There's a ship in the bay," Anne replied. "I know that."

"There are two ships, my daughter."

"May God protect them," Anne murmured. "If the efforts of a Christian woman can save them, Father, they shall not die."

"Noble child!" Dom Geoffroy said, putting his hand on Anne's shoulder. "The courage of faith is within you; but it is unnecessary to tempt Providence, and tonight you shall have an auxiliary."

"Who?" demanded the young girl, excitedly.

"Niel Roz de Kermor," Dom Geoffroy pronounced, slowly, fixing her with a piercing and troubled gaze.

Anne shivered at that name. A sudden blush covered her cheeks—which, thereafter, became whiter than freshly-fallen snow.

"Niel Roz de Kermor!" she repeated.

"He is coming," said Dom Geoffroy

"Here!" cried the daughter of Joël, agitatedly. "Niel Roz, here. Never!" Then, getting abruptly to her feet and making an effort to collect herself, she said: "Niel Roz de Kermor came in here once, Father. The door will never open to him again."

"Alas!" the holy man said to himself. "Who will save the sailors in distress?"

"Listen to me, Father," Anne of the Isles went on, in a calm but firm tone. "Niel Roz is a good sailor; let him embark in the convent's boat."

"The convent no longer has one, daughter. The pirates of Ouessant..."

"I understand. What do you expect of me, then?"

"I wanted," the old man said, "to strike a salutary terror into the hardened hearts of the inhabitants of the coast. Niel has not reappeared among them since the fatal day when..."

"I know that, Father."

"They believe that he is dead. If they saw him suddenly appear among them at the moment when they were occupied with their abominable task of stripping the wreck, perhaps they would be stricken by fear, to the extent of abandoning their prey."

Anne reflected for a while.

"They would abandon it," she said. "I believe they would. But it would be necessary to put Niel Roz in my boat."

"It would indeed be necessary, daughter."

They heard the noise of an iron-tipped staff knocking on the rock.

"Well?" said the monk.

Anne got up. "I'll take Niel Roz to dry land," she said.

On the evening when Niel Roz de Kermor quit the coast to seek out Anne, he left his ineffectively-moored boat to the mercy of the waves before scaling the cliff. The boat was detached by the rising tide and its debris carried back to the coast. What more was needed to set the rumor of his death in motion?

He climbed up and, after a long search, discovered the entrance to the subterranean dwelling. He was as strong as he was reckless; having violently broken down the door, he went in.

Anne of the Isles, whose father was not long dead, was then a pagan, performing the rites of her accursed religion in secret. At the moment when Niel came in, she was cutting magical herbs with the aid of her gilded sickle and composing a charm, following her father's instructions.

Rumor had it that it was dangerous to interrupt the witches of Sen in the course of their superstitious practices–for Sen had long been home to witches. In the time of their power, if a man were presented to their eyes, they would cause him to perish in the most atrocious torment. Anne was alone, but she had sworn an oath never to draw breath under the same roof as a man. We shall see in due course whether she was able to keep her vow.

Indignant at the sight of Niel, she threw herself forward. Her golden sickle plunged into the unfortunate young man's throat. He collapsed.

This happened in the evening. In the middle of the night, as she knelt beside Niel–whose breath was fading rapidly–Anne was suddenly struck by an idea. She went running out of her dwelling, descended the cliff in a few seconds, climbed the crag that served as the convent's base, and fell down exhausted at the door. With a final effort, she lifted the knocker.

Despite the precariousness of their situation in the midst of that hostile region, the monks opened their door in response to this signal. Anne, who had fainted, was soon surrounded by holy men. Several of them recognized her; they were obliged to call upon their charitable faith to repress the reflexive aversion inspired in them by the daughter of their most cruel enemy–but forgiveness is the virtue of the Christian, and besides, Anne was in need of help.

As soon as she returned to her senses, she pointed desperately to the path to her dwelling. "A man," she said. "I've killed a man."

The holy men recoiled in horror, but Anne, electrified by desperation, seized the hand of Dom Geoffroy and drew him toward her house.

Niel Roz was saved by the care of the good monks. He was carried to the convent, where he remained throughout his long convalescence.

At the end of a month, he was a Christian.

Anne also became a Christian. Her pure soul and strong and superior intelligence only needed to glimpse the truth to detest the lie forever. She was baptized. It was from that moment on that the people of the coast observed a marked change in the young virgin's habits. It was from then on that she became something like a patron saint to sailors in distress.

She was robust despite the graceful slenderness of her figure; she was even more skillful than she was robust. Accustomed since childhood to make the crossings between Ouessant and Sen or Crozon and Conquet alone and in a light vessel, she regarded the sea as her element. One could not have found a pilot more expert, nor a mariner more intrepid.

As priestess of Sen, she had taken a vow of perpetual celibacy. Once she was a Christian, she did not believe herself to be released from that vow. By a scruple of conscience, which Dom Geoffroy was tempted to regard as a vestigial leaven of paganism, she wanted to hold to the oath made to the Devil. And yet, in her long hours of solitude–whether spent in her dwelling, reading Joël's strange books, or in her frail skiff, struggling against the terrible storms of the Baie des Trépassés–the image of Niel Roz de Kermor sometimes troubled her thoughts. She saw him dying; she tried hard to remember a curse or a reproach, but Niel's eyes–in these visions as at the fateful moment–expressed nothing but forgiveness and thoughts of love.

Anne was proud. Her new faith had not been able to tame that vice of generous natures completely. She would have died rather than break her oath–and what she dreaded more than anything else in the world was the sight of Niel Roz.

Anne had promised to take Niel to dry land. At the noise of the iron-tipped staff rapping the rock, she gathered up her courage and went up to the clifftop, followed by Dom Geoffroy. She found herself face to face with Niel, who bowed his head at the sight of her and folded his arms across his chest.

The young man was pale and thin. An unhealthy jaundiced tint had replaced the warm colors that had formerly shone in his cheeks. He seemed to be out of breath, and was panting. Anne felt her own breath catch.

The storm had increased during her conversation with Dom Geoffroy. The sea was now breaking against the cliffs with unprecedented violence; the wind carried a bitter and briny rain as far as the clifftop.

Anne summoned her courage again, asked for the monk's blessing, and seized Niel's hand.

"May Providence guide you!" murmured Dom Geoffroy, kneeling on the ridge.

When he got up again, a lightning-flash showed him the boat more than a hundred fathoms from the shore; from afar, it resembled the shell of a nautilus in the midst of the waves pressing upon it from every direction.

The monk went slowly back along the path to the convent.

It is necessary to be born on the shore of the Baie des Trépassés to dare to confront such a sea by night. The frail boat of the daughter of Joël filled with water at every gust of wind; its very frailty and lightness were all that prevented it from being submerged. It went on towards the Bec du Raz, a redoubtable headland fecund with shipwrecks. It went on, guided by the perfidious lanterns that hastened the ruin of ships that had entered the bay.

Niel had tried to take the tiller, but Anne had pushed him back and pointed towards the bow of the boat. Niel sat down immediately, and the crossing proceeded silently.

Halfway across, a muffled sound, which was not thunder, passed over their heads and returned as an echo, resounding from the coast. Anne and Niel made the sign of the cross. It was the first shot of the cannon signaling a ship's distress.

"Time's pressing," Anne said.

The skiff took off then, skimming the foam in a manner that had to be seen to be believed. The whistling wind struck the sail and, weighing upon it, gave battle to the waves. Nevertheless, the boat remained steady on its keel; the Raz was doubled, and a comparative calm as soon felt. Anne turned her course towards the land.

"Anne," said the young man, anxiously anticipating the moment of separation, "must I leave you alone on this frightful night?"

"We each have our task," Anne replied, in a strained voice. "Here we must separate forever."

"Forever!" Niel repeated, taking a step towards her.

"Go ashore, Christian!" she cried, forcefully. "Go ashore, where your duty awaits you!"

Niel dipped an oar into the water, and touched bottom.

"Goodbye, then," he murmured.

Anne got up in her turn; a tear trembled on the long lashes of her eyelid. As Niel went to jump overboard, she held out her hand, to which the young man touched his lips respectfully. A shout soon announced that he had reached the shore.

Anne was then able to hear the celebratory songs and ferocious transports of joy of the people of the coast. Their bursts of laughter reached her as she rounded the Pointe du Raz for a second time. At the same time, her eyes were struck by the sinister beacons illuminating the cupidity of her compatriots. There were three of them, set very close to one another.

Anne allowed herself to drift, briefly skirting the shore, and arrived directly opposite the lanterns. Then she took up her bow, and took three arrows from her quiver. Three raucous lowing noises were audible on the neighboring cliff. Anne shot her three arrows. No lights were shining any longer on the shore.

The distress signals continued precipitately, however. The shots were coming from two different directions. One of the ships had to be in the open water, in the direction of Ouessant, while the other was coming closer and closer to the Île de Sen.

Anne hesitated momentarily. To which should she render assistance?

To the one closest to perishing.

She jerked the tiller, and turned her prow towards the Île de Sen.

In less time than it would have required for a gentle breeze to carry a quarter of the distance from the Pointe du Raz to the Sen causeway, Anne had passed the island and found herself in the wake of a fine naval brig–whose hull, ten minutes later, was almost upon the submerged rocks.

"Ho! Brig!" cried the young woman.

Her voice pierced the diverse clamor of the tempest better than any man's lower-pitched voice could have done. There was a general stir aboard the brig, which promptly came about.

There was a war in progress at that time. Of the two vessels that Dom Geoffroy had seen in the bay, one was a French merchant ship, while the other was an enemy–English, without doubt, for the English are always the enemy. The merchant ship had taken flight and had hastened into the bay; then, when darkness had come, it had changed course in order to give the brig the slip. The brig had continued on its original course. Its crew, who knew it to be a fine sailing-ship, would have been scornful of the tempest in the open sea, but the proximity of a coast bristling with reefs diminished their confidence. Without knowing the full extent of his peril, the commandant had ordered the cannon to be fired to request a pilot. On board, they assumed that the pilot had arrived.

Anne came alongside the brig. Before a rope could be thrown down to her, she had climbed up the shrouds and leapt on to the bridge.

"A woman!" cried the commander, with surprise and disdain.

"A woman!" repeated the sailors, bursting into a loud chorus of laughter.

Anne was not on her guard. She pushed through the sailors, snatched the tiller from the helmsman's hands and forced the rudder into an abrupt movement.

"Into the sea with her!" the crewman said. "This is madness, or treason!"

The helmsman, offended by Anne's usurpation of his authority, advanced to carry out the sentence, while the ship, obedient to the rudder, came into the wind, as seamen say, and began to tack. It threw itself forward in its new course, cracking under the weight of its sail, and cut across the long trail of foam that had been raised in its wake.

The crewmen, immobile, held their breath, awaiting the unpredictable result of this reckless maneuver.

At that moment, there was a flash of lightning. Anne was visible standing at the tiller. Her extended arm indicated a long line of dazzling white on the port side, which, curving within 20 fathoms of the rudder, seemed to be half-surrounding the brig. But the brig felt the wind; every second that passed drew it further away from that glittering line, which vanished into the shadows.

The sailors and their officers were all shivering silently, as one does at the sight of a frightful danger averted. It was the submerged rocks of the coast of Sen, tormented by the sea, that formed that arc of foam, towards which the brig had been impetuously heading a few moments before.

All through the night, Anne remained at the rudder. The commander and his mariners surrounded her. She tried to understand their language but could not make head nor tail of it.

Then she turned her gaze toward the place where the town of Audierne has since been built, as if her sight might penetrate the darkness of a stormy night. All was silent on that side. The sound of the warning cannon came no more to interrupt the voice of the tempest.

Anne shook her head sadly.

May God come to the aid of Niel Roz de Kermoz, she thought. *There's no longer a vessel in the bay now.*

She did not repent of having saved the enemy vessel, but she wept for her countrymen.

The people of the coast had gathered on the Bec du Raz. They were shivering with cold beneath their wretched rags, and accusing the tempest of failing in its duty. The cannon had fallen silent, but no debris came to run aground on the beach.

Sighing deeply with regret, the old men were telling stories of the fine shipwrecks they had seen in their youth, and the mouths of the listeners watered as they set their ears to the wind to catch all the sounds of the sea.

Nothing! Nothing but the sound of waves attacking the rocks; nothing but the howl of the wind in the fissures of the cliff.

Despair came to the people of the coast. They were hungry. Writhing on the sand, they invoked their forgotten gods.

"O gods whom our forefathers worshipped," they said, "answer our prayers, for we have rejected the new God who did on the cross.

"We have rejected him, we have persecuted his priests and dispersed the stones of his altars upon the ground.

"We have rejected him, because his law is mercy, and we must forsake pity in order to live.

"Gods, be propitiated. There is on Sen a priestess of the blood of your pontiffs; we shall make her our sovereign.

"We shall bring from her grotto the sacred knife of Joël and the gilded sickle of his daughter. When the new year comes, we shall kill men and cut the mistletoe from the oaks."

The demons were listening. As if the spell had worked, the tempest suddenly redoubled its violence. A plaintive cry was heard 40 fathoms out to sea. At the same time, the people of the coast saw a black form passing through the shadows, moving with a frightful velocity.

A joyous clamor emerged simultaneously from every throat.

"It's going to touch! It's going to touch!" they said.

It was the merchant vessel. It was moving haphazardly, virtually disabled. It wandered so close to the Bec du Raz that its topmasts ought to have brushed the formidable rock that overhangs the point and curves like an arched roof above the sea–but it did not touch.

The people of the coast, plunged into mute amazement, could not believe their eyes. No pilot could have followed that course without breaking up ten times over–and yet the ship was saved.

There was a sturdy man there, intrepid and wicked, whose name was Jean Cosquer. He leapt into a fishing-boat and cast off from the shore without saying another word.

The merchanter ran to starboard. After ten minutes, it came back, its crew in no doubt of the peril that they had just evaded. This time it passed on the other side of the point. Again, it passed without touching.

Jean Cosquer hailed it, and had himself hauled aboard as a pilot.

"Where are we?" asked the captain

"On the brink of death," replied Cosquer.

"Can you save us?"

"On one condition."

"Which is?"

"There," said Cosquer, pointing into empty space, "is the Pointe du Raz, the tomb of more *matelots* than there are in the King's entire fleet."

The mariners looked. Their terror showed them some frightful phantom of a rock. They shuddered.

"Here," Cosquer went on, this time pointing to the Bec du Raz itself, "a path remains open. I know it; I can guide you through it."

"Do it, in the name of God," said the captain.

"Whatever you might see, you will not interrupt me?"

"Be captain for half an hour, my man," said the commander–and he gave him his megaphone.

Cosquer seized this emblem of sovereign authority and changed course towards the Raz. The sailors soon heard the noise of the surf. They saw the phosphorescent spray. They even saw the gigantic black head of the rock itself.

"Don't be afraid," said Cosquer. At the same instant, the ship heeled, and its timbers screeched.

"Don't be afraid," Cosquer said, again. Then, releasing a savage burst of laughter, he jumped over the side.

Jean Cosquer's expedition had taken some time. The people of the coast, seeing nothing and hearing nothing, were in despair. It was a wasted night. They were setting out on the path to the village when they were halted by a joyous howl from the false pilot. Cosquer appeared in their midst, still dripping with sea-water. The crew's cries of anguish alleviated the need for explanation. Everyone–men, women, children and old people–raced to the shore.

The merchant ship had run aground at the uttermost tip of the Raz. Cosquer had chosen his spot; the ship was caught in such a way that not a single item of debris could be lost. The crewmen were only a step away from land; if some of them drowned during the shipwreck, it was because, in their complete ignorance of the locality, they swam into the open water in the belief that they were heading for land.

In a trice, a bright clarity replaced the obscurity of that frightful night along the strand. A hundred resinous torches were lit at once. What need was there to hide now? The hunter leaves his retreat when the prey has fallen into his trap.

The crowd–which included both sexes and all ages–presented a hideous spectacle as they went about their work of pillage. They snatched up the least items of flotsam. Those who were strongest leapt from rock to rock, going to plunder the very carcass of the ship, which was sustained in its entirety, nailed to the tooth of a reef. Others occupied themselves with the shipwrecked sailors, stripping them and choking them. The unfortunates, ten in number, were stretched out naked on the glacial sand; they did not realize, until it was too late, the fate that was reserved for them.

Where was Niel Roz de Kermor at that moment?

If he had shown himself in the torchlight, still pale from the after-effects of his wound, his eyes shining with anger and indignation, these savages—who were as superstitious as they were cruel—would have fled, howling like demons chased away by holy water or the sign of the cross. The people of the coast would have taken him for a vengeful specter; the unfortunate mariners would have been saved. Dom Geoffroy, in his charitable solicitude, had calculated correctly.

But where was Niel Roz de Kermor?

A few voices, it must be admitted, were raised here and there on behalf of the shipwrecked sailors; women asked that they might be spared. But the sea had done its duty; it was neither just nor prudent to deprive the sea of its prey.

"Equal shares!" said Jean Cosquer. "To us the gold and the brandy, to the sea the corpses!"

The corpses were given to the sea, and the orgy commenced.

Niel Roz had a good heart, and he was a Christian. He came ashore determined to complete the task imposed upon him by Dom Geoffroy, and to give his life, if necessary, to save the shipwrecked men. Such was his intention as he set foot on land, not far from the place where the town of Audierne would be built.

But he was in love, and love gives bad advice.

For long hours, he remained faithfully at his post, keeping track of the movements of the people of the coast, ready to appear at the fateful moment. The night wore on; no vessel appeared; there were no shipwrecked sailors to help. The distress signals had ceased; doubtless the ships had foundered in open water or on the shores of Sen. His presence was therefore useless.

Anne, he thought, *is perhaps in mortal peril herself. She is calling me, and I am far away from her. Her feeble arm cannot resist the force of the tempest—and I am here, safe and sound, waiting for an opportunity that might not present itself.*

These thoughts tyrannized his mind, perhaps weakened by long and terrible illness. He resisted as best he could, but a sort of delirious fever eventually took hold of him. He thought he could see Anne's boat in the distance, on the brink of the abyss and already half-full of water. He thought he could hear the young woman's voice calling his name and asking for help.

Niel Roz went slowly down to the strand; he was still struggling. At that moment, the ship—grazing the coast as a swallow grazes the ground on a rainy day—doubled the cape and disappeared. Niel thought that it was safe. He unhitched one of the boats on the shore and set off in search of Anne.

Because of that, ten poor mariners died unshriven, and Niel would no longer find happiness in this world.

Morning found Dom Geoffroy, the worthy monk of Sen, at prayer at the foot of the cross. The wind had dropped. A ray of the rising Sun, piercing the narrow stained-glass window of the chapel, threw a pale tint of gold over the old man's white hair. He got to his feet, left the convent and went to the cliff.

Out to sea there was a vessel sailing proudly, the conqueror of the tempest. The monk's gaze made a tour of the horizon. There was only the one vessel.

A thick fog covered the coast, the Bec du Raz and the place where the town of Audierne would be built. Dom Geoffroy had looked hard, but his eyes could not penetrate the vast vaporous shroud that concealed a scene of murder and pillage. A mournful presentiment took hold of him, which he immediately repelled.

"All is well," he said to himself. "My son Niel will have done his duty. May God reward him!"

The sailors on the brig, harassed by fatigue, were sleeping here and there on the bridge. The commander was awake;

he was standing next to Anne. The waves, no longer whipped up by the wind, were gradually subsiding. It was still dark.

"Woman," said the mariner, "you have saved one of the King's vessels; name your reward."

"I lost my boat in helping you," Anne replied. "Give me the smallest of your dinghies in return, and let me return to the coast. Others might perhaps have need of me."

"Your voice is soft, young lady. No, by my faith, you shall not return to the coast. Tell me, how much gold do you want?"

"Gold, sir?" Anne repeated, disdainfully. "I am the daughter of Joël Bras of the Isles."

"And what is this Joël Bras of the Isles, my girl?"

People who have studied in books would be able to tell how Anne replied, for they know the names of false gods. Those who tell the old stories by night, as their forefathers told them, have forgotten those accursed names

Anne replied that her father had been a priest of the old divinities of the region. The mariner recoiled.

"And you?" he said. "Are you a witch?"

"I am a Christian, sir."

"So much the better, child, for your voice is soft, and it would have been a pity to burn such an agreeable pilot alive. Now then, you shan't return to the coast."

Anne adopted a grave, almost imperious, tone. "I have come among strangers," she said, "to accomplish one of God's commandments. Be assured that I have more gold than would be needed to purchase your vessel. I shall stay with you until daylight, in order that you cannot accuse me of having deserted a task commenced. When it is light, I shall leave you."

In embracing the Christian faith, Anne had retained the vestments of her caste. She was wearing a flowing linen dress. Her bow and her quiver were suspended from her shoulder, and the tresses of her long blonde hair were retained by a gold diadem. The foreigner had not noticed it before, but the dawn that was just breaking allowed him to see the young woman's noble and beautiful face, to which the antique costume lent a strange and mysterious majesty. The commander found her so beautiful that he hardened in his intention to keep her aboard.

"Damsel," he said, assuming a humble and respectful attitude, "I am a gentleman and I can make you mistress of a noble manor. Leave this wild and tempestuous land and come with me. I would like to be your knight and your husband."

"This wild land is my home," Anne said, "and no man shall be my husband."

"I am influential in the King's court," the foreigner went on. "You will see feasting, jousting and tournaments; your beauty will make you the queen of the valiant games of chivalry."

Anne sighed. Perhaps she was thinking that there was a man nearby who was neither nobleman nor knight, but was the only one capable of causing her to regret the vows that bound her.

The foreigner heard that sigh. He thought that she was yielding.

He put on knee on the deck. "Be the lady of my dreams, beautiful damsel," he said.

Anne did not reply, lost as she was in her reverie. The foreigner, encouraged by this silence, reached out his arms. His hand brushed the young woman's clothing.

Anne drew herself up to her full height. "Get back!" she aid, lifting her hand to her bow. "Don't touch me, if you value your life!"

The commander, laughing at the threat, attempted to seize her. Anne, recoiling from the idea of murder, lowered her arrow. She leapt on to the gunwale, grabbed the rigging of the mizzen-mast and was soon out of the foreigner's reach. She bent her bow.

"Look!" she said, pointing to the other end of the ship at a trailing rope broken by the nocturnal storm. "Watch that cord."

The arrow whistled away, and the severed rope fell to the deck.

"Your life is mine," she went on. "You know that now—but I do not want to put to death one whom Providence has permitted me to save. I grant you mercy."

"You shall not escape me!" the commander cried, transported by wrath. He blew on his whistle. The crewmen, waking with a start, gathered around their captain.

"Someone seize that woman," he said.

Twenty sailors launched themselves in the rigging.

Anne saw that she was lost. She darted a desperate glance at the horizon. In the far distance, in the direction of the causeway of Sen, she perceived a little white sail glittering in the first rays of the Sun. Her heart beat forcefully; she pronounced the name of Niel Roz de Kermor.

Meanwhile, the sailors, urged on by the voice of their captain, were climbing rapidly. Anne fled from each sheet of rigging to the next, leaping as lightly as a bird and maintaining her advantage. The sailors, admiring her intrepid courage and remembering that they owed her their lives, were seized by pity, but the commander's voice pressed them relentlessly.

Anne paused from time to time to turn her gaze towards the sail that was growing on the horizon. Hope entered her heart. The boat was coming closer. It was now possible to make out the man who held the tiller. It was, indeed, Niel Roz de Kermor.

Anne, still pursued, had attained the highest part of the rigging. She suspended herself from a slender rope at one of the extremities of the crosspiece supporting the mizzen topgallant, and ceased in her flight. None of the sailors dared follow her to that perilous post.

"Someone grab her!" the exasperated commander shouted from the bridge.

"Wicked and ungrateful man!" said Anne. "God will punish you, who returns evil for good."

Niel's boat had now come within voice range, to windward.

"To me, Niel!" cried the young woman. Imparting a swinging motion to her rope, she swayed back and forth several times, then released the rope at the right moment, and fell into the sea.

Niel Roz had heard the cry and recognized the voice of Anne of the Isles. No longer trusting in his sail, he seized his oars, and his boat flew towards the brig.

The commander had lowered his boats, but Anne was a daughter of the sea. After having plunged deep into the water, she returned to the surface, shook her thick hair and started swimming. The distance between her and her savior was still considerable, but the brig's launches were gaining scarcely any ground. If Anne had not been exhausted by the fatigue of her aerial journey through the rigging, that final pursuit would have been a mere game to her.

Niel hauled on his oars. He finally reached the young woman and grabbed her clothing.

"Head for the open sea," she said, falling exhausted in the bottom of the boat.

The brig's launches were still approaching. They tried for some time to continue the pursuit of Niel's boat, but he laughed at their efforts. He was soon in the midst of submerged rocks, of which there was no shortage in the bay. The launches dared not follow him, and returned to the brig.

"I'll get that woman or die trying," said the commander.

Instead of heading out to sea, he tacked back and forth across that part of the Yroise all day, determined to attempt a landing under cover of darkness.

Old Dom Geoffroy was still at his observation post when he saw Niel's boat round the point of the Sen causeway. He recognized the white dress of Anne of the Isles and went down to the strand.

"Bless you, my children," he said to them.

Anne returned to her dwelling and Niel followed Dom Geoffroy to the convent. Anne spent the whole of the day praying at the foot of the crucifix. She asked God to guide and sustain her, for her courage was weakening; she was in love with Niel Roz de Kermor.

"Did Heaven hear the oath that I swore to the Devil?" she asked. Anne was about to answer in the negative when the holy man's customary signal resounded in her ears. She hastened to climb up to the clifftop.

Dom Geoffroy was pale, his limbs seemingly prey to a convulsive tremor. Niel Roz was behind him, his head bowed like that of a guilty man.

"We must go to the coast, my daughter," Dom Geoffroy said.

"Why?" she asked.

Dom Geoffroy glanced at Niel, whose forehead was running with sweat. Anne followed the glance and went pale.

"Why?" she asked, again.

Niel covered his face with his hands, and Dom Geoffroy lifted his arms towards the coast. Anne looked in that direction.

"Niel deserted his post," she said, in a strained voice. "The blood of shipwrecked sailors is on his hands."

The young man could only reply with a dull groan.

Night had fallen. Large fires were visible, burning on the Pointe du Raz, and a multitude of shadows, blackly silhouetted against that the dazzling background, seemed to be performing a bizarre and chaotic round-dance. There was still brandy to be drunk, and the orgy was continuing.

The scene left no room for doubt. A shipwreck was required to provision the people of the coast in such a fashion. Anne, Niel and the priest climbed silently into the boat. A few unfortunates might have survived; perhaps there was still time to save them.

The commander of the enemy brig was, however, still obstinate in his evil intent. He was determined to recapture Anne at any price. Darkness having fallen. he was approaching the coast.

Seeing a great fire lit on the Raz, the commander had a boat lowered into the water and steered toward the place, in-

47

tending to go ashore alone. He counted on impressing the good people merely by his presence, and to that end he had put on his best uniform, embroidered with gold and silver. This was a great miscalculation on his part.

The wind had changed; it was now blowing from the land. By a singular coincidence, the commander's launch and the boat carrying Anne of the Isles were sailing almost in convoy without either one perceiving the other. The foreigner reached the shore first. While Niel was searching among the rocks for a landing-place, he and his two companions were witness to a terrible spectacle.

They saw the foreigner go forward. With his embroideries sparkling in the torchlight, he resembled a golden statue brought to life and given the power of movement. The people of the coast, half-drunk and dazzled by that rich costume, immediately surrounded the newcomer with cries of joy. He was another item of flotsam that the sea had sent them.

When he saw that he was under attack, the commander discharged his pistols; then, drawing his large saber, he defended himself in the manner of a gentleman–but Jean Cosquer took up a long iron bar from the debris of the wrecked merchanter and plunged its tip into the fire.

The bar reddened. Jean Cosquer brandished it above his head and launched himself towards the mariner.

A sizzling sound was heard, as if the red hot iron had touched the water; then the noble costume decorated with gold and silver collapsed. The commander was no more.

Niel only just had time to push his boat back into the water. Within a minute, the shore was overrun. The members of the crowd, dazed by drunkenness, did not even try to defend themselves. Only Jean Cosquer, before being killed, made a few mariners feel the weight of his homicidal iron bar.

The commander was abundantly avenged.

In vain did the good monk Geoffroy, having recovered from his initial fear, try to step ashore; in vain did the daughter of Joël throw herself on her knees before the foreign mariners. They shoved the monk aside; they shoved aside the young woman who was their liberator. They killed, and they continued killing until daylight. When they stopped, it was because there was no one left to kill.

So died all the people of the coast. The place where the town of Audierne has since been built was deserted.

Niel did penance. It is thought that the holy men received him into their convent, where he died reconciled with God.

As for the daughter of Joël, this is what became of her.

Eight hours after the fatal event, she summoned the worthy monk Dom Geoffroy to her dwelling.

"Dom Geoffroy," she said, "there has been a treasure in our family for centuries–the treasure of the priests of Sen. I have sworn, according to custom, only to reveal its existence to a single person–and I have chosen you, Father."

As she spoke these words, she unhooked Joël's harp–which sounded a plaintive chord, as if to deplore the annihilation of the last privilege of the priests of the false gods. Behind the place where Joël's harp had hung was a movable stone, which immediately yielded to the pressure of Anne's hand. The old man stepped back, astounded. Anne had told the brig's commander the truth; she possessed more gold than it required to purchase his ship, and ten others like it besides.

"When you no longer see me," Anne went on, in a voice full of emotion, "go to Brittany, Father. Exhort poor and benevolent Christians to follow you, and build a temple to the Lord."

"You will be with us for a long time yet, if it pleases God, my daughter," said the monk.

"If it pleases God, Father... and now, I must go out in my boat. Will you execute my will?"

"I will execute it, my daughter."

"Farewell, then," Anne of the Isles went on. "Tell Niel Roz de Kermor that I shall pray often that God will pardon him... and that perhaps, if he had acted as a good Christian on the night of the storm... But no, don't tell him that, Father."

49

A tear glittered in Anne's eye. She received the monk's blessing, and went down the cliff slowly, without looking back.

From that time on, she was never seen again on Sen.

Dom Geoffroy waited for her for a year. Then he took up his white staff and commenced his tour of Brittany. In every village, he asked poor and benevolent Christians to follow him. At the end of another year, he came back to the coast, to the place where the town of Audierne has since been built.

Anne's gold served to build a temple to the Lord. When the temple was finished, some gold still remained. Seeing that, those who had followed the good monk began to build houses. Soon, instead of the miserable village of the people of the coast, a beautiful town began to emerge.

Its inhabitants were always humane and charitable towards the victims of the Yroise shipwrecks. They remembered their origins for a long time, and the name of Anne of the Isles was blessed thereabouts for many centuries.

Now, it is all forgotten. There are only a few old men left who can tell how the town of Audierne was built, in Finistère, in Brittany.

The White Lady of the Marshes

There is, it is said, a noble châtelaine–Madame Ermengarde de Malestroit–who comes to revisit her former domains by night, gliding over the tranquil waters of the Oust marshes without a raft or a boat. She is tall, beautiful, majestic. Her body is supple, and undulates gracefully as the breeze blows. Her long hair cascades around her like a capacious cloak. On autumn evenings, when the air is calm and warm, she is sometimes seen to grow so large that her forehead touches the stars. If the wind rises by night, she begins to sway slowly, as Madame Ermengarde did in her mortal life when she danced the good Duc François de Bretagne's minuet. The folds of her dress become diaphanous then; the moonlight pierces the long waves of her hair. Then again, if the wind increases, she hangs tremulously upon its wings, and climbs with it towards the firmament.

The place where she is normally manifest is situated in the heart of the marsh. Near there, the currents of the Oust and another river intersect, their combination being exceedingly dangerous at any time, becoming a veritable whirlpool when the waters are in flood. By day, its turbulence is visible at a distance, hurling a white spray tinted with the colors of the rainbow high into the air.

By night, one only sees the *White Lady.*

Some people pretend that the White Lady is nothing but the spray of the Trémeulé whirlpool, but they are mistaken if they think so–and to say so is a temeritous act. Madame Ermengarde has, in fact, avenged herself cruelly on more than one occasion against the incredulous, and doubters are well-advised never to entrust their boats to the current of the Oust once the north star has risen over the black trees of the Forêt-Neuve.

I. The Château de Malestroit

There was a time when Monsieur de Rohan [14] became a Huguenot–which was a great pity, for a scion of such a fine family. It was in the second half of the 16th century. Monsieur de Mercoeur [15] was the leader of *la Ligue* in Brittany; Catholics and Protestants were fighting fiercely wherever they encountered one another.

It came about that the followers of Monsieur de Rohan– who was then in Paris–were defeated by Messieurs de Guer and de Malestroit, worthy gentlemen and fervent Catholics, who drove them out of both the Château de Rohan and the Château de Guéméné. The defeated parties fled through the greater part of the Vannes region, only stopping at the Château de Roche-Bernard, whose lord was in favor of Reform. [16]

The leader of de Rohan's men-at-arms was named Guy de Plélan. He was a tough soldier, believing neither in God nor the Devil, who lived by plunder, always ready to do evil. He immediately formed an alliance with the master of la Roche-Bernard, and their combined forces set out to hold the surrounding countryside to ransom. These two miscreants made no distinction between gentlemen and serfs; they pillaged cottages and châteaux alike, and there was soon nothing but misery and desolation for ten leagues in every direction.

Before leaving his château to make war against the Huguenots, Monsieur de Malestroit had confided his wife, Marguerite de Guer, to the care of a faithful servant, a commoner by birth, named Toussaint Rocher. Toussaint had never worn a sword or carried a military arquebus, but he was brave, and he would have been a dangerous adversary in a fight because he was a hunter by vocation, equally skilled with a crossbow and a wheel-lock rifle. He was a man of the marshes. He had spent his childhood on the banks of the Oust, in a little manor-house on the Malestroit estate, where his father held a fief. Summoned by his lord to the château, where he had filled the of-

52

fice of huntsman for several years, Toussaint had not forgotten the pastimes of his youth. He remembered his companions who remained simple peasants, and often came to visit his aged mother, who was now a widow. She still lived in the little manor-house of Gourlâ, whose cracked walls were reflected in the clear waters of the marsh.

Pursuing the course of their success, however, Messieurs de Guer and de Malestroit drew further and further away from their domains. They traversed the greater part of southern Brittany, always victorious, and made plans to lay siege to Quimper. Only one idea sometimes troubled the joy of their triumphs; both of them thought about the beautiful Marguerite, who was de Guer's only and beloved daughter and who had just given an heir to the noble house of Malestroit. They thought about her, and about her infant, but that did not prevent them from putting more long leagues between themselves and the château containing the precious treasure with every day that passed.

What was there to fear, in any case? Rohan's men had been defeated, and Toussaint Rocher, the faithful servant, had ten of Guer's men-at-arms with him, who would give up their lives, to the last man, to defend their master's daughter. That was what the two noble lords thought, as they went forth with light hearts and swords unsheathed, ever-ready to do battle with the Huguenots, cursing Dame Fortune every time the heretics did not present themselves two-against-one, at least.

In the time when Marguerite had been a maiden, a number of gentlemen had competed for her hand. Among the losers was Guy de Plélan. One could not exactly say that he loved Marguerite, but he certainly loved the handsome château de Guer and the old lord's inheritance with a sincere and ardent passion. Rejected by the young woman, who preferred Amaury de Malestroit, Plélan had conceived a mortal hatred against the two spouses, and had become a Huguenot for the express purpose of going to war against his fortunate rival.

Vanquished by Amaury on the field of battle, as he had formerly been in Guer's noble drawing-rooms, he felt his rage increase twofold, and swore to avenge himself or die. The Devil usually heeds such impious oaths, and makes sure that one or other of the two alternatives is realized sooner or later.

Retrenched in the Château de la Roche-Bernard, which was reputed to be an impregnable fortress, Plélan held dominion over the entire sector of the Vannes region situated between Redon and Ploërmal. After having primed his men with the pillage of a few stray villages, he set out one night with 50 horses to take Malestroit by surprise.

At about midnight, the young Comtesse was awakened by the echo of maces hammering on the thick oaken doors, and by the piercing cries of the sentinels patrolling the ramparts. Within an instant, all was tumult and disorder within the château. The garrison, discouraged by its weakness, set out nevertheless to confront the enemies which were coming from every direction. Every man-at-arms, without any hope of victory, died at his post, as befit soldiers of Guer. Plélan, having taken the walls, threw himself into the interior at the head of his men.

"Watch the doors!" he cried. "No one must leave the château. The looting will only begin when Madame Marguerite has been found. Ten ounces of gold to the one who brings her to me!"

The victors dispersed–in every sense of the word–within the château. Plélan, meanwhile, lit a fire in the great hall. Stretching himself out in an armchair embroidered with the Malestroit coat-of-arms, he demanded wine. The great hall was decorated, as was usual, with a smoothly-finished tapestry depicting the heroic feats and deeds of ancient members of the family. In addition, a long rank of family portraits extended around the walls.

"She will come!" Guy de Plélan thought, drinking his first glass of wine in little gulps.

As he replaced his empty goblet on the tale, he directed his gaze at the stern and proud faces of the old lords of Malestroit. A brutal and self-satisfied smile opened his lips.

"Milords!" he cried. "You would bid me welcome wholeheartedly, if you could talk, wouldn't you? Here you are, my noble hosts, whose escutcheon wears a Comte's crown, prisoners of a very poor gentleman. To your health, milords!"

He emptied a full goblet at a single draught, and added, while losing his insolent smile: "But she's very late coming!"

Impatience took hold of him. To counter that impatience, he seized a torch and made a tour of the room, stopping briefly in front of each portrait in order to hurl some vile and coarse sarcasm at it.

After taking some 20 paces, he came to a halt. A fleeting and involuntary shiver shook his arm.

"Ermengarde!" he murmured, hesitantly spelling out the name inscribed in gold beneath one of the portraits. "That one was said to be a witch!"

The canvas depicted a woman who was still young and admirably beautiful. Her eyes were lowered. A profound sadness tempered the austere expression on her face. It was one of those haughty and melancholy faces, which are supposed to presage a short life in Breton belief.

"Witch or not," Plélan cried, ashamed of his momentary fear, "I'll empty a cup to your health!"

He went back to the table and filled his goblet to the brim. Just as he lifted it to his lips, though, his eyes happened to fall upon a part of the tapestry where a strange scene was embroidered.

Madame Ermengarde—for it was certainly her, there was no mistake about that—was standing upright in the stern of a boat, which seemed to be borne along by a current. She was smiling, and beckoning with her hand to another boat full of men-at-arms. In front of her skiff, so close that the foam was already whitening its prow, the vortex of a turbulent whirlpool was yawning.

Plélan shivered again, more violently than the first time, for he thought he saw the Comtesse's gaze respond to his own. It seemed that she was addressing her gesture to him, and that she seemed to want to draw him into the whirlpool, a vast and inescapable tomb.

"Yes, yes," he said, seeking to reassure himself, "I've heard talk of that. The witch drew a brave King's officer into the abyss, and by dying in that fashion saved her rebellious father's life. What has that to do with me? To your health, noble lady!"

Plélan did not drink, and retreated to the fireside. Perhaps because he was already drunk, or perhaps for some other reason, he thought he saw the Comtesse's head reply to his toast with a grave nod.

He sat down, with his back to the terrible tapestry, seized the pitcher and drank directly from it, demanding courage from the wine. The wine did, indeed, cause him to forget Ermengarde, and reminded him of the real reason for his presence in the Château de Malestroit.

"Marguerite!" he exclaimed, abruptly. "The wretches have let her escape!"

He thumped the table violently with his closed fist. The veins stood out on his forehead. His eyes became dull and bloodshot. "To ruin her," he murmured, "I'll need more than one life!"

At that moment, the noise of footsteps sounded in the corridor, and the men-at-arms came in one by one. None of them had seen the young Comtesse.

"Who shall I hang?" Guy de Plélan wondered.

The last man-at-arms came in. He was dragging a prisoner, whom he shoved roughly into the middle of the room. Unable to withstand the brutal thrust, the latter fell at the feet of the angry captain.

It was a youth, barely out of childhood. He wore the costume of the peasants of north Brittany, but his long jacket and his felt breeches displayed his delicate figure in a seemingly coquettish fashion. His symmetrical and remarkably handsome features were almost hidden behind the tousled curls of his long black hair. He got up, crossed his arms on his chest, and darted a rapid and furtive glance around the room.

While the glance lasted, his physiognomy expressed a rare finesse, but when he lowered his eyelids a dull and apathetic indifference took over his features.

Plélan had not noticed the change of expression. "Is this all that you've found?" he said, addressing his men. "Words fail me! This wolf-cub will be hanged–but some of you shall keep him company!"

A dull and fearful murmur went around the men of Rohan. It was well-known that Guy de Plélan always kept promises of that sort.

"What's your name?" the captain went on, shaking his prisoner's arm roughly.

"Chantepie," the latter replied.

"Chantepie!" the captain repeated, with a loud laugh. "Well, Chantepie, my friend, I'll send you where the pie sings soon enough, when you hang from one of the trees in the avenue!" [17]

The soldiers greeted this brutal wordplay with exaggerated hilarity. They were eager to help the captain's anger pass. Two men-at-arms came forward hurriedly to take hold of Chantepie.

"That's all right, masters!" the youth said. Swiftly leaning over to whisper in Plélan's ear, though, he added: "Milord, it's a foolish hunter who kills his bloodhound as soon as it gets the scent..."

"What are you saying?" the captain exclaimed, excitedly. "Do you know where Lady de Malestroit is hiding?"

Chantepie had resumed his apparent indifference. "If I find her for you," he said, "what will you give me?"

"Your pardon."

"What else?"

"Whatever you want. Your cap full of money."

The youth took off his cap and extended it, in both senses of the word, as if to make more room within it. "It takes bushels of water-chestnuts to make a Nantais *écu*," he said, "and my boat's beginning to let in water like a sieve. I accept." [18]

"I recognize this young comedian now, sire," said one of the soldiers, in a low voice. "He's Noël Torrec, the water-chestnut fisherman. He's reputed to be the craftiest fellow in these parts. Don't trust him!"

"That's all right," said the captain, puffing himself up. "Are you afraid that I'll let this child tell me tales? Now, Noël Torrec, or Chantepie, why don't you ask me what awaits you if you don't keep your promise?"

"Because I already know."

"Good! So you're not afraid of death?"

"Milord, one winter night, I was trapped by the ice in the midst of the water-chestnuts. That was death–a slower and more cruel death than iron or the rope can dole out. I offered my heart to God and I went to sleep, milord."

"And what happened?"

"A southerly wind melted the ice." As he spoke these words, Chantepie lifted the pitcher, with some difficulty, and drank a small swig in a boastful fashion.

"You're an intrepid little fellow," Plélan murmured. "Well, what guarantee do I have, since you don't fear death?"

Chantepie showed him the cap. "I like Nantais *écus*," he said."

"That's fair–agreed! The bargain's made–bark, hound!"

Chantepie looked at the captain slyly, and began without requiring any further persuasion. "The Château de Malestroit has extensive underground workings, which Madame Ermengarde excavated–so it's said–to hide her father, who had taken up arms against the King of France. These subterranean passages have one exit on the heath..."

"And that's how she's escaped?" Plélan put in.

"If she has escaped," the water-chestnut fisherman continued. "Personally, I believe she's still here..."

"Quickly!" Plélan cried. "Search the cellars!"

The men-at-arms looked at Chantepie questioningly.

"Do you want to know how to get into them? There's more than one entrance, and one of them is much closer than you imagine... mind out, sergeant, sir!" As he pronounced

58

these words, Chantepie struck one of the floor-tiles smartly with his heel, and a trapdoor opened almost beneath the feet of the sergeant–who stepped back in alarm, murmuring: "There's something diabolical down there."

"Quick march!" commanded Guy de Plélan, imperiously. "Bring her to me, dead or alive!"

"Wait a minute, masters," Chantepie said. "If you don't find her in the underground passages, mount up and take the Pontivy road at the gallop." He turned to Guy de Plélan, adding in a knowing manner: "Her father's making war in the Cornouailles; she'll want to join him."

Plélan gave him a little tap on the cheek and smiled benignly. "Do as he says, the rest of you," he cried. "This baby has spirit enough for a hundred–which is to say, twice as much spirit as all of you put together."

"Alas, sire," Chantepie murmured, "what have I done to you that you should underestimate me so?"

The men-at-arms scowled, but Plélan burst out laughing. A minute later, the trapdoor fell back into place after the last soldier had descended into the cellars. No one remained in the hall but two sentries, the captain and Noël Torrec, alias Chantepie.

While this was taking place, two horses were running off the bridle, with their backs turned to the Pontivy road, heading cross country towards the Oust marshes. On one of the horses was Toussaint Rocher, who was carrying the heir of Malestroit in his arms; on the other sat the beautiful Comtesse de Guer.

Toussaint had been at his post at the moment when the Huguenots had attacked the château. He was alert, but what could vigilance and courage do against such numbers? One other thing had prevented him from fighting to the death: Marguerite and her son no longer had anyone but him to protect them.

Thus, while the last of Guer's soldiers were still holding the walls, Toussaint, assisted by Noël Torrec–a young orphan whom he loved like a son–had hastily saddled two horses and taken flight by a secret exit, with his master's wife and son.

"Get up behind me," he had said to Noël.

"No," the boy replied. "The horse has ten leagues to go. Besides, they're already in. In a moment or two, perhaps, you'll be pursued–and that mustn't happen, Toussaint, my old chap. Hup!" Striking the two horses with a switch that he was holding in his hand, he shoved them outside and closed the postern behind them.

"Noël!" cried Toussaint, trying to turn back. "Silly boy!"

But the victor's cries of triumph filled the château just then, and the distraught Marguerite pronounced her son's name.

"God will have pity on poor Noël," Toussaint said to himself, "and I must put my master's son before everything." At the same time, he pricked his mount with both spurs, drawing the Comtesse in his wake.

II. The Legend

Noël Torrec–or Chantepie, as he had been nicknamed because of his cheerful character–was the son of one of Toussaint's childhood friends. He lived close to the latter's aged mother, in the little fief of Gourlâ, on the other side of the marsh,

Although Gourlâ was a considerable distance from the Château de Malestroit, Noël often mounted an old nag to carry water-chestnuts–the produce of his fishing, or, more accurately, his harvesting–to Lady de Malestroit, who was so beautiful and so good to her vassals. On these occasions, he spent the day with Toussaint, his Mentor, whose straightforward mind–serious and a trifle timid–was sometimes astonished by the precocious intelligence and child-like intrepidity of his pupil. Noël left the château at dusk, went back to the boat he moored to the willows on the river bank, and crossed the marsh in the deepest darkness of the night as he would have in broad daylight. The marsh was his domain; with his eyes shut, he could have pointed out the exact location of every hollow and every turning. He alone, perhaps, would have been able to tell, to an arm's length, the distance at which one could approach with impunity the terrible whirlpool of Trémeulé, above which floated the gigantic specter that the peasants called the *White Lady*.

As he was galloping along the Redon road, Toussaint's thoughts remained in Malestroit. He brooded anxiously about the perils hanging over Noël, still at the mercy of Guy de Plélan, for whom murder was a pastime and a pleasure. Even Marguerite, preoccupied as she was by her misfortune, sometimes thought about the intrepid youth who had devoted himself to her salvation.

"We can relax our pace, Madame," Toussaint said, finally. "Noël Torrec is between us and the Huguenots. He'll prevent them from following us."

"Poor young man!" Marguerite murmured. "Rohan's men are pitiless... what if they kill him?"

Toussaint shivered, and sensed himself going pale. "They're pitiless, indeed," he murmured, dully. "Madame, we must concentrate our minds, and pray from the bottom of our hearts, for God alone can save that generous child now."

Toussaint bared his head and began to pray in a low voice. Lady de Malestroit did likewise. Then they both continued on their way in silence, in the middle of a moonless night, guided solely by Toussaint's perfect knowledge of the country.

Meanwhile, once the last of the men-at-arms had passed through the trapdoor, Chantepie said to Guy de Plélan: "Milord, the search might take some time. Would it please you to empty a few flagons, to keep boredom at bay while waiting?"

Guy tapped the pitcher that was beside him on the table.

"Fie!" Noël Torrec exclaimed, smiling scornfully. "That's vassals' wine. I know the hidey-hole where Guibert de

Malestroit, Milord Amaury's father, put his Gascony wine. I can furnish you with a vintage flagon momentarily."

"Gauthier," Plélan said to one of the two sentries, "take this honest lad by the arm and take him to find the flagon he's told me about. Go, Chantepie, my friend; I'll willingly drink your health in that good wine."

Noël held out his hand to the sentry, smiling. Although Plélan was watching him attentively, the captain could not discover any hint of ill-humor or disappointment in that cheerful visage.

"The boy is sincere," Plélan said to himself, as he followed him with his gaze. "He's put me on the trail of Madame Marguerite, and I'll finally have that proud châtelaine in my power. Ah, Malestroit, Malestroit! You, who have humiliated me, vanquished me, dishonored me—what would you give me to return your wife and heir?"

Chantepie came back then with the sentry, who was carrying a basket of dusty and moist flagons. Plélan's eye lit up at the sight of them.

"Boy," he said, "you're fit to serve a gentleman. Would you like to be my page?"

Noël bowed respectfully. "Your page and your cup-bearer, milord," he replied, pouring Plélan an ample measure.

Plélan drank. Chantepie poured again, and Plélan drank again. When the first flagon was empty, Plélan drew his cutlass and broke the neck of the second bottle. "Oh yes!" he said, in a voice already rendered hoarse by the commencement of drunkenness. "That papist rogue Guibert de Malestroit was a connoisseur of wines, on my oath! Pour, Ganymede—for me, first, then for these brave men—as much as they like—and then for yourself, my son... then for the Devil, if he so desires! Speaking of the Devil, did I not see the portrait of that accursed witch move?"

He pointed at Ermengarde, whose severe and melancholy features did indeed seem to be animated by the flickering lamplight.

"Be quiet, for pity's sake!" murmured Noël Torrec, manifesting a sudden anxiety.

"Why be quiet?" the Huguenot demanded, roughly.

"Have you never heard talk of the White Lady of the Marshes, milord?" Noël asked in his turn, instead of answering.

"Of course—but what does that matter to me?"

"Ermengarde has always found a means to protect her family," the youth said, earnestly, "and many bones are scattered on the sand beneath the Trémeulé whirlpool."

Guy de Plélan burst out laughing.

"Perish my flesh!" he cried. "I'll allow the witch to add my bones to those of which you speak when the fancy strikes me to engage her in a naval combat. Until then, let's drink! Now then, Chantepie, my joyful page, I'll wager that you know a ballad or two?"

"I only know one, milord."

"Which one?"

"An old legend that one of Milord Amaury's servants told me."

"What's your legend called?"

"The story of the White Lady of the Marshes."

"Still harping on about the White Lady? No matter! I'd like to know what kind of face Madame Ermengarde will pull as she listens to the story of her feats and deeds. Fill the cups, and tell us your ballad."

"As you wish, milord!"

Chantepie filled the goblets of the captain and his two men-at-arms to the brim. Then, on Plélan's orders—the latter was still fearful of an escape—he placed himself between them and began the recitation, in a slow and monotonous voice, of the rhythmic but rhymeless prose to which some rustic poet had consigned the story of Madame Ermengarde de Malestroit: *The Legend of the White Lady.*

"The people of Malestroit are saying masses, praying in the chapel and praying at the parish church, all draped in black–for Madame Ermengarde is dead, has died at the Trémeulé whirlpool.

"Hervé, our overlord, is the son of Alain de Malestroit; his daughter, when she was still in this world was named Ermengarde.

"There was none in Nantes, the great city of the rich Duc, nor in Rennes, the capital of the Breton lands, either dame nor demoiselle, who could compete with the beauty of the daughter of Malestroit.

"The lords watched her ride by on her black horse from a distance, saying *Who will be her spouse*? Then they looked at one another with wild eyes, and their steel gauntlets clinked as they touched the hilts of their dirks.

"Duc François died; Madame Anne inherited Brittany.[19] French men-at-arms rode through the Breton countryside.

"Hervé had said *I will not suffer it!* He buckled on his fine sword, and gathered his vassals about him.

"They went forth, 100 men bearing lances, as far as the town of Redon, where the river Vilaine runs. There were French men-at-arms at Redon, who received them valiantly.

"There was a battle. Malestroit was defeated. It was the eve of Candlemas.

"Ermengarde had quit the château and crossed the marshes. She awaited her father at the fief of Gourlâ. Malestroit returned, closely followed by the King of France's men.

" 'Sire,' the French captain said to Hervé, 'you are weak and we are strong. My soldiers have taken your château and I shall overwhelm your last refuge. Give me your daughter, Ermengarde the Fair, whom I shall take as my wife, and my men-at-arms will take the Redon road again–and I shall return your château to you.'

"Hervé had climbed up on the wall of the manor-house to hear the French captain out. He went to find his daughter and said to her: 'The Frenchman loves you, and he is the stronger, but your decision is final.'

" 'Milord,' replied Ermengarde the Fair, 'no man shall have my hand, because I have given my heart to God.'

"The Frenchman became furious. He made a breach in the manor's feeble wall and came in. Malestroit's servants died, to the last man.

"Then Ermengarde seized her father's arm and drew him toward the marsh.

"There were three boats on the bank. Hervé climbed into one and Ermengarde pushed it into open water with her foot, despite her father's protests. She climbed into the second and came away from the bank. The captain and his men, who were running in pursuit of the fugitives, threw themselves into the third.

"Hervé's boat had neither oars nor a pole. Ermengarde had taken them. The boat drifted away towards the shallows of the broadest part of the marsh. The daughter of Malestroit blew her father a farewell kiss and steered toward the current of the Oust, which formed a white line in the middle of the green waters of the lake.

"The Frenchmen hesitated. Which should they pursue? Ermengarde was seated in the stern of her boat. She smiled, seeming to summon the Frenchmen with her gaze. The French went after Ermengarde the Fair.

"Ermengarde's smile widened. She plied her oars for a few strokes more. The prow of her boat encountered the current of the Oust and was immediately caught. The vessel set itself to follow the rapid river. 'Pull hard on the oars!' the Frenchmen cried. 'Let's gain the current too!'

"They gained the current. Dusk was falling. A dull sound was audible in the distance, incessant and inexplicable. 'What's that noise?' the Frenchman asked. No one at his side could answer him.

"The sound was the Trémeulé whirlpool, above which the White Lady was not then yet afloat.

"Ermengarde the Fair's boat cleaved the waters as an arrow cleaves the air. The Frenchman's boat pressed close behind. The noise of the whirlpool was no longer dull nor distant; it was clear and terrible.

"All of a sudden, the Frenchman saw Ermengarde the Fair kneel down to pray. Then she made the sign of the cross, and remained motionless. 'Pull those oars hard!' cried the Frenchman.

"His boat surged forward, almost touching the vessel of Ermengarde the Fair. But at that moment the vessel of Ermengarde the Fair spun around and vanished. It had touched the lip of the Trémeulé whirlpool, whose white and luminous spray was already surrounding the Frenchmen. 'Pull back!' cried the captain.

"There was no time. The whirlpool seized the boat, caused it to pirouette momentarily, and precipitated it, crushed, into the depths of the vortex."

Chantepie stopped. The further his ballad advanced, the more monotonous and muffled his voice became. He had a plan.

The three Huguenots had continued drinking. Completely drunk, they had lowered their heads on to the table. Before surrendering to sleep, however, Plélan, with a final glimmer of reason, had ordered each of his two sentries to seize one of Noël's hands. His own hand had grasped the youth's belt.

Noël, closely held in this fashion, wanted to see how just profound his guardians' sleep had become. He stopped talking–but a groan from Guy proved to him that his new master was still in need of rocking, and he continued immediately.

"That is why the people of Malestroit are praying and weeping in the chapel draped in black. It is because Lady Ermengarde is dead, dead at the Trémeulé whirlpool.

"The Frenchmen perished, and Lord Hervé was saved.

"Ever since that day–who has not seen her?–Lady Ermengarde has come back every night to float above the vortex that was her tomb. She comes back because her death was voluntary, and she therefore saved her father by means of a sin.

"She still comes back. The people of Malestroit have been praying for her for a long time—but who can say what sentence God has measured out for the expiation of her crime?

"She comes back—and if a Malestroit should find himself in peril in the marsh on a tempestuous night, she deflects his boat away from the Trémeulé vortex. But if an enemy of the house approaches, and dares to brave her terrible vicinity after the setting of the Sun, she extends her long arm of mist, and draws his vessel with an invincible strength. Then she twists it with a fist of foam, and hurls its deformed debris into the abysmal depths of the whirlpool.

"The people of the marsh fear her gigantic form, and salute it from a distance. Those who approach close enough to touch her diaphanous dress are bold and reckless men. They never see the green grass of the river-bank again, and their bones are strewn like pebbles on the bed of the Oust.

"That is the legend of the White Lady, who guards the Trémeulé whirlpool by night."

For several minutes, Noël's voice had been fading imperceptibly. After pronouncing these last words, he continued to emit an indistinct and ever-decreasing murmur.

During the second part of his recitation, the cunning youth had not remained in the least idle. Gently bringing together the hands of the two soldiers who held him to the right and the left, he had disengaged his own with infinite precaution and put in their place the two hands of Milord Guy himself, who was sleeping leadenly. That accomplished, he borrowed a dagger from one of the guards and slit his belt, which remained dangling from the hand of the Huguenot captain.

He was free, and could not prevent himself jumping for joy. Fearful of the imminent return of the men-at-arms who had gone into the cellars, however, he repressed any more imprudent manifestations and went to the stables, where he saddled a horse and, soon, departed at a gallop.

When Guy de Plélan woke up the following morning, he was extremely surprised to find both his hands clasped, as if in a vice. His two men-at-arms, for their part, were more than slightly astonished to find themselves face to face with their leader, in front of a dozen decapitated flagons. Their thoughts, as vague and indecisive as thoughts usually are on the morning after an orgy of drunkenness, obstinately resisted every attempt to put them in order. They looked at one another, all three of them dumbfounded.

Eventually, Guy de Plélan recovered his memory of what had happened the previous evening.

"What have you done with Chantepie?" he asked, suddenly.

To the soldiers, this was a ray of light. They looked around the room, and lowered their heads.

"Perish my bones!" Plélan cried. "The clown's escaped! I see it all now. He was in league with Lady de Malestroit, and our men-at-arms will return empty-handed..."

Dawn was just breaking when Toussaint and Marguerite de Guer reached the edge of the Oust marshes. Their horses, racked by fatigue, lay down exhausted on the moist grass.

As soon as she set foot on the ground, Lady de Malestroit hurled herself towards her son, whom Toussaint still held in his arms, and pressed him passionately to her heart.

"What can Amaury de Malestroit do to repay your devotion, Toussaint?" she said, gazing thankfully at the faithful servant. "You have saved everything that is dear to him in this world."

"Saved..." Toussaint echoed, with an air of doubt and hesitation. "May God's will...!"

He leaned over and set his ear to the ground.

"That's the hoofbeats of a horse!" he murmured. "It'll catch up with us within ten minutes."

"What are you saying?" Marguerite exclaimed, fearfully.

"We must embark immediately, Madame. When we're on the other shore, and I've closed the door of the secret room at Gourlâ upon you, you may say that I've saved you, not before!"

He took a hundred paces along the bank, and soon discovered a boat moored among the willows. It was old and seemed to have outlived its usefulness; water had seeped through its badly-fitting joints. Toussaint hesitated momentarily, but the horse's hoofbeats were now quite distinct and were approaching rapidly. Toussaint leapt into the boat and baled out the water as best he could. After taking Marguerite and her child aboard, he began to punt with all his strength.[20]

Scarcely had they left the bank, when the horse emerged from the stony path that led to the waterside and ran silently over the thick grass, which muffled the noise of its hoofbeats. The daylight was still very weak. Toussaint saw the blur that was the horse and its rider glide swiftly through the shadows, following the curve of the river-bank–then they disappeared behind a clump of willows.

Marguerite de Guer let out a long sigh of relief. Toussaint shook his head sadly.

They went forward slowly. The boat was heavy and was taking in water at every seam. Toussaint wondered whether the water might not win before they reached the other bank.

The part of the marsh where our fugitives had embarked is the most difficult to cross, because of the tongues of land and promontories that must be doubled. Toussaint punted without pause for a full half-hour, but the dark line of the shore that they had quit seemed scarcely a thousand yards distant. On one side, the daylight illuminated nothing at all. In the distance, in the direction of the open water, the colossal form of the White Lady stood out as it did in the dead of night, but the darkness was too profound for the flow of the Oust to be distinguishable.

Many years had passed since Toussaint had left the marsh to become one of the château's servants, but he had not entirely forgotten the characteristic and striking signs that announced the advent of autumnal fogs. Within some anxiety, he saw cottony wisps of pale grey vapor running along the sides of his boat, disappearing momentarily only to return, denser and more undulant than before. At the same time, the stars that still shone in the firmament seemed to increase in size and take on a sallow tint. The wind suddenly dropped. The White Lady enlarged her proportions, in every dimension, to an immeasurable extent, eclipsing the greater part of the horizon in the blink of an eye.

Toussaint stopped plying his pole and folded his arms.

"What are you doing?" Marguerite cried. "Do you think it's prudent...?"

"Audacity and prudence are equally useless to us henceforth, Madame," Toussaint said, interrupting her. His expression was one of bleak despair. "Heaven is my witness that I would gladly give every last drop of my blood to save you, but God alone can help us now."

Lady de Malestroit looked up at him in frank astonishment. The waters of the marsh were calm, as smooth as a mirror.

"What new danger can threaten us now?" she asked.

Toussaint pointed towards the place where the form of the White Lady had been distinguishable a short while before.

"Look," he said.

Marguerite looked, and smiled. "I see nothing," she replied, "except for a curtain of fog–which, according to the proverb, promises us a sunny day."

Toussaint shivered and lowered his eyes. His mistress's trust, in that supreme moment, squeezed his heart.

"Alas, Madame" was all he said, in a low tone, "the sunlight will arrive too late for us to see it."

"Is it possible?" the poor mother cried, passing abruptly from security to terror. "My son! Can you not save my son, at least?"

Toussaint made no reply. Throwing down his pole, however, he set about baling out the boat with his straw hat. While he concentrated on that task, the wall of fog drew ever closer. Soon, the boat was enveloped by a thick veil, which hid the water, the land and the sky alike.

"I understand–I understand now," cried Marguerite de Guer, clasping her son convulsively in her arms.

Toussaint continued baling out the boat without pause, but new cracks were appearing at every instant, and it was possible to make an approximate calculation as to the moment of the boat's inevitable submersion.

"It's all over!" Toussaint murmured, finally, as he fell back exhausted.

While Marguerite de Guer had watched her faithful vassal laboring, she had conserved a vestige of hope. This final statement was, for her, like a death-warrant.

She knelt down and prayed.

Then, looking at her son, who was sleeping peacefully at her breast, she said: "Dear God, I was a happy wife and a happy mother–but Thy will be done!"

Then she shut her eyes again and waited for death.

For his part, Toussaint, driven to distraction by his mistress's peril, studied the marsh-water with bleak eyes. It was already brushing the gunwale of the boat.

At that moment, a clear and child-like voice–perhaps the voice of a shepherd grazing his ewes on the banks–cut through the fog, carrying the joyful notes of an improvised song to the agonized unfortunates.

III. Chantepie

The voice was singing these words:

Whether it's warm or it's cold,
Whether there's thunder or wind
Over the narrow shallows,
I am the stray water-chestnut;
And if someone somewhere
In the tempest is singing,
That's me!

Toussaint held his breath in order to listen harder. His entire soul seemed to be concentrated in his hearing. "It's Noël!" he cried, bringing his hands together. "I recognize his song."

Marguerite lifted her head slowly. She dared not yield to hope.

Toussaint, however, made a megaphone with his two hands and called out.

Noël presumably did not hear, for the voice went on:

Nothing other than a boat,
Needs little Chantepie,
For he looks without desire
On the pomp of the château.
Living on the water,
Scornful of catching cold,
Seeing nothing in life
But good!

"Noël! Noël!" Toussaint shouted again.

The voice began a third verse. It seemed to be much further away, for the words now arrived indistinctly, like a confused murmur.

"Dear God! Dear God!" sobbed Marguerite de Guer. "Will you not have pity?"

Toussaint gathered his strength again and forced out one last shout, prolonged, heart-rending and full of despair. Then he collapsed on the benches of the boat.

This time, the song ceased abruptly. Toussaint pricked up his ears avidly, and a distant cry reached him through the fog.

The good servant replied immediately. Mad with joy, he knelt down in front of his mistress, whose hands he kissed rapturously.

A few minutes later, Chantepie's skiff, guided by the expert hand of the young fisherman, appeared out of the fog. It glided lightly and rapidly over the water, like a sleigh on ice.

Marguerite and Toussaint climbed into the other boat. "If the pie had not sung," Noël murmured, "your old mother would have been weeping tonight, père Toussaint."

"Noël, Noël!" cried the faithful vassal. "Kneel down and thank God, child, for you have been the savior twice over of your master's dearest treasure."

Noël obeyed, and touched his lips to the hand of Marguerite de Guer. She leaned over to kiss him on the forehead, and uncovered the face of her sleeping son so that Noël could kiss him in his turn.

"Noël, Noël!" the awestruck Toussaint repeated. "You have earned, my son, a glorious and noble reward. I would not be astonished now were you to become a gentleman and put on gilded spurs."

Noël tried to smile, but he had tears in his eyes.

"Thank you, my lady and mistress," he murmured. "Some day, if it pleases God, I shall give the last drop of my blood for you."

The Oust marshes, formed by the conjunction of various watercourses of unequal importance, are some four or five leagues in extent, between two amphitheaters of verdure, which crown the tall trees of the Forêt-Neuve and the Forêt de Rieux on one side, and the arid slopes of the heathland of Saint-Vincent–pierced here and there by the heads of grey and mossy rocks–on the other. They run from east to west.

In summer, when their waters are low, the marshes' basin is a vast grassland cut through by innumerable streams. As soon as autumn arrives, though, each stream suddenly swells, overflows its banks, and mingles its waters within those of the recently-augmented Oust. The grassland becomes a lake; nets and fishing-lines are cast in places where the châtelain's horses, the mayor's cattle and the poor hut-dweller's dwarfish sheep were wandering a little while ago, mingling as hectically and good-humoredly as in the Golden Age.

In the 16th century, there were no mayors as yet, but sheep were already familiar. When the waters were in flood, all the flocks disseminated over the surface of the marsh moved unthinkingly to the lower slopes to either side and re-grouped everywhere that a thin line of greenery remained dry. It was said in olden times, and it can still be seen in the present epoch, that they resembled two interminable ribbons of raw cloth left out to dry and bleach in the sun.

When the waters are in flood, while the days are still warm and the white morning dews are still frequent, the waters of the marsh, warmed by the rising Sun, sometimes give off mists at the end of the night. There are doubtless other circumstances, which we cannot specify, favoring this sudden disengagement of vapor, for the entire lake is covered within a few minutes with a thick, white, almost solid veil, of which the word "fog" can only give the slightest idea to the inhabitants of cities. It is a sort of *bright night*.

This opaque veil, radiant with a light of its own, brightly illuminates objects within arm's reach, while hiding everything else completely. When you see, for instance, a large tree whose branches sparkle with diamantine prisms of frost, you see one branch or two, but the third disappears in the fog and you have to take a step forward to perceive it.

In this season, the fog is dangerous and causes frequent disasters. Some sort of lighthouse is in fact, necessary to the navigation that seemingly tranquil lake, criss-crossed by innumerable currents. By day, one steers straight toward its shores; by night, the colossal specter of the White Lady, perceptible from all parts, can serve as a compass–but the fog confounds everything with a dense, complete and uniform obscurity. It is necessary to stay in place and wait.

If the boat is good, the Sun arrives to chase away the fog, and one can resume one's course. If the boat is old and leaky–which is more common than not in those poor regions–the Sun still arrives, but it arrives too late. At the place where the boat was, the waters of the marsh have closed in, as calm and smooth as the surface of a mirror, cheerfully reflecting the Sun's rays. There is nothing to testify to the sinking and dying; it is the white sepulchre of the scriptures.

It is understandable now why Toussaint felt his courage wane and stopped plying his pole. There might have been ten currents between him and the bank, of which one led straight to the bed of the Oust, then to the Trémeulé whirlpool. To strive against the peril was to hasten the moment of death.

Once they were in Noël's skiff, however—which was new and sat well upon the water—our fugitives found shelter.

"Lay down your pole, Noël, and wait for daylight," Toussaint said.

That was not Chantepie's estimation of what the situation required. "Père Toussaint," he replied, "is there not a great deal of gold in his lordship Amaury's château?"

"Undoubtedly. Why?"

"Because Plélan, who is an accursed Huguenot, faithless and lawless, and who never hesitates over a wicked act, will say: *Here's gold! A lot of gold! Search out Madame Marguerite and bring her to me...*"

"That's true," Toussaint murmured.

"When the Sun shines, there are open eyes on both sides of the marsh—and when the eye has seen, the tongue wags."

"Where we're going," Toussaint said, "there are none but faithful vassals..."

Noël interrupted him. "Have you never heard the parish priest tell the story of the Passion from his pulpit? Jesus was betrayed, père Toussaint, for 30 pieces of silver, by one of his own apostles."

"That's true," Toussaint said again, "but what's your point?"

"Judas would not have betrayed anyone, père Toussaint, if he had not known where Our Savior was to be found. Let's profit from the fog, so that Madame Marguerite may cross the threshold of the manor of Gourlâ before anyone has been able to see her."

Toussaint looked at his pupil with frank admiration. "Noël, Noël," he said, "if God preserves your life, my son, you shall become a great lord."

Lady de Malestroit herself could not help admiring Noël's precocious sagacity and devotion. "When you come of age, child," she said, smiling, "Monsieur Amaury will make you a knight. If God permits me to see him again, my first word will be for you."

"Me, a knight!" cried Chantepie, bursting into laughter. "Who, if you please, would then fish for water-chestnuts for the château?"

So saying, he set his pole on his shoulder, went along the entire length of the boat, and shoved off vigorously.

"The bottom's giving way," he murmured. "We're about to enter the Oust."

At the same moment, the boat took off by itself, and the fugitives felt themselves carried rapidly away by the current.

"Are we far from the whirlpool?" asked Marguerite, in alarm.

"We'll hear it any minute, but you hear it long before you see it." Noël set down his pole and came to kneel in front of his suzeraine. "And now, my noble lady," he said, "I beg you to grant me a favor."

"Fie, Noël, fie!" Toussaint murmured.

"Let him speak," said Marguerite. "I swear by Notre-Dame de Guer to refuse him nothing."

"You heard her, père Toussaint!" Noël cried. "I ask for the ring that Milord Amaury de Malestroit gave you on the blessed day of your betrothal."

Marguerite de Guer sat up straight, and assumed a stern expression. "Vassal," she said, "I have sworn by Our Lady, and I shall keep my oath come what may, but what do you intend to do with my nuptial ring?"

"I intend to put it on my finger, noble mistress..."

"Wretched child!" said Toussaint the huntsman, attempting to interrupt.

"I intend," Noël went on, "to display it as a proof of an important mission, which I'm perhaps unworthy to undertake, but which, with God's help, I pledge myself to follow through to the end."

"What mission?" asked Marguerite and Toussaint, simultaneously.

"Is it not necessary," Noël went on again, "that Milord Amaury be informed of the danger to Madame Marguerite and the heir of Malestroit?"

Marguerite de Guer's forehead suddenly cleared. "Is it not perilous to assume responsibility for such a message?" he asked, as she slid the ring along her white and delicate finger.

"I don't know," Toussaint replied, his joy giving way to anxiety, "but my boy Noël fears no danger when it is a matter of serving Malestroit." And he patted the child's shoulder proudly.

Marguerite de Guer paused momentarily for reflection.

"Here is my ring," she said, "and I shall say not one word to you about a reward, Noël, for you have the heart of a gentleman."

Chantepie took the ring and got up cheerfully, while Toussaint wept tears of joy.

"Listen," said the youth. "There's the song of the White Lady; it's time to get to work."

The vortex was indeed bellowing not so far away. Noël seized his pole, but he could not find the bottom and was obliged to have recourse to his oars. In a matter of seconds, the boat turned sideways and, cutting across the current of the Oust, soon came into tranquil and sluggish water. Noel took up his pole again then, and did not relinquish it until the moment the boat touched the bank.

He had not hesitated once during the crossing. As we have said, the marsh was his domain. Scarcely perceptible signs, which would have been mute for anyone but him, showed him the way. The color of the water, its depth, the consistency of the bottom and the direction of the currents, all enabled him to steer his skiff in a sure and rapid manner.

When the three fugitives disembarked on the shore, the fog was only just starting to dissipate. The Sun's disc was visible, reddened and diminished by refraction, but its rays were still only able to pierce the misty mass imperfectly. Lady de Malestroit was able to cross the threshold of her Gourlâ fief without being seen.

Guy de Plélan, furious at having lost Chantepie, on whom he had been counting to serve as a bloodhound in picking up the trail of Marguerite de Guer, gave the matter profound consideration. As he reflected, he went to sleep.

When he awoke, the sunlight was streaming through the high stained-glass windows of the hall of Malestroit. His first glance fell upon Madame Ermengarde's portrait.

"Infamous witch!" he cried, angrily. "It's your accursed history that's the cause of all this! Well, here's your wages!"

Seizing the empty pitcher, he hurled it with all his strength at the unfortunate portrait, which received considerable injury therefrom.

Following this legitimate vengeance, the valiant captain went into the courtyard of the château, where his men-at-arms were to be found.

"Where are Gauthier and Corentin?" he said. These were the names of the two sentinels who had woken up with him in the hall.

Corentin and Gautier came forward.

"You've got long arms, Gauthier," he continued. "Drive two nails into the lintel of that doorway for me–two strong nails, with a reasonable distance between them."

Gauthier fetched a hammer and drove in the nails.

"You, Corentin," the Huguenot went on, "find me two pieces of rope about three feet long... two good cords capable of bearing a reasonable weight."

"It's done," said Gauthier, throwing his hammer aside.

"Here you are," said Corentin in his turn, holding out the lengths of rope,

"Good! Now, kneel down and say a prayer, if by chance you know one."

The two men-at-arms went pale; they had divined Plélan's intention.

"Have pity, in the name of the Virgin!" cried Corentin.

"Have mercy, on your salvation!" cried Gauthier.

Plélan burst out laughing.

"Who speaks of the Virgin here?" he said. "Don't you know how to die like good Calvinists, without invoking saints and other mummeries? As for my salvation, perish my blood! That's my concern, and I suggest that you give it no more thought than I do."

He gave a signal. The two cords were firmly knotted, and the two unfortunate men-at-arms, suspended by the neck, were soon swaying over the threshold.

"Now," Guy de Plélan resumed, "is anyone among you a clerk, comrades? Don't be afraid—I shan't hang anyone else today. Who among you can write?"

A soldier emerged from the ranks. Plélan had a leaf of parchment brought, and dictated as follows:

Guy, knight, Lord de Plélan, to all those presently living, greetings!

Ten gold écus *of 30 Tournois* livres *are promised to whomsoever brings to the aforesaid Chevalier de Plélan the wife and son of the papist Amaury de Malestroit.*

So it is written!

The valiant captain sealed this placard with the aid of his sword-hilt, and had it attached to the door of Malestroit church, taking care to post one of his men-at-arms beside it—to defend it if necessary, but primarily to explain it. Then he gave his sergeant a duplicate of the proclamation, and instructed him to take it around the surrounding villages, so that no one might be ignorant of his munificent intentions.

Satisfied with his morning's work. he sat down at the table of the Lords de Malestroit, and had dinner served. At the first gulp, he threw his goblet away. "Pooh!" he said. "Someone go find me the wine that young clown Chantepie had me taste yesterday."

The remaining 46 men-at-arms hunted high and low, but it was the unfortunate Gauthier who had acccmpanied Noël to the Malestroit wine-cellar on the previous evening. The others did not know the way. "Someone cut Gauthier down!" cried Plélan, suddenly recalling this circumstance.

It was too late; Gauthier was no longer breathing.

"Perish my flesh!" cried Guy de Plélan. "The clodhopper should have waited to render up his soul until we knew where those papist dogs put their choice wines... but he was never good for anything in his entire life, and I surrender him to the Devil with all my heart."

Such was the funeral oration of the unfortunate sentinel.

A few hours later, Plélan mounted his horse and abandoned the devastated Château de Malestroit to retake the road to Roche-Bernard, where his general quarters were.

Marguerite de Guer was in the secret room at Gourlâ, slumped in an armchair beside her infant, who was awake and smiling, ignorant of the dangers he had recently run. Around them stood Noël, Toussaint and Marthe Rocher, the aged mother of Malestroit's huntsman.

"So, young man," Marguerite was saying, "the perils of the adventure have not weakened your courage? You are determined to carry a message to my husband?"

"Quimper's a long way from here," sighed old Marthe, who was dividing her maternal tenderness equally between Toussaint and Noël. "The child will die before reaching it."

"Perhaps it would be better if I went myself," said Toussaint the huntsman.

"No, no, no," Chantepie said, three times over. "To each his role, père Toussaint! Watch over the deposit entrusted to you; I'll go in search of help... and I'll bring it back."

"It's a sin to tempt Providence," Marthe went on, in a low voice, smiling and weeping at the same time, "but if the child says so, he'll do it."

"So he must go," Toussaint said, sadly.

"For that matter," the old lady continued, by way of an aside, "you'd have to go a long way to find his equal."

Marguerite de Guer seemed troubled. She had been seized by tenderness towards this youth, so devoted, so intelligent and so courageous. Having a vague idea of the terrible perils of the journey, she hesitated to dispatch him on an enterprise in the face of which a man in the prime of life might have recoiled–but a single glance darted at her son put an end to her irresolution. "He must go!" she said, in her turn.

Chantepie was only waiting for that word. He embraced Marthe and Toussaint, kissed Marguerite's hand, and ran to the door, saying: "Keep watch by night on the white rock that stands out in the midst of the forest foliage on the far bank. When you see a fire lighted there, come to look for me in my boat, père Toussaint. I'll have seen Milord Amaury."

He went out. Toussaint followed him.

The châtelaine and her vassal leaned out of the window. Noël was mounted on a little horse and Toussaint was marching beside him, his carbine on his shoulder. Instead of going down towards the marsh, Noël took a path leading to farmland and soon disappeared behind the trees that lined the road. Marguerite de Guer came back to her baby's crib and kissed him on the forehead. "May you resemble him one day!" she thought aloud.

"Amen!" replied the old woman proudly. "One could not wish for anything better."

It was scarcely ten minutes after Noël had quit the manor-house. Toussaint was making his last farewells and recommendations, not forgetting to slip a well-furnished purse into his hand, when a man-at-arms appeared at the end of the road.

Noël was not on his guard. He received the huntsman's final accolade, and spurred his horse. Toussaint retraced his steps.

"God be with you, sir!" Noël said, as he passed by the man-at-arms.

The latter raised his eyes; they recognized one another at the same moment. Chantepie turned back and the soldier followed him at full tilt.

"Rascal! Accursed imp!" cried the latter, spurring his horse. "I'll get you this time! You're the cause of two honest lads being hung this morning and I've spent the night in a damp cellar with no exit. By holy Calvin, you'll pay for all that!"

Toussaint turned round on hearing the noise. He saw that the mercenary, whose horse was a powerful Norman beast, was gaining ground with every stride. He also saw that the horseman was wearing the Rohan colors on his cap.

"Help!" cried the youth, on the point of being overtaken.

Toussaint primed the wheel-lock of his carbine and shouted to the soldier to halt.

Far from obeying, the latter, who had almost caught up with Noël, brandished his long sword above his head. The youth fled towards Toussaint, who was unable to fire because the two riders were too close together.

"Help!" Noël repeated.

At that moment, his horse stumbled.

The soldier stood up in his stirrups in order to strike; Toussaint saw his head above Noel's and squeezed the trigger of his weapon.

IV. The Challenge

The gun fired. The soldier, Noël and Noël's horse rolled in the dust.

"I've killed him! I've killed my son Noël!" murmured the distraught hunter.

"Well aimed, père Toussaint!" replied the youth, rising briskly to his feet. "But for you, I wouldn't have got far on the road to Quimper."

He tried to get his horse to his feet, but found that its legs had been sorely wounded by the gravel of the road. He turned towards the man-at-arms, who had taken Toussaint's bullet in the middle of his forehead.

The soldier was dead; he was none other than Guy de Plélan's sergeant, instructed by the captain to advertise the reward for Marguerite and her son in the towns and villages. He had been on his way to Saint-Vincent to accomplish his mission at the moment when Toussaint's bullet had struck him dead in the saddle. He still carried, suspended by a silken thread around his neck, the sheet of parchment containing the promise of ten gold *écus* to the person who delivered the Lady and heir of Malestroit.

Noël broke the silken thread and read the proclamation. As he read the first lines, his blood curdled in his veins. He crumpled the parchment convulsively and leapt into the saddle of the soldier's well-trained horse, which had remained motionless at the spot where its master had fallen. "I guessed as much!" he said. "They will tempt Judas, and I must make haste if I don't want to arrive too late."

He made a gesture of thanks and farewell to Toussaint, who was running towards him to make sure that he had not been injured. When the powerful Norman horse on which he was now mounted felt his spurs, it departed flat out.

Toussaint came to a halt beside the sergeant's corpse and put a hand to the man's heart, which was no longer beating. The worthy huntsman was pale; sweat was trickling down his forehead. "The man was a Christian," he murmured, "and I'm the one who killed him!"

He knelt down, said a brief prayer, and–as a matter of habit–reloaded his rifle. "I'll think about that for a long time," he went on, shaking his head. If it were a matter of saving my own life, I wouldn't do it again... but it was for my son Noël!"

Beyond the marshes that retain its name, swollen by numerous tributary streams, the Oust runs more rapidly, framed between two escarpment slopes. Several bridges have now been built along its course, but in the time of our story, there was nothing between the marsh and the confluence with the river Vilaine but a few ferries, tenanted according to feudal custom and subject to tolls.

The Vilaine itself had no bridge other than the one at Redon, but at Rieux, the lords of that name had established a passenger ferry that was free to all those wearing military armor. Guy de Plélan, wishing to profit from this generosity, was following the course of the Oust at walking pace, at the head of his 46 men-at-arms. The daylight was already beginning to fade. He had passed the thin bell-tower of Questembert, on his right, and was looking ahead towards the flat and monotonous countryside through which the meager river Vilaine flowed, on which crude Breton frankness had unwaveringly inflicted a name that suited it.

"Blaise," said the captain to the old cavalier who, in the sergeant's absence, was the most important person in the troop, "have you ever heard of this damned thing the people of the marsh call the *White Lady*?"

"I've seen it," Blaise replied.

"You've seen it?"

"At too close a range. This isn't the first time that the men of Rohan have gone to war with Malestroit. One night, when 60 good men were crossing the marshes to surprise the manor of Gourlâ, I suddenly heard its infernal roar. I looked up... on my honor, milord, I saw its white arm, as long as the mainmast of a caravel, reach out towards us and open its claw to seize our boat."

"What did you do, Blaise?" the captain asked, his curiosity mingle with terror.

"I shut my eyes, captain."

"And what happened?"

"Our lookout knew the marshes. He sang some magic charm, and when the White Lady's hand closed, it seized nothing but a fistful of foam from our wake."

"That was lucky, Blaise," said Guy de Plélan, in a speculative tone. "Do you think that a volley of arquebus-fire might send her back into her hole forever?"

Blaise looked at him in amazement. "Arquebuses?" He murmured. "Heavens above! Who'd be bold enough to set light to his tinder within range of the White Lady? Then again, milord, unless you know better, it's not easy to kill phantoms, because they've already died once."

"Ignoramus!" muttered the captain, shrugging his shoulders. Then, addressing the entire troop; "Now then! Do you all recall that young clown who promised us yesterday to put Madame Marguerite into our hands?"

The soldiers replied affirmatively.

"And do you remember," the captain went on, "the generous reward that he was promised?"

"A cap full of Nantais!" cried Blaise. "That's more than an honest soldier would have asked for risking the gallows,"

"Well, my sons," Plélan continued, "remember this and profit from it if you can: the one who brings me Chantepie's head and cap will receive, in exchange for the head, the cap full of Nantais."

At the exact moment when Plélan pronounced Chantepie's name, a shrill and youthful voice, which our readers would doubtless have recognized, burst into song on the far bank. The 46 men-at-arms and their leader turned their heads as one, but they were unable to see anyone; they were facing a dense thicket, which extended as far as the eye could see.

Guy de Plélan brought his horse to a halt and placed his hand over his eyes like a visor, striving to penetrate the greenery interposed between himself and the object of his curiosity. It was in vain. The war-weary detachment resumed its course—but Plélan did not lose sight of the other side of the river and kept watch for some hazard of the terrain that would permit him to glimpse the singer.

"If it's him, as I believe," he murmured, furrowing his bushy brows, "I'll send him running like a badger." All of a sudden, he cried out: "Perish my family! He's on horseback! Wind up your crossbows and get ready!"

Plélan's soldiers were armed for an ambush. Instead of arquebuses, they carried shortened crossbows, and had no other armaments but their pistols. Scarcely had Plélan given the order than all the crossbows, their strings pulled back, were ready to fire. At the same moment, a youth mounted on a sturdy warhorse emerged from the thicket, still singing, and trotted across a little clearing.

Plélan gave a signal, and 46 bolts went whistling across the river.

Chantepie–for it was him–shook himself, and urged his mount to a gallop, but he did not pause in his song.

"Fire again! Fire!" cried Guy de Plélan, furiously.

The soldiers discharged a second volley, too hastily. It was similarly fruitless.

"Perish myself!" howled the captain. "Will this demon always escape us?"

As if he intended to maximize the wrath of the aggressors, Chantepie, before plunging back into the thicket, lifted his cap and gave them an ironic salute from afar.

Plélan, in his impotent range, raised his fist and offered himself to the Devil, as was his habit–but Satan took no account of the offering, for he had regarded the good captain as his legitimate property for some time.

Darkness had fallen. The Rohan men-at-arms had arrived half an hour earlier at the Rieux ferry, and were becoming hoarse cursing the ferryman–who was presumably asleep, or turning a deaf ear, for he had made no reply to their clamor.

"Rohan! Rohan!" cried the captain. "Attend to your duty, wretched vassal!"

No voice replied to this last appeal, but the sound of chains on the far bank announced that the ferry was finally about to come across the river.

"Like master, like vassal," Plélan grumbled. "The people of Rieux don't like Rohan any better than Calvin, and it will give me real satisfaction to box the ears of that sleepyhead who's coming across."

"With respect, unless you know better," Blaise said, in a low voice, "it might be better to delay boxing the ferryman's ears until he's set us down on the other side."

Guy de Plélan sensed the justice of this advice and remained silent.

"How many are you, masters?" the ferryman asked, at that moment.

"Forty-seven," Blaise replied, gently.

"On foot or mounted?"

"Mounted."

"In that case, it'll take six trips; the ferry can only carry nine horsemen."

The first nine men-at-arms got into the ferry and crossed over.

"Blaise," said the captain, "I believe the Devil's whispering in my ear. I can't stop thinking about that accursed imp who escaped us again two hours ago, to the point that the boatman's voice sounds like his."

"The ferryman's voice is deeper and hoarser," Blaise replied.

"A voice can be disguised..."

"Nine more horsemen!" the ferryman's voice said, at that moment, as he reached the bank.

Plélan started on his horse. "Blaise," he murmured. "It's either him, or it's the Devil!"

The old man-at-arms thought that he ought not contradict his leader. He only thought: *That's very unfortunate—milord Guy's gone mad.*

"Nine more horsemen!" the boatman repeated, on returning from his second crossing.

He made that journey, and two others besides. The sixth time, no one remained on the right bank but Plélan and Blaise. Forty-five horsemen were waiting for them on the other shore.

The captain and his confidant dismounted in their turn. Blaise went aboard first. Guy de Plélan, holding his fine horse by the bridle, then set foot on the ferry. The ferryman was positioned on the near side, standing motionless, leaning on his pole. As he passed close by, Plélan darted a sideways glance at him, but the night was dark and all that he could make out was that the ferryman was short in stature and seemed very slender for someone engaged in such heavy labor.

Once we're on the other side, he thought, holding on to the bridle of his horse, *I'll find out what's what.*

Guy de Plélan was mistaken; he did not have to remain in uncertainty for so long.

Before his fine horse had quit the bank, the boatman lifted his pole. Unleashing a violent blow upon the bridle, he forced the captain to let go. At the same time, the captain felt a slap on his face. Then, quicker than a lightning-flash, the boatman jumped on to the bank and shoved the ferry away with his foot.

"Guy de Plélan!" he said, no longer disguising his voice. "In the name of Amaury de Malestroit, my lord and master, I have put my hand on your cheek, which is that of a discourteous and disloyal knight. In the name of the aforesaid lord, I insult you and challenge you, dastardly oppressor of women. God alone can say what the day and place of combat will be, but if Malestroit cannot or does not deign to redeem this pledge, I, Noël Torrec, will kill you, Guy de Plélan! In the meantime, remember that Madame Marguerite is under the protection of the White Lady, and that neither serf nor gentleman shall attack her without mortal peril."

As he spoke these final words, Chantepie threw a little packet into the boat, which was drawing away. Mounting the captain's horse, he departed at a rapid trot.

It was as if Guy de Plélan had been petrified. Astonishment, fury and fear divided his soul and paralyzed his will. His intelligence, violently unsettled, momentarily confounded the witch Ermengarde with Noël Torrec, compounding them into a fantastic enemy that was ungraspable, invincible, ever-ready to pursue him and ever-capable of reaching him.

After a few seconds, he lifted his hand to his cheek, which was still burning from the outrage it had suffered. "Perish my beard!" he said, in a plaintive tone. "Do you think, Blaise, that a slap on the face from the Devil can dishonor a gentleman?"

"If that's the Devil," Blaise replied, "he's not as black as he's painted, for he could have drowned us both. Hang on, milord captain–here's something, Devil or not, that he threw into the boat."

Guy de Plélan took the object that was offered to him and lifted it to his nostrils to see whether or not it gave off a sulphurous odor.

"It's a glove," he said, "and something with... push the boat, Blaise, or the current will carry us off."

Blaise obeyed, and the two latecomers were soon reunited with the 45 men-at-arms waiting on the opposite bank. Little by little, Guy de Plélan recovered his normal disposition, and let all his customary insolence and intrepidity return.

"Well, my sons," he said, as he came ashore, "the Rieux ferryman is a miscreant papist. He's just played us a trick worthy of a hanging. What do you think he deserves in return?"

"The rope!" replied the Huguenots.

"Fie!" cried Plélan. "We've already had a hanging this morning. As good as a dish may be, one tires of it... Blaise, my friend, break down the ferryman's door, tie a stone around his neck and... Are you listening to me? Get on with it!"

With a single blow of his heavy boot, Blaise knocked down the worm-eaten door of the Rieux ferryman's hut. A lamp was lit in the interior, and two women were on their knees, weeping, beside the bed of a dying man.

"Where's the ferryman!" he cried.

The two women gestured mutely, pointing to the moribund man.

"Then who's the man who came to look for us on the other shore?" Blaise demanded.

"I don't know," replied one of the women. "He came to ask for a passage, and when he found us in tears, he took the key to the ferry."

All that's quite natural, Blaise thought. *The Devil has nothing to do with it.* In order to let the poor ferryman die in peace, he threw a large stone into the Vilaine, noisily.

"Is it done?" Plélan demanded, from a distance, having mounted a horse taken from one of his men.

"It's done," Blaise replied.

The detachment resumed its march, and went into Rieux.

When Guy de Plélan had installed himself next to a good fire in the town's only inn, he took from his jerkin the glove and the other object Chantepie had thrown.

"Strike me dumb, it's the parchment!" Blaise cried. "I thought I recognized the sergeant's horse out there in the thicket–no doubt about it now!"

"Do you think that anyone would dare to kill one of Rohan's sergeants?" the captain demanded.

"I don't know–but the hand of one of Rohan's sergeants doesn't open to give up what has been entrusted to him until his heart has stopped beating."

"That's true," murmured Guy de Plélan, putting his head in his hands. Then, as if talking to himself, he repeated Noël Torrec's last words: *The White Lady! Neither serf nor gentleman shall attack her without mortal peril!"*

After encountering the men of Rohan on the bank of the Oust, Noël Torrec had pressed his horse in order to gain speed and arrive at the Rieux ferries before them. We use the plural because there were two of them, one above and the other below the confluence of the Oust and the Vilaine–with the result that, in order to cross the former river, it was necessary, so to speak, to make a tour of its mouth and cross the Vilaine twice.

The youth had not premeditated the audacious deed that we have just seen accomplished, but the opportunity, the desire to punish Plélan's odious proclamation, and the desire to procure a better horse to hasten his course and minimize the danger to Madame Marguerite had determined it. He had heard the repeated call of Rohan's soldiers from the left bank, and had taken the place of the dying ferryman.

All that night he raced full tilt along the road to Vannes, intending to go from there to Port-Louis, then Concarneau, then Quimper, following an itinerary that Toussaint the huntsman had given him. For all his intelligence and intrepidity, however, Noël was still a child. In his reckless impatience, he pressed his horse too hard, and arrived in Vannes on foot, sustained by a staff of holly, which he had cut on the way.

At Vannes, he encountered a brave man to whom he confided that he was in need of a mount and that he possessed the means to buy one. The brave man to whom he spoke thus suddenly remembered that he had to make a pilgrimage to Saint-Anne d'Auray, halfway between Vannes and Port-Louis, which would allow him to accompany the young master for part of his journey. Chantepie was talkative and liked company; he accepted. The brave man procured two horses, and attached a long rapier to his belt, for fear of thieves. They set off together for Auray.

Two leagues from Vannes, the brave man set himself sideways across the road and drew his long rapier.

"What are you doing?" Chantepie asked.

"Accursed papist!" his comrade replied. "Any means is justified to dispossess damned souls like you. I feigned a pilgrimage, because such stupidities inspire confidence in your peers, but I'm a Calvinist! Your purse!" [21]

Chantepie had nothing but a little dagger and bitterly regretted the two long-barrel pistols that he had left hanging from the sides of the captain's saddle. He took out his purse and threw it in the middle of the road.

"Don't move," said the Huguenot, who immediately got down from his horse and grabbed the bridle of Noël's by way of precaution. "Now give me that little gold cross that's hanging round your neck."

"My mother gave it to me," Chantepie murmured, with tears in his eyes. "My mother, who is dead!"

"That's touching, my young master! Give it to me anyway."

Noël lifted up the cord from which his mother's cross was suspended around his neck and gave it to the bandit.

"Now," the latter continued, "I shall only ask for one thing more: that ring shining on your finger."

This was the Lady de Malestroit's ring.

"Never!" cried the youth, forcefully. "Rather die a thousand times!" Drawing his dagger, he prepared himself resolutely for defense.

V. Poor Noël

On seeing Chantepie strike a bellicose pose, the bandit burst out laughing. "Do you think you can pit yourself against me?" he said.

Noël leaned over and tried to strike him with his little dagger, but the Huguenot disarmed him effortlessly.

Poor Chantepie was not in his element here. In the middle of the marsh, with a stout pole in his hands and his new boat beneath his feet, he would have had no fear of the bandit's long rapier, but here, on the highway, mounted on a shabby horse, which he had not yet mastered, he felt despair welling up and took refuge in prayer.

"Leave me my ring," he said. "Let me keep it, for pity's sake."

"You value that ring highly, then?"

"More than my life."

"Then it must be precious and I intend to have it."

A fight began–an unequal fight, whose result was easily predictable. Noël felt his hand crushed by the iron hand of his antagonist, but he would not let go and continued to defend his treasure.

Suddenly, the brigand stopped and cocked his ear.

"Wretch!" cried the youth. "Someone's coming to my aid."

"They'll come too late," replied the Huguenot–and, wanting to put a end to the struggle with a single blow, he struck Noël with his sword.

The poor boy fell, bathed in his own blood–but the bandit was unable to gather the fruit of his cowardly blow. A numerous cavalcade came around a bend in the road, so he only had time to pick up the purse and make off with all possible speed.

The cavalcade was composed of pilgrims on their way to make their devotion to Saint Anne. It stopped at the sight of Noël, who was lying in the middle of the road. The pilgrims all dismounted and gathered around the wounded man, who was put on a hastily-improvised stretcher and carried to a nearby farm. Then, the good pilgrims deposited an offering in the hands of the farmer and continued on their way, glad to have found an opportunity for a charitable deed.

When Chantepie recovered his senses, after a long period of unconsciousness, he found himself lying in a bed. His memory returned, and he lifted up his hand.

"It's there," he murmured, kissing the ring with a kind of passion. "I haven't lost it!"

Exhausted by this effort, he fell back on his bed and went to sleep.

On his return to the Château de la Roche-Bernard after his expedition to Malestroit, Guy de Plélan sent forth his emissaries to find out where Marguerite de Guer had gone. Henceforth, he regarded it as a matter of honor to pursue the war to the death that he had declared against Malestroit. Unintelligent, but possessed of the indomitable courage of the man of war—which has nothing in common with the intelligent intrepidity that is the bravery of heroes—he felt drawn all the more powerfully towards whichever enterprise presented the most terrible dangers. He was firmly convinced, in fact, that his sword, in this instance, would not have to combat mortal men formed like him of flesh and blood. The White Lady of the marshes presented herself incessantly to his excited imagination, and permitted him to divine new and mysterious future perils.

Guy de Plélan, a braggart by nature, braved from afar these perils which he did not understand, forgetful of the terror that had been inspired in him not so long before by a weakling youth whom he had believed to be clothed with a supernatural power.

"Perish me!" he said. "Let this ancient Ermengarde and her page Chantepie come and I'll cut them both up!"

He said that by day, for the most part; at night, when the north wind moaned in the window-frames of la Roche-Bernard, when the woodwork was creaking and cracking, when the ospreys loosed their strident and funereal cries from the roofs, to which the grinding of the weather-vane replied, fraying its rusty axle, the valiant captain summoned Blaise or some other man-at-arms to his side, in order to have someone to talk to. On those occasions, he swore less and drank more, until the point at which, having drunk enough, he recovered the courage to swear properly.

He often spent long hours with Blaise in this fashion. No matter what he did, his preoccupation always ended up taking hold of him, and the names of Ermengarde and Chantepie, which he united in his hatred as in his secret dread, emerged continually from his mouth, accompanied by a variety of maledictions, for which the blasphemers of our times have not retained the recipes.

Blaise, who was a skeptic, let his captain talk or joined in the chorus, but within his private thoughts, he was persuaded that Chantepie and the White Lady were, on the one hand, a bold and clever youth, and on the other, a pinch of dust at the bottom of a tomb and a wisp of fog on the marsh.

Despite his efforts, Gut de Plélan's search bore no results. He spent two months idling at la Roche-Bernard without learning anything regarding the hiding-place of Lady de Malestroit and her son. Becoming desperate in consequence, he resolved to conduct the search personally, and departed one morning for Malestroit, assuming that if Marguerite had not rejoined her husband, she must have taken refuge with one of her vassals.

"Milord Guy," Blaise said to him, as he took off his boots, "there's a peasant in the outer courtyard who claims to be in possession of important secrets. He's asking for an interview with you."

"Have someone bring my supper," the captain replied.

"And the bumpkin?"

"What bumpkin?"

"The one who's asking to see you."

"Tell him to go to the Devil–and have someone bring my supper."

"So be it," said Blaise. "The peasant might know where Lady de Malestroit is hiding, though."

Gut de Plélan darted a sly glance at the portrait of Madame Ermengarde which he had brutally mutilated during his previous visit to the château. Half of Ermengarde's face had been torn away, but the one eye that remained to her seemed to have taken on a threatening expression. The narrow slit beneath its half-closed eyelid emitted such a sinister gleam that the good captain felt a shiver. He had no recourse but wine to conquer his superstitious fear.

"Have someone serve my supper!" he repeated, for the third time, in a voice that he intended to be imperious, but which was shot through with secret distress.

Blaise hastened to obey.

Left alone, Guy de Plélan began to pace back and forth along the length of the hall, taking large strides. He was pale; his lips moved convulsively. Every time he passed in front of the part of the tapestry where the image of Ermengarde was reproduced, he shut his eyes and increased his pace. A mysterious and invincible attraction seemed to draw him towards that fearful image, however; he always came back to it.

Finally, his forehead suddenly reddened. He seized a torch and advanced resolutely upon the tapestry, staring straight at it.

"This is the legend that demon Chantepie recounted to me," he murmured. "The witch smiles and beckons, while the poor French knight..." He interrupted himself abruptly. "Perish my blood! The Frenchman looks like me, feature for feature!"

He lifted up his torch and examined his reflection in a little square looking-glass suspended between two window-panes. Whether there really was a resemblance between the Frenchman and himself, or whether his disturbed imagination had confused his sight, the mirror showed him, instead of his own image, that of the knight represented on the tapestry. The torch slipped out of his tremulous hand.

"Help!" he cried, in a choked voice. "The accursed woman is strangling me! The vortex will open and close again on my crushed bones! Help!"

The torch had gone out. Guy, suddenly plunged into darkness and prey to a veritable delirium, drew his sword and engaged in a furious combat against his imaginary enemy.

"Take that, witch!" he said, eventually, and plunged his sword into the tapestry all the way to the hilt.

The reappearance of Blaise, who returned with a valet carrying wine and foodstuffs, immediately dispelled the captain's hallucination. Nevertheless, as he withdrew his embedded blade from the tapestry, he saw with a certain horror that instead of piercing Ermengarde he had run the Frenchman through the heart.

"Perish my bones!" he groaned. "All this is the Devil's work—but never let it be said that Guy de Plélan recoiled before a nightmare. Drink!"

He downed several cupfuls of wine one after the other, and soon recovered the haughty manner appropriate to one of Rohan's lieutenants.

"Didn't you say something about a serf asking for an audience?" he said to Blaise. "Have him brought in."

Blaise went out and returned almost immediately, followed by a peasant of coarse and cunning appearance, who came forward with his eyes lowered, twisting the brim of an enormous linen hat in his hands. He was a man of about 50. His greying hair hung down over his forehead, almost reaching his bushy eyebrows, giving his physiognomy a villainous appearance that gave the lie to the complaisant smile sustained by a large mouth furnished with false teeth.

Plélan, who was just emptying his tenth glass, had recovered his uncouth cheerfulness.

"Here's an ugly fellow!" he cried, bursting out laughing. "What do they call you, my friend?"

"Renot, if it pleases you, milord."

"It pleases me. Where are you from?"

"Gourlâ, in Saint-Vincent, on the far side of the marsh."

"Oh yes? And what do you want?"

Renot scratched his ear and reinforced his smile. "It's been put about over there," he replied, "that milord would give a good deal to find Madame Marguerite..."

"You know where she is?" Plélan cried, excitedly.

"Not exactly, by my faith," the rustic replied, with equal vivacity.

Plélan, who had come to his feet, sat down again in an ill humor.

"That's the exact truth," the peasant went on. "Who would have told me? But I have my suspicions."

"You've guessed it?"

"Not exactly. With all respect to you, master, I didn't say that... except... the gossip over there is that milord would give a capful of Nantais *écus*..."

"I have promised it; I shall keep my promise!"

"A cap like this?" Renot asked, his grey eyes suddenly raised, shining with a wild and extraordinary avidity." And he spread out his hat, whose brim unrolled as far as the ground.

"Heavens above!" cried Blaise. "Here's a cunning fellow! One could easily fit three heads like his into his hat, and his donkey's as well."

Plélan imposed silence with a gesture. "Your cap is broad and deep, my man," he said. "No matter—I'll fill it with Nantais."

The peasant did a little dance, and winked his eye.

"Speak," said Plélan. "Where is Lady de Malestroit?"

"Where is she?" repeated Renot, with seeming astonishment.

"Don't you know anything?"

"Not exactly–I'll tell you no lies! But I have my suspicions."

Guy de Plélan had no more patience than the average fighting man of his time. Renot's shrewd simplicity made him very angry, and he felt a powerful urge to have him hanged from one of the nails that had previously served the two men-at-arms–but he restrained himself. He was used to the crafty attitude that Breton peasants adopt with regard to their superiors, and restricted himself to saying, coldly: "This brave man is in no position to earn the promised recompense. Have him shown out of the château!"

Renot bowed awkwardly and took a few steps towards the door–but he turned round before reaching the threshold. "If it pleases milord," he said. "We might make an agreement."

"Speak–but hurry!"

"This is what Milord should do. He should place a sentinel on the edge of the marsh–on this side, mind, for it's necessary not to frighten the prey that one wants to catch in a snare. This sentinel may sleep by day, if it suits him, but he should keep watch all night. When he sees a fire lit on the heights of Saint-Vincent, that will be the signal that milord can cross the water with his men-at-arms–and that he'll need the Nantais to fill my poor cap."

"You'll deliver Marguerite to me?"

"Not exactly–but I'll tell you where she is."

Plélan smiled, and nodded his head by way of consent. Renot climbed back on his donkey to return to the marsh.

A long time had passed since Chantepie had departed. Marguerite de Guer lived alone in her little manor-house at Gourlâ, never leaving her secret room, because Toussaint the huntsman had got wind of Guy de Plélan's promises. He knew that the people living on the edges of the marsh were very poor, and that poverty advises evil in every land; he feared everyone and trusted no one.

One man in particular excited his suspicion. It was a field-digger [22] of rather bad repute who lived in the village of Saint-Vincent. This man—who was none other than Renot—wandered past the manor-house more often than he needed to, and sometimes passed whole days nearby, under the pretext of sharpening his mattock, watching the windows of Gourlâ. Toussaint had threatened him with his carbine more than once, But Renot, guided by an instinct that we can only compare to the nose of a bloodhound, was suspicious, and continued his inquiry.

"Don't be so hard on the poor, master," he said to Toussaint. "In these accursed times, with the heretics roaming the fields, one likes to rest close to the house of a servant of the Holy Church. What harm do you see in that?"

Toussaint shook his head. Something told him that the wretch was a traitor, a spy—having no proof, though, he dared not chase him away by force for fear of exciting suspicion in the neighborhood. To ward off the danger that he could not directly oppose, he became increasingly watchful over his mistress. Marguerite de Guer never had permission to go outdoors, except, occasionally, on the darkest of nights. On such occasions, she dressed in peasant costume and walked on the edge of the marsh, supported on the huntsman's arm. They both watched the other shore avidly, in case a flame might be ignited in the midst of the darkness, among the trees of the Forêt-Neuve, to announce that the hour of deliverance was nigh.

But no flame appeared on the other side of the marsh. Days passed, then weeks, and there was no hint of an end to that perilous captivity.

What had become of Noël Torrec? Could the poor youth have survived the fatigue and the perils of the journey? He was brave, but he was frail, and in these unhappy times there were many obstacles that a man in the prime of life might not be able to overcome.

"Poor Noël!" thought old mère Toussaint. "He was so handsome, so good, so generous!"

"I should have gone in his place," the huntsman told himself.

"The unfortunate child has perished in trying to serve me!" Lady de Malestroit thought.

And all three repeated, tearfully "Poor Noël!"

It had been the week of All Saints [23] when the young messenger had departed, and the end of the year was approaching. It was Christmas Day. Scarcely any hope remained that the youth would come back.

Madame Marguerite spent that day—which the Church celebrates cheerfully as one of the most important of its festivals—quite miserably. She could not go out to mingle her voice with the songs of the Catholic villagers singing the Lord's praises. The sound of the bells of the parish of Saint-Vincent, silvery and joyful, reached the manor-house, but she was forbidden to respond to their pious appeal.

"Toussaint," she said, when dusk fell, "I would like to go pray to God at the foot of the cross in the marsh."

"Noble mistress," the good servant replied, "the Moon is shining in the sky; to go out at this hour would be imprudent."

"Who will be able to see me?" cried Marguerite, impatiently. "Who will recognize me in my vassal's costume? It's Christmas Day, Toussaint; the poor child named after it is probably dead. I want to kneel in the dust of the road and pray for him—I need to."

Toussaint did not reply. Respect might not have been sufficient to close his mouth, but the name of Noël, whom he loved as much as any father had ever loved a son, softened his heart. He shook his head sadly and kept silent.

"Thank you, my noble lady, thank you!" murmured old Marthe, whose eyes were full of ears. "Thank you for having thought of Noël, our beloved. Go! God will grant your prayer, and Noël, if he is no longer..." She could not finish the sentence. "No, oh no," she went on, "Noël is not dead. My poor eyes will see him again before they close forever."

Marguerite de Guer hid her delicate figure beneath the folds of a monastic cloak and went out, supported on Toussaint's arm.

As they crossed the threshold, the huntsman thought he saw a shadow slip behind the hedgerow. He went back in and picked up his crossbow.

As they went along the road, Lady de Malestroit rejoiced and breathed the pure country air delightedly. The wind was cold and sharp. Toussaint felt anxious; he paused occasionally, and his eye interrogated the tall palisades of stone that border almost all the cultivated fields in that part of Brittany. Two or three times more, he thought he saw a human form moving furtively behind the walls.

When they arrived at the foot of the marsh cross, Lady de Malestroit knelt down and said a short prayer. Then she got up, and Toussaint, whose turn it was to be glad, hurried back to the manor-house.

"My reliquary!" Marguerite said, all of a sudden. "I've lost my reliquary."

They were 200 paces from the cross. When Toussaint turned around, he could see an object on the steps reflecting the rays of moonlight and sparkling in the shadows. He immediately turned back–but before he had crossed half the intervening distance, a man climbed over the wall of the neighboring field, ran to the cross and seized the reliquary.

"I suspected as much!" muttered the thief, as he fled as fast as his legs could carry him.

Toussaint had recognized Renot, the field-digger, at a glance. He shouldered his crossbow immediately and the bolt whistled away.

Renot let out a sharp and plaintive cry, but he must only have been wounded, for he reached the heathland slope before Toussaint could take aim again, and vanished into the gorse.

"Madame," said Toussaint gravely, as he rejoined Marguerite, "is the Malestroit coat-of-arms engraved on your reliquary?"

"It was a gift from my husband Amaury," Marguerite replied. "The enamel on the lid bears the seven gold mascles of Guer, quartered with the red rose of Malestroit." [24]

"May God help us, then!" Toussaint said, dispiritedly. "our secret is in the hands of a traitor, who will probably sell it tomorrow for a pinch of gold."

VI. Two Signals Instead of One

In the meantime, Noël Torrec had continued his journey. He had been ill for more than a month in the farm near Auray, where he had been accommodated after his misadventure. This delay made him very impatient, but he consoled himself with the thought that he still had Lady Marguerite's ring on his finger–the ring that would guarantee the credence of Lord de Malestroit.

One morning, therefore, still weak and feeling the after-effects of his wound, he took his leave of the good people who had helped him and went on his way. He no longer had a horse and his purse was empty, but as compensation, he had a light heart and savored the sense of well-being that follows a successful convalescence.

He sang as he went along the road. When he felt hungry, he begged a morsel of bread; when he needed sleep, he made his bed in a barn. Occasionally, when he stopped at the home of some rich laborer, he earned a place at the table and a good bed by singing his merry village songs or reciting the story of the White Lady of the Marshes. They listened to him and fêted him then; the housewives, as he departed, slipped a few provisions into his bag and a few pennies into his purse. He sang so well and told stories so fluently! Then again, the unaccustomed pallor that his wound had conferred on his face went so well with its frame of black curly hair.

Eventually, marching in stages and going astray from time to time on deserted roads, he arrived within view of the city of Quimper. It was a moment of great joy, for that was the destination of his journey–but the joy was of short duration. Noël's eyes searched for the tents and armorial pennants of Messieurs de Guer and de Malestroit, but no matter how hard he looked, he saw nothing.

There was arid heath everywhere, cut by narrow bands of stubble in cultivated enclaves, a few stunted and leafless trees scattered here and there, and–in the distance–grey mountains confused with the grey clouds on the horizon. There was, however, no sign of the movement that a troop of men of war produces. Nowhere in the plain were there groups of foraging mercenaries, pursuing and being pursued; nowhere could he discern the sparkling reflections that aristocratic armor disperses in sheaves, even beneath the pale sun of Cornouailles.

Chantepie lowered his head sadly. He would have given a year of his life to hear the bellicose sound of the Malestroit horn; he would have heard ecstatically, as one listens to delightful music, the roar of the town's culverins or the dry strident rattle of an arquebusade. Just as he saw nothing, though, he heard nothing.

"Has Milord Amaury met his death, along with all his vassals?" Noël asked himself. "Or shall I find him in the leisure of triumph in the city of Quimper, which lies so seemingly bleak and silent where the road turns?"

As he formulated this question, leaning on his staff, he saw the gate of the city open. A few old men, mounted on mules, came out; then the gate was closed behind them. As the old men came closer, Noël made out their cowls and their large tonsures. He recognized them as monks, and ran joyfully to ask for their fatherly blessing.

"May God bless you, child," said the first of the monks in a slow, sad voice. "May God bless you, if you are within the bosom of the Holy Church; may he bless you still, if you are a Huguenot, for we are constrained to return good for evil."

"I'm a Catholic," Noël replied, "and I'm going to Quimper to deliver a message to Malestroit, my liege-lord."

The first monk had not reined in his mule; the others passed by in silence, limiting themselves to making the sign of the blessing above Noël's head. They all did so until the last, who was a lay brother burdened with infirmity and old age. This one was even more mournful than his superiors. His bald head hung forward almost to the neck of his mule; he was sighing deeply, and a tear was suspended from the whitened lashes of his eyelid.

"Turn your back on Quimper, my son," he said to Noël, "if you are a servant of the Church. The heretics have been masters of the city for two days, and here we are–us!–chased out of our retreat and going forth at hazard, not knowing where we shall rest our weary limbs when night comes."

"And Monsieur de Guer? And Lord de Malestroit?" Noël asked, his heart filled with anguish.

"They were good Christians and valiant lords!" relied the monk, shaking his head.

"Are they dead, then?"

"Three days ago, Monsieur de Guer quit this life and died within the walls of our convent... Our convent, alas, which I shall never see again! As for Milord Amaury, it's said that he was able to retreat at the head of a few cavaliers."

"And where shall I find him, father?"

"I don't know... May God protect you, my son! The road is long, and I am very old."

With these words, the monk pricked his mule in order to catch up with his superiors.

Noël sat down on the dewy grass on the verge of the road. Bitter sobs racked his breast; he felt his courage becoming numb.

"Vanquished!" he murmured. "Vanquished, fugitive... Perhaps dead."

Then he added, despairingly: "Who will save Madame Marguerite now?"

Noël fell asleep. He had a strange dream.

He saw Madame de Malestroit abandoned in the middle of the marsh, pursued by a hideous monster. He, Noël, was too feeble to fight the monster. He called to the White Lady and showed her Marguerite, who was dying.

The White Lady stretched out her two long arms. With one hand, she seized Marguerite, whom she set in the shelter in one of the folds of her robe of mist; with the other, she choked the monster, whose crushed bones she hurled into the whirlpool.

Then he awoke with a start. The heavy footfalls of war-horses were shaking the ground. Noël rubbed his eyes, and by the dim light of dusk, which had fallen while he was asleep, he saw horsemen coming towards him. They were coming from Quimper.

Chantepie hurriedly jumped off the embankment on which he had fallen asleep, and crouched down behind the hedge.

The horsemen were laughing, singing and chatting; the barrels of their arquebuses were visible here and there.

"Now then, my sons," said the man who marched at their head, "we'll have to hold our tongues soon, if we want to surprise the wild boar in his lair and lay him low without his making us feel his horns."

"Bah!" replied another. "His horns are cropped, and we'll get the toothless prey cheaply."

"Take care!" the first countered. "No matter how far we have cast him down, Malestroit is cornered, and before we sound his death-knell, more than one of among you will have been unhorsed."

Chantepie put his hand on his heart to contain its precipitate beating. He ran noiselessly along the hedge in order to follow the horsemen, and cocked his ears avidly.

"He'll die as old de Guer died... a valiant soldier."

"A valiant soldier, yes... How many men-at-arms has Malestroit conserved?"

"I don't know, exactly," replied the leader of the detachment, laughing. "His camp, two leagues from here on the Faouët road, consists of four tents."

The Huguenot cavaliers let loose a chorus of laughter. "With our 60 arquebuses," one of them said, "and the advantage that surprise will give us, Malestroit won't stand a chance."

They continued chattering noisily and uninhibitedly for half an hour; then silence was established in their ranks. Noël was still following them. He did not know the precise spot at which Amaury de Malestroit was camped and could not go on ahead to warn him.

"Hide your gun-barrels!" said the leader of the Huguenots abruptly, as they reached a junction in the road,

Chantepie threw himself forward along the embankment beside the road, risking discovery, and perceived a fire burning in the fields. Then he picked up his pace and tried to force himself ahead of the detachment—but the nearer the horsemen came to their objective, the more they increased their own pace, and Noël was very tired. All that he could do was remain level with the foremost of the Huguenots. He despaired, sensing that he would arrive too late.

Fortunately, the horsemen had no suspicion of his presence. Within arquebus-range of the camp, they came to a halt in order to arrange their final disposition at their leisure. Malestroit's soldiers were now easily discernible, seated or lying around a large fire. Standing up, to one side, a dozen men-at-arms were holding council. This was all that remained of the army that had recently swept victoriously across southern Brittany under the command of the bastard of Lorraine, Monsieur de Mercoeur.

Chantepie, exhausted by fatigue, recovered his strength at that moment. He rapidly crossed the distance separating him from the camp, and fell breathless at Malestroit's feet.

"Flee!" he said. "There's no time for self-defense. Sixty arquebuses are pointed at you at this very moment."

"Who are you to tell a Malestroit to flee?" the other demanded.

"Alas, milord," Noël said, setting one knee on the ground, "I am your humble vassal, and I have come on behalf of Madame Marguerite, who requires your help."

"Marguerite!" cried Lord de Malestroit, going pale.

"Flee! For pity's sake, flee!" Chantepie repeated. "Who will protect Madame Marguerite and her son if you succumb?"

Amaury passed his hand over his face. Involuntarily, he turned his gaze towards the Quimper road and saw a dozen luminous points gleaming in the shadows.

"There are arquebuses out there, for sure!" he said. Then, turning towards the soldiers lying beside the fire, he cried: "On guard! Crawl to the tents and grab your weapons."

In response to this movement, the Huguenot soldiers set off, covering the distance that separated them from Malestroit's men at the gallop.

"Raise your weapons!" cried the leader.

Sixty detonations followed close on his command.

"Malestroit! Malestroit! For Notre-Dame de Bruc!" Amaury cried in his turn, having leapt up on his horse.

A few soldiers got up here and there; the greater number had been felled by the arquebusade.

At the very moment when the Huguenots were rejoining and crying "Form up!" however, Amaury—emerging from the shadows at the head of his dozen men-at-arms—fell upon them unexpectedly. There was a horrible mêlée. Every time Malestroit raised his heavy sword, a man fell. After 20 minutes, some 20 Huguenots, bruised, lamed or wounded, were returning full tilt along the road to Quimper.

"Where's the boy who raised the alarm?" Amaury demanded, wiping his sword on the mane of his horse.

Chantepie presented himself. He too held a sword in his hand—a bloody sword.

"Good lad!" cried Amaury, joyously. "It seems to me that we've got an extra man-at-arms! How old are you, valiant champion?"

Chantepie did not reply and lowered his head sadly. "I wish to Heaven, milord," he said, "that all those brave soldiers who are lying in the dust were standing in my place, still capable of mounting a horse. I can't replace them, and Madame Marguerite..."

"Marguerite!" said Malestroit, interrupting him. "I did not want to let you speak before the battle, because there are words that soften the heart of a knight, but now... What has happened?"

Chantepie took Marguerite's ring from his finger and held it out to his lord. Amaury lifted it to his lips. "If I had seen this," he murmured, "I would have departed without drawing my sword."

"And you would have done well, milord."

Chantepie told him about the taking of Malestroit and Marguerite's flight. The further his story went, the darker Amaury's complexion became. The poor lord ran his gaze around the camp scattered with corpses, and counted despairingly the few men-at-arms that remained to him.

"No matter," he said. "Mount up."

"There's something else I have to tell you," Chantepie went on. "Once, during my journey, I found myself face to face with Guy de Plélan."

"And what did you do?"

"I struck him in the face and called him a traitor and a coward."

"You!" Malestroit cried, astonished.

"Then," Noël continued, "I threw my glove at him, challenging him in the name of Amaury de Malestroit, my liege-lord, to a duel to the death without quarter."

"Well done, child! Well done, by Our Lady! You have performed the act of a noble man, and I thank you for your great heart. Mount up! Mount up!"

The remainder of the little troop gathered around its leader and they departed at a gallop along the Vannes road.

Marguerite de Guer returned sadly to the manor-house of Gourlâ. She was distraught at the loss of her reliquary, solely because it was a gift from her husband, and was quite oblivious to the dire consequences of that unfortunate occurrence.

Toussaint's reaction was quite different. The worthy huntsman had suspected Renot for some time of being one of Plélan's spies, or at the very least of being a wretch intent on discovering his mistress's hiding-place in order to sell the information to the Huguenots. The eagerness with which Renot had hastened to seize the reliquary, risking his life, and his presence in the environs of the manor at that hour, combined to turn Toussaint's doubts into certainty.

If only, he thought, striking his crossbow, *I had had my good carbine instead of this child's toy, the fool would not now be holding the fate of a noble house in his hands. In the meantime, we must find another hiding-place from tomorrow on... And God alone knows what retreat we shall be able to find!*

This was the object of Toussaint's meditations when, just as they were leaving the rich grass of the march to take the rocky path that climbed towards Gourlâ, Marguerite suddenly stopped and released an exclamation.

"Look! Look!" she said, pointing at the other bank.

"The signal!" cried Toussaint, suddenly passing from misery to the most extravagant joy. "Thanks be to God, who has come to our aid in our moment of peril!"

A flame, feeble at first and veiled by smoke, was glimmering amid the trees of the Forêt-Neuve. Soon it was throwing forth jets of purple, illuminating the leafless branches.

"Saved! Saved!" cried the châtelaine and the faithful servant, in unison.

They returned in all haste to the manor. Toussaint's first impulse was to have Lady de Malestroit and her son climb aboard the boat, without wasting time going to look for Noël on the far shore, but he remembered the perils his mistress had already run during a similar crossing. Since that time, the waters had grown considerably; the marsh had become a vast lake, whose rapid and changeable currents would test the practical skills of a professional boatman. The huntsman resolved to go in search of Chantepie. Hastily exchanging his crossbow for his heavy wheel-lock rifle, he ran to unhitch the young water-chestnut-fisherman's skiff, and immediately quit the bank.

Chantepie and the master of Malestroit were waiting for a response to the signal, hidden within the trees of the Forêt-Neuve. The Moon was hidden behind thick clouds; nothing was visible but the lake, save for the immense outline of the White Lady, whose contours stood out vaguely from the dark horizon, seemingly radiant with a pale and phosphorescent gleam.

As if he were anxious to pierce the darkness, Noël was darting avid glances in every direction; he could see nothing.

"If we have come too late...!" said the master of Malestroit, whose voice betrayed a poignant emotion.

"Shh!" said Noël, instead of replying. He had just heard a noise on the marsh that was not the sound of the Trémeulé whirlpool. "He's coming," he said.

The master of Malestroit pricked up his ears, but one needs to be a child of the marsh to catch the sound of an oar cleaving the water a thousand yards away in the midst of the thousandfold clatter of a furious inundation. Lord de Malestroit could not hear anything.

"Listen!" said Chantepie, again.

Putting both his hands, formed into a horn, in front of his mouth, he made that strange and prolonged cry, particular to the countryside around Vannes which, muffled at first, increases into two dissonant cadences, and dies away into a guttural bass-note.

The effect was entirely different from what he intended.

Two similar cries replied at the same time. One came from the open water; the other came from the depths of the forest.

"We're not the only ones on watch," Chantepie said, in a low voice, "and that approaching boat might not be for us...

110

but may I die if that isn't the oar-stroke of my father the huntsman."

As he completed this speech, a sudden gleam of light sprang up, drawing a line of illumination across the lake. Noël and the master of Malestroit raised their heads, instinctively following the angle of reflection and saw a fire lit on the summit of the Saint-Vincent hill, several hundred yards to the left of the little manor-house of Gourlâ.

"What's that?" asked the knight.

"I don't know," the youth replied, "but strange things are happening here tonight, milord."

An arquebus shot resounded in the forest, close to the spot from which the second cry had come—the one that had astonished Chantepie. Almost immediately, the hoofbeats of several horses became audible, descending towards the marsh.

"Perish my bones!" cried one of the horsemen, passing so close to the master of Malestroit that he could have reached out and touched him. "We'll have her his time, my sons, and the peasant shall have his capful of Nantais!"

"That's Guy de Plélan," Chantepie murmured.

Malestroit put his hand on his sword and was about to throw himself in pursuit, but Noël restrained him.

"When I bring Madame Marguerite back to the shore," he said, "it's necessary that she find a husband, and her son a father. Milord, guard your life dearly, so as not to leave those who are dear to you without support."

Amaury groped in the darkness for the youth's hand, to shake it like a friend's.

Since Renot's expedition to the château, Plélan had established a sentinel in the forest, and a detachment of his men in a guardsman's hut a short distance away, ever-ready to cross the water as soon as the signal was given. He often came to visit the sentry-post himself, and swore by the death of all his limbs that the clown Renot would pay dear for too long a delay. He happened to be at the guard-house when the fire appeared on the hill of Saint-Vincent; warned by the arquebus shot fired by his sentry, he hurried to the shore of the marsh.

While he was embarking very noisily on a vessel much larger and more artfully-constructed than the poor boats of the region, Toussaint's skiff silently came aground on the bank.

Chantepie, who had been waiting for that moment, leapt to the side of his adoptive father and took up his pole. Then, as if they had been given the word of command, the two vessels left the shore at the same time.

VII. The Trémeulé Whirlpool

A dying light was still visible in the forest: the fire lit by Chantepie. Renot's threw off red sparks, and drew a purple trail across the lake.

The master of Malestroit, left alone on the bank, tried to assuage his anguish by thinking about the happiness of the ardently-anticipated reunion; he imagined Marguerite's joy, and extended his arms as if to clasp his son to his breast–but the anguish returned, tenacious and ineradicable. It clutched at his heart, changing hope into dread and happiness into torture.

That fire, whose reflections took on the color of blood in traversing the humid atmosphere of he marsh, was a signal. That signal had put Plélan and his soldiers in motion. Was it not a new danger for Marguerite? But if it were a new danger, Malestroit's sword would play no part in the struggle. He must stand and wait–wait, at the moment of peril!

The two boats were not traveling with equal velocity. Plélan's, carrying six men-at-arms and steered by two local boatmen, moved haltingly through the utter darkness enshrouding the lake, losing time in avoiding the currents. Chantepie's sped in a straight line, like an arrow loosed at a target. When the depth permitted it, Noël left the oars to the huntsman and leant on his pole; then he seized the oars again, and the skiff flew, skimming the water with its flat keel-less bottom.

"Keep going, Noël my son!" Toussaint said. "That fire shining over there is a Judas signal, and here, just behind us, are those who will pay the 30 pieces of silver."

"The White Lady is behind us," Noël replied. "We have a quarter of an hour in hand, and only need five minutes to reach the manor. Madame Marguerite will be with us before they've touched the bank."

"It won't be enough, Noël."

Toussaint pronounced these words slowly. Touching the youth's shoulder, he pointed at the sky.

A large mass of cloud covered the entire southwestern reach of the firmament. The air was calm; that immense curtain, immobile and cut cleanly at the zenith, left half the heavens exposed.

"The Moon's in its second quarter," Toussaint went on. "In a quarter of an hour, it'll turn the edge of that cloud silver. In 20 minutes, we'll see the ruddy ring surrounding it appear– and then..."

"Are you quite sure that it's as high as that already, père Toussaint?" Noël exclaimed.

"I can see it," the huntsman replied. "I sense it behind the cloud that yet covers it. Keep going, Noël my son, for the salvation of Madame Marguerite and her son is in your hands again."

"We shall save her, père Toussaint, we shall save her!" the youth said, forcefully.

They could no longer hear the other boat's oars, but Plélan' voice reached them, urging and rebuking his oarsmen.

When they reached the bank, the Moon was still behind the cloud, but the light vapors floating at the zenith were whitening, seemingly illuminated by a mysterious radiance. Toussaint threw himself forward and raced along the path to Gourlâ. As he entered the manor-house, he raised his head and saw a ruddy semicircle in the sky, cut in the middle by the edge of the cloud.

"Quickly, my noble lady, quickly!" he cried from the threshold.

Marguerite was ready. Toussaint took the child in his arms, and they both ran at full speed back down the path that led to the marsh. As they came out on to the grass, the Moon's narrow edge came clear of the cloud and the tips of the lake's little waves began to sparkle in the distance. Chantepie, whose eyes were peeled, saw Plélan's boat some 200 or 300 yards to the left, forcefully propelled by its oars. Marguerite crossed the grass. As she set foot on the skiff, the Moon's disc was gradually being unmasked, inundating the marsh with its rays.

"Hide!" exclaimed Noël. "Lie down in the bottom of the skiff."

Marguerite obeyed, but it was too late; her white dress, suddenly and vividly illuminated, had attracted the attention of the men of Rohan. If he had not recognized her, Plélan had guessed who she was, and a cry of rage rose from his lungs.

"Row, clowns!" he said, in a broken voice. "I must have my prey, or die trying... row!"

The boat came about. Instead of continuing toward the bank, it maneuvered in such a way as to bar the passage of Noël's skiff, which had taken off, as mariners say, and was in full flight.

The Oust marsh had changed its appearance completely since Lady de Malestroit's first crossing. Two months had passed in the meantime; the waters had grown, covering the various islets and promontories that had still shown their heads at the beginning of autumn. Only one point remained uncovered on the entire surface of the lake. This was a kind of cape formed by the prolongation of the chain of small hills on which Gourlâ was situated. It extended quite a way into the marsh, and was known as the *Pointe-aux-Halbrans*. In winter, when the waters were at their highest, the isthmus disappeared; nothing remained but the point itself–which, retaining half of its name, was then called the *Île-aux-Halbrans*.[25] It reared up at the point where the Oust marshes attained their greatest breadth, located on a line perpendicular to the course of the river as it passed the Trémeulé whirlpool.

The two boats were running parallel to the shore. Noël was waiting for a favorable opportunity to change direction and head for his true goal, to which his flank was turned—but it was soon obvious that no such opportunity would present itself. With every minute that passed, he lost some of his advantage. Plélan's boat, impelled by four oars and better-constructed than his own, grew in the moonlight and threatened to drive him into the bank before much longer.

The two enemy crews could see one another almost as well as in daylight. Chantepie had counted six men-at-arms in Plélan's boat, but the latter could no longer see anyone in the skiff but Toussaint and Noël. Lady de Malestroit, distraught and more dead than alive, was still lying on the damp boards of the hull.

"Blaise," Plélan said to his usual confidant, "look at that young clown over there in the skiff, who plies the oar so skillfully."

"I see him," Blaise replied.

"Don't you think he resembles that accursed imp who stole my horse at the Rieux ferry?"

Blaise peered attentively, then silently stood erect.

"Well?" said the captain.

"Milord," said Blaise, shaking his head, "my opinion is that the youth is flesh and blood, like your lordship and myself—but that youth is worth as much as a man. To tell the truth, I'd even rather see a man in his place."

"So you recognized him?"

"Yes, milord."

Plélan tugged on the cord that secured an enormous gourd about his neck, and lifted the gourd to his lips.

"Well, Blaise," he said, when he had got his breath back after drinking, "here I am facing both my enemies: the imp there, the witch here." He extended his hand toward the White Lady of the Marshes. "Perish me!" he continued. "I'll strangle the imp and spit in the witch's face."

"Neither one, nor the other!" replied Noël's voice in the distance.

Plélan felt himself shiver.

"Blaise," he said, going pale, "did I speak so loudly just now that a human ear could hear me at such a distance? No matter–even if he's the Devil, I'll wring his neck. Row, all of you!"

Plélan's boat had gained ground. It was now scarcely 200 yards from the skiff. The two vessels were at the two bases of an isosceles triangle whose tip was the Île-aux-Halbrans. It seemed highly probable that the skiff would have to double the islet on the shore side and the boat on the side of the open water. Now, because the shore on the far side of the islet became narrower and more steeply-sloped, forming a sort of funnel that terminated the lake to the west, the dénouement was approaching rapidly.

"Put your pole down and get your carbine ready, père Toussaint," Noël said, in a low voice. "Speed can't save us."

The huntsman laid down his pole dispiritedly.

"Let's see if you're as good a shot as you say," Noël said.

"What good will it do to kill one man?" the huntsman said, sadly. "I have but one charge."

"With God's help, that will suffice. Listen, père Toussaint. Their boat's turning; it's coming toward us–so much the better! Get your weapon ready, and take aim at the oar on the right at the moment when it emerges from the water. Ready... fire!"

The shot was fired, and the bullet struck the oar at the outset of its blade. The oar did not break on the impact, but when the oarsman plunged it into the water again, it cracked under the force of his pull. The boat, lamed, turned about on itself and took some time to recover its course.

While Plélan cursed and his oarsmen tried to repair the damage, Noël doubled the Île-aux-Halbrans.

"Père Toussaint," he said, rapidly, "it's necessary for us to part here."

The huntsman looked at him in astonishment. Chantepie went on, in a firm, almost imperious, tone: "We must separate,

I tell you. I'm not strong enough to compete with Rohan's oarsmen, and Madame Marguerite's salvation is not in this skiff. Get up, go ashore, and hide in the willows."

"But..." the huntsman attempted to object.

"Time's pressing," Noël put in, impatiently. "I can hear the boat–it's doubling the isle. Farewell, père Toussaint! You and my noble lady are not required for the battle I must fight against the Huguenots."

Toussaint, submissive to the empire that the youth had taken upon himself, obeyed without further reply. He took Marguerite de Guer in his wiry arms, deposited her on the ground and leapt after her.

"Farewell!" Chantepie repeated, hauling on the oars and heading back into the marsh.

Plélan's oarsmen were undoubtedly waiting for this final maneuver, for they were ready to continue the chase in this new direction.

Once he was alone in his skiff, Chantepie took a deep breath, like a man relieved of a crushing burden. Then he leaned on his oars to test his lightened boat; he knew, without a doubt, that he could now escape Plélan's pursuit–but that was not his plan.

Far from continuing his efforts, he set himself to float nonchalantly, in such a manner as to allow the distance between the boats to diminish gradually.

Plélan, who thought that Marguerite de Guer was still in the bottom of the boat, gave voice to his joy in excited exclamations. "We have them!" he cried. "Shall I wring the imp's neck straight away, Blaise, or should I wait until we're back on land to hang him?"

"As you please, milord," Blaise replied.

The skiff's situation did indeed seem desperate. Always closely pursued, it had crossed the distance it had previously covered in the reverse direction, and had regained the environs of Gourlâ. Now, on this side as on the other, the lake became noticeably narrower, in such a manner that the skiff had no other alternative but to run aground on the shore or to cut across the breadth of the marsh, which would inevitably bring it within range of the other boat.

It was the latter course that Noël took. Making use of the actual superiority of his speed, he avoided running aground and succeeded in putting the larger boat between the shore and his skiff. That was doubtless all that he intended to do, for he immediately resumed floating gently, careless of the incessantly diminishing distance between his own boat and Plélan's.

"We must finish this, Blaise," said the latter, whose deceptive hope was changing into anger. "In the absence of their arquebuses, do our men have their pistols?"

"I have mine," Blaise replied.

The others had departed so precipitately that they had brought nothing but their swords.

Plélan seized the pistols that Blaise held out to him, promising the rest of his men to have them hanged as soon as he had the leisure; then he set himself comfortably to take aim.

The first shot produced no other effect than to alarm a flock of aquatic birds, which took flight noisily.

By way of reply, Chantepie sent a couplet from his favorite song.

"Demon!" murmured Plélan, bringing the second pistol to bear.

"You'll waste your last shot, sire," Blaise said. "We're out of range."

Plélan sat down again, muttering.

Meanwhile, Chantepie had reached the Oust. The two vessels, drawn by the current, followed one another with frightful rapidity. A quarter of a league in front of the skiff, the gigantic figure of the White Lady loomed up above the terrible roar of the vortex.

"Where's he leading us?" the oarsmen asked one another.

"Perish me!" Guy de Plélan finally cried. "Do they want to repeat that farce of Ermengarde's? On my faith, I'll follow them–to Hell if necessary!"

Two hundred yards from the whirlpool, the skiff turned and quit the course of the Oust, then disappeared into the mist.

"Follow it," the captain said.

The oarsmen leaned into their oars harder and began to steer a course around the whirlpool. They caught an occasional glimpse of the skiff, but it was immediately lost to view, and the pursuit had nothing to guide it but Noël's voice, which had finished intoning its verse and was repeating the chorus over and over, in a slow and monotonous voice.

Plélan said nothing more. He remained seated in the bow, his teeth clenched and his brow convulsively furrowed.

If I die, he thought, *Marguerite will follow me, and I shall die avenged.*

Noël was still singing.

The circle around the White Lady was diminishing. The fearful oarsmen crossed themselves. The men-at-arms trembled and dared not blaspheme.

Noël stopped singing. "Guy de Plélan!" he said, in a ringing voice. "In the name of Malestroit, my lord, I challenged you once to a duel to the death, without quarter. I said to you: *If my lord does not deign to come on the day and to the place that God will fix, I will come myself.* Here I am!"

"Row, row!" cried Pélan, prey to a kind of delirium.

Noël narrowed the circle once more, and his skiff vanished into the misty folds of the White Lady's dress. Then he continued: "Madame Marguerite is under the protection of the White Lady of the Marshes. Neither serf nor gentleman shall attack her without mortal peril!"

Noel interrupted himself to deliver one last stroke of his oar, which carried his skiff to the very lip of the vortex.

"Row! Follow him! Row!" cried Plélan. And when one of the oarsmen hesitated, he put the pistol to his throat.

"Serfs and gentlemen, you have all attacked Madame Marguerite," Noël continued, "and you are going to die."

"You lie, demon," howled Guy de Plélan. "I'll get to you and your lady and, perish my blood, I'll wring your neck!"

As he spoke these words, the skiff, propelled with new vigor by Chantepie, skimmed across the rim of the whirlpool and, immediately ceasing its circular motion, came out of the mist. The other boat tried to follow it, but, being heavier and less skillfully steered, was seized by the vortex.

Plélan was heard to give voice to one last blasphemy, followed by his crewmen's cry of distress; then the vortex rendered up a dull sound.

Chantepie wiped the sweat from his forehead and returned to the Île-aux-Halbrans.

When Toussaint and Madame Marguerite exhorted him to hurry during the subsequent crossing, he replied: "Guy de Plélan is no longer to be feared, and the White Lady has protected her family."

The following day, at the Château de Malestroit, Amaury said to Noël: "You have saved my wife and my son; would you like to be my squire?"

"Shall I be a knight one day?" Noël asked.

"On my oath as a gentleman, you shall be."

Noël reflected and lowered his head. "Knights do not fight on the water," he murmured, sadly.

"Indeed they do, Noël," said Lady de Malestroit. "There are valiant men-at-arms who fight on the decks of vessels in the open sea."

"The sea!" cried Chantepie, his young face radiant with enthusiasm. "The sea! I have seen it on the coast of the Cornouailles. It is huge... even larger than the Oust marshes..."

"Well, Noël," said the master of Malestroit. "Would you like to be a knight of the sea?"

"I would!" replied Noël, joyfully.

"Tomorrow, then, I shall send you to my cousin de Tinténiac,[26] who is the master of one of the King's ships... and if God assists you, child, you shall be a nobleman."

A long time afterwards, on the ruins of the little manor-house of Gourlâ, an old gentleman built a fine château, in which he made his home with his wife and children.

The old gentleman was a captain in the navy of His Majesty King Louis XIII. He was named Noël Torrec.

As for the château, he named it–and it is still named–*Chantepie*. Its high walls overlook from afar the whole of the Oust marshes, and it is in the Great Hall with its vast portals that we heard the legend of the White Lady of the Marshes told for the first time.

The Lovely Château

I. Master Luc Morfil

This is a very old story. Good people tell it on evenings by the fireside, when they cannot remember a better tale. Nurses, whose arms are wearied by rocking the cradle, make use of it as an opium substitute to send little children to sleep. It is a rudiment of a novelette, a short story of the kind people were able to make up in the depths of poor regions 100 years before the *feuilleton* was invented.

There was once a gentleman named Monsieur de Plougaz. He was the lord of Coquerel, Coatvizillirouët, Kerambardehzre and other places. His Château de Coquerel was the most beautiful to be seen for ten leagues around and more. It was talked about in Paris as well as in Brittany. The King often said: "I would really like to see Monsieur de Plougaz's château." But the King had things to do and the château was a long way from his home, because it was built on a charming little hill, verdant and covered with flowers, between the towns of Dinan and Bécherel. The combination of these two factors ensured that the King never came to Monsieur de Plougaz's château.

Although the King never came, there was no lack of visitors. Old Plougaz, hospitable by nature and maintaining a very well-stocked table, did not like eating the fish from his lakes and the game from his park on his own. There was a new feast almost every day at the Château de Coquerel. There was drinking, laughing and dancing there. The main door was always open, and Plougaz boasted of only ever having refused one guest in his life. That guest was gloom.

The master of Plougaz had no family. His wife, Nannon Le Brec de Batz, had been dead for ten years or so, and his only son, Arthur de Plougaz, was Heaven knows where—perhaps in Palestine, dead or captured by infidels, which was all one. The worthy lord had lost hope of seeing him again and, it must be admitted, scarcely spared him a thought. Hunting, dining and gambling—for he was a skillful and relentless gambler—left him little leisure for such trivial indulgences. He had no time to think about his business affairs either. Master Luc Morfil, his steward, thought about them for him, and spared no effort in doing so.

This Master Luc was a short man, a Norman by birth, who was always smiling. He charmed everyone with his straightforward and easy-going demeanor. He might have been in his forties. Around his little grey eyes, his habitual cheerfulness had engraved a multitude of slight wrinkles, which converged in the corner of each eyelid and extended from there to the temple and cheek to form the kind of joyous fan that is commonly called a "goosefoot." His cheeks were rosy, and plumpness had covered up any rough angularity that his prominent cheekbones might once have had. Their flesh was slack and softly-contoured, harmoniously matching his double chin. His short curved nose seemed only to have been roughly drafted by the Creator's hand. His superabundantly indented nostrils, in fact, allowed the interior cartilage to descend in isolation, forming an obtuse angle with the upper lip and seemingly making a effort to diminish, so far as was possible, the enormous distance separating two features that are normally friendly neighbors: the nose and the mouth. His mouth was entirely Norman—thin, flat and pale—but a circular wrinkle, a second result of Master Luc's cheerful gaiety, corrected the slight formal defect, and gave the lower part of his face a more attractive appearance.

Such was Monsieur de Plougaz's steward, in physical terms. In moral terms, he had the best heart in the world. He was always making promises, but never kept them. He offered his services to everyone, begging people to have recourse to his purse, but reserved the privilege of turning away those who chanced to yield to his insistence. He lied like a pagan, was as fearful as a hare, and was a thief to the tips of his fingernails.

After gambling, dining and hunting, what Monsieur de Plougaz loved most in this world was his Château de Coquerel. After the château, it was his steward, Master Luc Morfil.

"Master Luc," said the old lord, "is a pearl among stewards. He tells me, over and over again, that I overspend my income every year by about 20,000 *livres*. At Pentecost, he has me authorize the sale of a fief or a forest. That's all right. I sign what he gives me to sign without reading it. Another man would batter my ears with annoying complaints, telling me ten times a day that I'm ruining myself. Master Luc ruins me and never says a word–and that's a notable plus."

As you can see, Monsieur Plougaz was a commonsensical old fellow.

In addition to the châtelain, Master Luc and an army of valets, the manor had one other resident of some importance, whose name was Pluto. He was an old wolfhound of gigantic stature, whom the steward had adopted as his guest and companion. Unlike the general run of dogs, Pluto showed not the slightest gratitude towards his benefactor. He growled gruffly every time the steward stroked his coarse fur, and his large eyes glistened in a terrible fashion. Because of this, Master Luc loved him, and said to himself: *This animal has his good points. The better I treat him, the more he hates me, just as I do with respect to Monsieur de Plougaz. We're two of a kind, Pluto and me.*

Master Luc was mistaken, and did Pluto a great injustice. Pluto was not an ingrate at all; he was merely a dog disgusted with the way of the world, made misanthropic by disenchantment.

In the days of his adolescence, Pluto had been a dog to be envied. In that era, his master, the young Monsieur Arthur de Plougaz, had taken him for long walks on the high hills of Bécherel, or towards Dinan, along the enchanted banks of the river Rance. Pluto had no worries then. He ran joyously through the fields of stubble and leapt up madly at larks in flight. He chased rabbits into thickets and fought long and exciting duels against badgers. It was the Golden Age; Pluto was two years old.

While he frolicked in this manner, his master let his horse off the bridle and wandered at hazard. Arthur was a valiant and robust young man; at 20 years of age, he had already taken the honors in more than one passage of arms, and the noble ladies greatly admired his gallant manner when he made his horse cut capers beneath their massive granite balconies. Arthur was handsome, noble and rich. He was the sole heir to Coquerel and Coatvizillirouët, and also Kerambardehzre, not to mention Monsieur de Plougaz's other fiefs. He seemed melancholy, though; his lips were not often seen to smile, and his large black eyes were surrounded by bluish circles, which one might have imagined to have been hollowed out by tears.

He wandered, solitary and pensive, over the wooded hills of Bécherel or the white sandy shores of the Rance; he went with his head bowed and his body slumped. Pluto might bark and bound, but Arthur did not see him, lost as he was in his reverie. Of what was he dreaming? No one knew.

Some said that he had disturbed the Sabbath of the *chats-courtauds* on the Evran heath, and that those malign demons had pierced his heart with a needle. Others claimed that he had wrung the diabolical linen of the *laveuses de nuit* the wrong way.[27] Finally, others suggested that the Devil in person always followed him everywhere, in the guise of his wolfhound Pluto. Whatever the reason was, young Monsieur de Plougaz became more and more melancholy every day.

One morning, he had his finest horse saddled and went to his father. "Monsieur," he said, "I want to go to war against the Saracens."

Old Plougaz thought the matter perfectly straightforward, and replied: "Go find Master Luc and ask him to give you 1500 *livres*. I give you my blessing."

Master Luc counted out 500 *livres* and gave them to Arthur. "You're leaving us then, Milord!" he said, with a tear in his eye.

"I must," Arthur replied, in a somber tone.

"If I might ask the question, milord, why is that?"

"Because... it's strange but true... a terrible voice bursts forth every night at my bedhead, commanding me to go fight the Saracens."

"Bah!" said the steward, incredulously.

"I have disobeyed too long... I leave today."

Master Luc smiled covertly, and appealed to Heaven to bless his young lord.

When Arthur had gone, Master Luc rubbed his hands together. "It's said that the infidels have strong arms and excellent scimitars," he muttered. "Our young lord will leave his bones in Judea; me, I'll have the lovely Château de Coquerel." As he pronounced the last word, his grey eyes lit up with a sudden flash. "The Château de Coquerel," he repeated, stroking his chin. "That's well worth the trouble I went to getting up every night for six months to play the role of phantom and order the young fool to go get himself killed in Palestine! Luc Morfil, master of Coquerel–tee hee!"

As Arthur crossed the threshold of the château's courtyard, Pluto's plaintive howl made him turn his head. Pluto was tied up.

"Adieu to you too, poor Pluto," Arthur murmured. "The road is too long for me to take you with me." He spurred his mount, and the fine horse departed at the gallop.

Pluto became agitated and pulled at his chains with all his might, trying to grind them with his teeth. When his neck was bloodied by the force of his pulling, and his broken teeth were falling out of his gaping mouth, he lay down and wept silently. After that, he was never seen to leap after larks or run joyfully over the heath. He became gloomy and churlish. Monsieur Plougaz's valets would certainly have treated him badly had they not been afraid of the red glare that sometimes shot forth from his irritated eye.

Twelve years had passed since Arthur had departed. Pluto was still sad. He had loved his young master, and he remained faithful to Arthur's memory.

During those 12 years, Master Luc had fulfilled his duties as a steward as required. Monsieur de Plougaz had never found his coffers empty. From time to time, though, a piece of land held by his ancestors had fallen into foreign hands, to the extent that he no longer possessed any but the three fiefs whose name he bore.

"Which would you prefer to sell, of Coatvizillirouët, Kerambardehzre and Coquerel?" the steward asked him, one day.

Plougaz went pale. "Have we come to that already?" he murmured. But he collected himself immediately, and added cheerfully: "What good are three good chateaux, Master Luc. Sell Coatvizillirouët–that manor has a ridiculous name; I don't want it any longer."

When the manor was sold, Master Luc, as was his custom, divided the price into two equal parts. He put one in his master's coffers, and the other in an old iron chest in which he accumulated the fruit of his embezzlements. When he had spent long enough studying the heap of gold glimmering in the old chest, he took up his account-books and lost himself in lengthy calculations.

Darkness stole upon him while he was engrossed in this occupation. He put his hand on his ledger, whose figures he could no longer make out, and fell into a profound reverie.

"Coquerel!" he murmured. "My beautiful Coquerel! My lovely château! When shall I be master of Coquerel? Plougaz is ruined, it's true–but I'm getting old myself. If I should die before possessing Coquerel..."

At this thought, a deep wrinkle creased the steward's forehead. His features suddenly changed their appearance, expressing a passionate desire sustained by an indomitable determination.

"I shall have it," he went on, animatedly. "Oh, I shall have it! I haven't spent 30 years of my life nourishing myself with that dream to see it flee before me like some vain illusion. I shall have it, if I have to sell my soul!"

That was a Norman expression, for Master Luc's soul had been sold and paid for a long time ago. Nevertheless, he shivered as he pronounced those final words. The darkness that surrounded him made him afraid, and he groped for his lamp.

There was a storm raging outside. The wind was crying in the tall oaks of the Forêt de Coquerel, and shaking the strong window-frames violently.

"My soul," muttered Master Luc, as he struck a light. "I'm a good Christian, after all, and the Devil has no business with it."

The lamp was lit, and Master Luc's terror evaporated.

"Hee hee," he said, mockingly. "Must I believe myself damned forever for the few gold coins I've set aside? As for sending young Arthur to die overseas..."

He did not finish. At the sound of Arthur's name, Pluto–who was lying by the fireside–stood up on all fours, stretched out his neck and stared fixedly at Master Luc. Then he let out a long and plaintive howl.

"Doubtless, doubtless, my lad," said the steward. "You understand better than many a man, and if your tongue could talk, I wouldn't give sixpence for my neck... but you're mute, my friend. You won't be the one to let on that the mysterious voice whose advice drove the young idiot out of his paternal home was the voice of honest Luc Morfil. You won't be the one to tell the tale of my innocent pranks. You've seen me put all the money that old Plougaz intended for his own in my chest, but you'll be discreet, Pluto–as discreet as the tomb where young Monsieur Arthur is resting in peace."

Pluto released a second howl, mournful, prolonged and menacing. Then, lowering his head, as if in recognition of his impotence, he lay down again next to the extinct fire.

II. The Devil's Tower

Master Luc Morfil was sitting in his retreat. Old Pluto was asleep, with his paws in the ashes of the fire.

Now and again, the steward cocked an ear to listen to the sounds of the storm; the rest of the time, he devoted his mind entirely to his ambitious dreams, calculating how many months or years he must wait to possess Coquerel.

His love for Coquerel was tender and sincere. He loved nothing in the world except Coquerel.

It must be admitted that the lovely château was worthy to inspire such passion. It was a model manor-house. Its main part rose up between two wings in the Saxon style, topped coquettishly by a little belfry, grey with age but neither wrinkled nor cracked, like an aged knight still wearing his armor proudly. There were turrets at its four corners, pierced with narrow loopholes, looming over the high walls, whose pointed roofs extended symmetrically. Three hundred and sixty-five windows opened on its four façades, encouraging the belief that Coquerel would have been a good source of revenue for today's Treasury.[28] Above the main gate, two archangels armed for war supported the Plougaz coat-of-arms, which was *gules* with seven silver crescents in *orle*, and carried above that device the golden lion *passant* of Plougaz, from which Plougaz claimed to be descended.[29]

The interior reflected the frontispiece. There were none but hangings of fine linen and silk anywhere. The flagstones were hidden beneath thick carpets made from animal-furs. The paneling of carved black oak shone as brightly as the polished granite of the immense fireplaces. When the chandeliers were lit up on the eves of feast-days, and a fire fed by seven or eight tree-trunks burned in the vast concavity of the hearth, and the table tottered under the weight of its foodstuffs, and a decorated crowd filled its noble drawing-rooms, and the golden goblets were clinked in a feast's final toast, what a pleasure it was, by Saint Malo, to see the old place sparkle resplendently!

Not a single recess remained dark, nor was there a single vaulted ceiling that did not send back sonorous echoes to mingle with the joyous hubbub of the feast.

Oh, it's true: if Plougaz was the paragon of hosts, Coquerel was the king of châteaux.

And Master Luc, hidden in some solitary corner, contemplated all that joy morosely. It was for someone else that Coquerel displayed all her beauty. Master Luc was jealous, like a vassal who casts an audacious eye upon a noble lady, and goes pale with rage in seeing her smile upon his liegelord. "When?" he said to himself, then. "When shall I be master of Conquerel?"

He asked himself that question on the evening of which we are speaking, perhaps for the thousandth time, and his response was not at all satisfactory, in the context of his impatience. In fact, Monsieur Plougaz, reduced to his three principal fiefs, was far from the point of ruination. One of the fiefs was sold, but the price remained to be dissipated, and that price seemed to Master Luc to be an inexhaustible treasure. Then again, even when that sum had been dissipated, the towers of Coquerel would not have reached the same point. There was still Kerambardehzre, with its immense forests and fertile fields.

It was still a matter of years that he had to wait!

Now, waiting is a cruel martyrdom for an imagination as active as Master Luc's.

Partly to distract himself from his somber thoughts, partly to give himself a foretaste of proprietary joys, the steward plunged both his hands into a dusty chest, which had served the lords of Plougaz as a deed-box since the Saxon invasion of Brittany, and brought them out full of parchment manuscripts. From the midst of these veritable grimoires, the sight of which would have made one of our archaeologists blush with pleasure, he plucked a scroll at random. He unfurled it slowly and distractedly.

The parchment was covered with writing in the Breton language, and carried this title at the upper extremity, which was bound to excite the curiosity of the future master of Coquerel: *How the northern tower of the lovely château of the lords of Plougaz came to be called "the Devil's Tower."*

"The Devil's Tower!" Luc Morfil repeated. The oldest members of Coquerel's staff did, in fact, still give that name to the northern tower. He began reading avidly.

The manuscript related that, some 80 years previously, the Devil had taken possession of the northern tower and had established a sort of pied-à-terre there. The Evil One had played a number of nasty tricks, so effectively that the master of Coquerel had been obliged to desert his manor-house to make his domicile in Kerambardehzre. When the master had gone, Satan declared a truce, but every time anyone returned to Coquerel, Satan resumed his pranks.

This state of affairs endured, the manuscript said, *throughout the lifetime of Simon Troarec, Monsieur de Plougaz's steward.*

Master Luc paused at this passage, and became profoundly pensive. After a full half-hour, he lifted his head again and said: "This state of affairs endured throughout the lifetime of Simon Troarec, Monsieur de Plougaz's steward." Then he resumed reading.

After the death of Simon Troarec, the apparitions and devilries ceased. The rooms in which Satan had held Sabbaths were purified with great ceremony, and order was fully restored. In memory of this occurrence, the tower where these rooms were located was named the Devil's Tower.

Master Luc rolled up the parchment and threw it back in the chest.

"Well, well!" he said. "The Devil's Tower! That state of affairs endured throughout the lifetime of Simon Troarec, Monsieur de Plougaz's steward. Ha ha!"

This second exclamation was pronounced in the equivocal tone that observers regard as an infallible symptom of intellectual infantilism. Indeed, Master Luc added immediately afterwards: "Well, there's a marvelous story. This Simon Troarec must have been a clever fellow. Let's go! Within three months, I'll be master of the lovely Château de Coquerel." So saying, after rubbing his hands vigorously together. he seized his lamp and went through the long corridors that led to the Devil's Tower. Pluto got up and followed him meekly.

Master Luc walked at a lively and joyful pace. He took no notice of the gusts of wind rattling the windows. His rotund figure expressed the most perfect contentment, and his little grey eyes shone and blinked like the eyes of a stroked cat. Having reached the end of the main gallery, he turned a heavy key in the north tower's rebellious lock and went in.

The first room he passed through had the same appearance as the château's other rooms; it routinely served as a retreat for one of Monsieur Plougaz's guests. The second presented a sadder aspect; it was only ever used when the château was overfull on the eve of some great feast. The third was dusty, dark and sinister. Master Luc had an immense amount of trouble forcing back the bolt of the rusted lock. When he finally got in, he could not help feeling a constriction in his heart.

This room, abandoned for 12 years, had served as young Monsieur Arthur's bedroom. The damp tapestries were hanging in tatters. The wind was whistling through broken panes in the windows.

Pluto, who had come in behind the steward, opened his large nostrils and seemed to be taking delight in breathing a familiar atmosphere. He made a circuit of the walls several times over, pausing each time beside the empty bed.

"This will be hard work," muttered Master Luc, whose forehead was considerably clouded. "I don't like this room, and I'm sure that I shall see the phantom of that young fool Arthur here more than once."

Pluto stopped circling and let out a long howl.

"What! You're here, are you?" As if the company of the dog had moderated his vague terror, he added, in a boastful tone: "If he comes, we'll receive him, and if he doesn't come, we shall send Monsieur his father to join him... isn't that so, Pluto?"

Pluto, according to his habit, replied to this amicable interpolation by displaying two rows of white teeth, long and sharp, which would have done credit to a wolf in the prime of life.

"Good, my lad, good!" Master Luc, went on. "I'm familiar with your teeth. Unlike the good people of my native land, though, who bite without making threats, you make threats and never bite."

Pluto seemed to recognize the truth of this reproach. He lowered his head, growling.

Master Luc then began a detailed examination of the three rooms that he had just passed through. Young Plougaz's room was moderately high-ceilinged and nearly circular in form, which comprised on its own the first story of the north tower, or Devil's Tower. It had only one evident entrance, but near the bed that Arthur had abandoned there was a secret staircase, about which none of Coquerel's other inhabitants knew, leading to the courtyard. Master Luc opened the hidden door, and tipped a little oil from his lamp on to the hinges.

"That's good!" he murmured. "That's the door of which the legend speaks. That's the way that my predecessor, Simon Troarec, got in. It seems that the Plougazes have always had a happy knack in the choice of their stewards. Silence, Pluto! Hee hee! The Plougazes hire none but clever fellows. Master Luc's the equal of Master Simon, and had no need of the grimoire to find this nice little stairway. Master Luc got in that way too, but instead of playing the role of Satan, we chose that of an angel, preaching the crusade. Hee hee! That's not to say that we're scornful of the Devil's role–on the contrary. Peace, Pluto! Having been an angel, we shall be a demon–that's the story of the King of the Inferno–and I hope that the Devil will be as successful in respect of old Plougaz as the angel was in respect of Monsieur Arthur."

Throughout this long monologue, which Master Luc pronounced in a low voice, toying all the while with the hinges of the hidden door, Pluto devoured him with his eyes and growled gruffly. At the pronunciation of the name of Arthur, he stretched out his neck for the third time and intoned a prolonged plaintive howl. At the same time, the increasing storm outside sent forth a powerful gust of wind, which entered by the door and the damaged windows at the same time, extinguishing the steward's lamp and filling the room with debris.

A profound silence followed this tempestuous outburst. Pluto fell silent. Master Luc groped fearfully in the darkness. His hand suddenly encountered the dog's furry head, whose hair bristled at the contact. His eyes met Pluto's, which were round and wide open, shining in the gloom like two burning coals.

"Holy Mother of God!" he murmured, instinctively trying to make the sign of the cross.

A flash of lightning showed him the door. He hastened back to the corridor.

A few days afterwards, the servants of Coquerel were assembled in the château's immense kitchen. It was evening, between dinner and bedtime. Beneath the mantelpiece of the chimney-breast, sitting on a smoke-blackened bench, mechanically turning the handle of a spinning-wheel, was a woman at the extreme limit of old age. This was Anne Parker, who had been Monsieur de Plougaz's wet-nurse.

Anne was at least 100 years old. Her dead eyes saw nothing, except for visions of the future. Her long bony face, dappled with countless wrinkles, resembled a sheet of parchment hardened by the fire. Her lips moved incessantly without making any sound. Her hand continued to turn the handle of her spinning-wheel, where there was no longer any hemp. Next to her, a large space remained empty. She was said to be a witch, and people were afraid of her.

On the other side of the chimney-breast, the somnolent and sluggish Pluto was warming his paws and dreaming about hunting in the fields of stubble.

Then came all of Plougaz's servants. The circle was numerous. There was Alanic, the shepherd; Corentin, the little

135

gooseherd; fat Michel, who grazed the cattle; Yaumi, the crop-cutter; and Francin, the master of the cider-press. There were also the grooms who looked after the dogs and the grooms who looked after the horses, the seamstresses and the scullions, the gardeners and the laborers. As for the men-at-arms, they were in their armory-cum-guardroom, just off the vestibule. We must not forget Dame Marthe, the woman in charge of the farmyard girls. The whole of this subaltern population was meagerly illuminated by two resin candles supported by two cleft sticks fixed into the masonry of the hearth.

Such periods of nocturnal rest were normally lively and joyful at the Château de Coquerel. There would be plump chestnuts roasting in the embers and enormous pitchers full of foaming cider, with which everyone, in their turn, proposed earnest toasts. There would also be the pleasure of seeing the young people laughing, and the old ones prattling by the light of crackling resin lamps. This evening, however, the assembly was silent and morose. No one took the trouble to retrieve the chestnuts, which were burning; the pitchers remained full, their foam evaporating without anyone moistening his lips with it.

What had come over the Château de Coquerel?

What indeed? Alas, it is terrible to describe, and we shiver even to think about it. Monsieur de Plougaz no longer knew which way to turn; his valets and servants were visibly growing thinner; everything was desolation and despair. Coquerel was a *haunted house*! The Devil was up to his old tricks there. There were ghosts. For an entire week, sleep had not closed the eyes of Monsieur de Plougaz's commensals.

That was what had come over the Château de Coquerel.

The vigil had already proceeded in silence for some time when the belfry sounded 8 p.m. Everyone shivered, then everyone collected himself. Alanic extended his forefinger timidly and pulled a roast chestnut out of the fire, which he nibbled with evident pleasure. Emboldened by his example, Corentin the gooseherd set his hand to work foraging in the ashes. Fat Michel, while releasing a melancholy sigh, slowly

136

raised a pitcher and drank Yaumi's health; the latter could not do otherwise than return the compliment. Then Francin found the courage to blow his nose, in a fashion that we dare not specify, but can declare to be simple, primitive and convenient for people who lack handkerchiefs. One of the kennel-grooms coughed. Pluto yawned, and Dame Marthe sneezed weakly. The ice was broken.

The stools drew closer together. Yaumi passed the pitcher to his neighbor, and the foamy liquid made a tour of the circle.

"It's good," Michel said. "It's good, strong cider... but who knows how many more times we'll be drinking it beneath Coquerel's chimney-breast?"

"Who knows," Francin the press-master went on, "Whether I'll be pounding milord's apples next year?"

"Alas, alas!" said the assembly in chorus.

"You see, my lads," Michel said, in a pompous tone, "there's no remedy for it. A house that's haunted is a house that's lost... It might as well be the plague!"

"That's the truth," Francin replied. "It's the pure truth."

"If only Monsieur de Plougaz had replaced the late Dom Maurice as the château's chaplain–but no!"

"But no!"

The pitcher made a second circuit, and the voices took on a slightly less lamentable tone.

"For this, Master Francin," Alanic said, "you've not left the best cider in the vat."

"It's good...good, strong cider... Yes, that's true... But what did you hear last night, the rest of you?"

This question darkened all their faces.

Dame Marthe, being a woman, found her tongue first. "I heard chains rattling in the northern tower," she said. "I heard strange mutterings in the air, and I slid my head beneath my bedclothes."

"That was prudent, lady."

"At midnight, the racket was redoubled. I thought the château would be swallowed up. I fainted."

137

"How convenient it is to have the ability to faint when one's terrified!" said the little gooseherd. "Me, I saw the loopholes in the Devil's Tower..."

"Silence, fool!" cried the assembly.

"That's right–I meant to say the northern tower. Anyway, the loopholes were shining with a ruddy light, and the late Monsieur Arthur's room..."

This time, it was Pluto who interrupted, releasing the plaintive howl with which we are familiar.

"Well, what was in the room?" Yaumi asked.

"I don't know–but it was properly lit up, that's for sure."

"That's strange!" murmured Dame Marthe. Then, shaking her head, she added: "There's someone here who could tell us all about that."

"Who? Who do you mean?" The question came from every direction.

"Old Anne Parker," Marthe replied.

This supposition seemed so risible that they could scarcely prevent themselves from bursting into laughter.

"Old Anne!" Francin repeated. "It's almost 50 years since she last said a word."

The woman in question remained in her corner, inert and impassive. She did not appear to have heard. Her hands were still turning her spinning-wheel, as if to draw off an imaginary thread. Her lips moved slowly, in silence.

"She's seen strange things in her time," Marthe went on.

"She no longer remembers them."

"Perhaps... In any case, she can't tell us, since age has rendered her dumb."

"Dumb and deaf. She's a living corpse."

It was Michel who had spoken last. Monsieur de Plougaz's old nurse slowly turned her fleshless neck and fixed him with her eyes, dull and deprived of thought. "Does any of you," she said, in a halting voice, "remember Master Simon Troarec, Plougaz's handsome steward?"

The assembly could not have been seized by a more profound astonishment if Pluto himself had begun to speak. Everyone there had virtually forgotten the sound of Anne Parker's voice. Her question, strange in itself and stranger still in the mouth that proffered it. sent a shiver of fear running from each person to the next.

"She's recovered her speech!" murmured Dame Marthe. "What will she say?"

Everyone opened his eyes and ears–but Anne Parker soon reverted to her original position. She resumed threading her non-existent distaff, silently moving her lips, as she had done for more than 20 years.

III. Master Roch Requin

The Plougaz servants remained mute with surprise for some time. Eventually, though–because the whole point of an evening gathering is to talk–they resumed their interrupted conversation.

"I'm willing to bet that's the last time old Anne speaks in this world," said Michel.

"Me, I pray God that it's not an omen of misfortune," Marthe replied. "But what have we to fear, after all? Hasn't misfortune arrived already?"

"The fact is that the good times are over. Plougaz has become sad and morose."

"You can say that again!"

"I can't deny it. Even Master Luc seems overwhelmed."

"He's a faithful steward," said Dame Marthe, with conviction.

"A steward who fears God–and the Devil even more so," added Yaumi, not without a certain calculated mockery.

Anne Parker ceased tormenting the handle of her spinning-wheel and said, as if she were talking to herself: "The steward doesn't fear the Devil." Then, turning slowly towards the assembly, she said: "Does any of you remember Master Simon Troarec, Plougaz's handsome steward?"

"Respectable lady," Marthe replied, "Plougaz's steward is named Luc Morfil."

The old woman shook her head incredulously. "Are you trying to tell me my own fiancé's name, my dear?" she said, severely. "I never heard mention of Luc Morfil, and that's not a Breton name. Besides, Plougaz has but one steward–and that's quite enough, believe me!" Anne pronounced the final phrase emphatically. "That's quite enough," she went on, "especially when the steward doesn't fear the Devil...and Master Simon isn't afraid."

"She's mad," murmured Dame Marthe.

"He's the one who's the Devil," Anne Parker went on again, her voice becoming weaker and more halting. "Plougaz doesn't know what's going on. Don't tell him anything... If no one talks, Plougaz will leave his château and the steward will become the master."

"If that were Master Luc!" cried Yaumi, struck by a sudden thought.

"Peace, boy! I'm the only one in the world who knows what happens by night in the Devil's Tower!"

"What did I tell you?" Dame Marthe put in, thoughtlessly. "The witch knows everything!"

Anne Parker shuddered slightly, and slid her dry and wrinkled hand over her brow. "I must be mad!" she muttered. "It's 80 years since all that happened."

Her head slumped again. Her fingers clenched around the handle of her spinning-wheel; she resumed her pretense of spinning a thread.

"Venerable lady," said the disappointed Marthe. "May we not know what happens in the northern tower?"

There was no response. The old woman had become a mummy once again.

"I shall know it!" cried Yaumi, resolutely. "I'll know it this evening!"

This exclamation attracted less attention than it might have, because every gaze was fixed on Anne Parker, whose entire body was slowly sagging, and who ended up slumped on her stool: an inert, lifeless mass.

"The poor old lady's not long for this world," said Michel.

"I knew that someone in the château would die this week," replied Francin. "I saw the *candle* as I was coming back from the village." [30]

"The poor woman's fate is clear, then," Yaumi said.

Someone was indeed fated to die, but Yaumi would have been greatly astonished had anyone told him the doomed individual's name.

It was 10 p.m. The steward had just completed his customary round, supervising the locking of the doors. He was pale and seemed to be tired; even so, before retiring to bed, he took hold of Pluto's iron collar and led him to the courtyard, where he tied him up with the aid of a doubly-padlocked chain.

Master Luc never neglected this precaution, but he never carried it out without saying, as if in felicitation: "If Pluto had not been secured by that double chain 12 years ago, young Arthur would still be at the château. As for me, I'd be...the Devil knows where."

Once Pluto was chained up, Master Luc went back in. When the last servant had left the place where the evening gathering had taken place, however, he opened the exterior door discreetly. As he was about to slip outside, he heard a noise behind him. The steward paused indecisively.

"Bah!" he said, after a brief hesitation. "It must be old Anne, fallen asleep by the fireplace."

He went out.

Yaumi, who had not lost sight of him for a single instant since a vague suspicion had crossed his mind, ran after him on tiptoe.

After locking the kitchen door, Master Luc walked along the façade of the château and went back in by a hidden postern situated at the foot of the northern tower, which connected by

141

means of a little staircase with the room formerly occupied by young Plougaz. Yaumi, astonished but now sure of his facts, continued to follow him.

Having arrived in Arthur's room, the steward took some chains and a packet of resin candles from under the bed, where he had hidden them. Then he waited patiently.

At the moment when midnight sounded, he let out several screams, struck a light, lit his resin candles and ran around the room, shaking the chains noisily. The cunning Norman had probably been doing gymnastic exercises, for he made as much noise all by himself as an entire legion of demons.

Suddenly, though, he stopped. His rubicund face took on a livid pallor and the chains slipped from his hands. A profound silence followed the awful din that he had been making. He had just perceived a tall man standing in the middle of the room, who was watching him in action with his arms folded across his chest.

Master Luc was not brave. He was afraid, at first, that he had evoked Satan in person. When he finally recognized Yaumi, his fear did not diminish at all, for the scythe-wielder had a well-established reputation for strength and intrepidity.

"Ho ho!" said the latter. "So you're the Devil, honest Master Luc?"

"Don't give me away, Yaumi, my good friend," the Norman replied. "I'll give you anything you want."

"I want to see you hanged, Master Luc, that's all," the lad said, moved by that instinctive hatred that has existed since the world began between the servant of the lowest rank and the master's favorite.

Luc Morfil mustered the courage of desperation. A rapid glance convinced him that his adversary was unarmed. He slid his right hand discreetly beneath his doublet. "I'll give you ten *écus*... 20 *écus*... 30 *écus*!" he cried.

"None of that, master. I wouldn't spare you the rope for 50 *écus*."

"A hundred *écus*!" the steward said, in response.

Instead of replying, Yaumi placed a strong hand on his shoulder.

"Mercy!" murmured Master Luc. As he pronounced the word, though, he suddenly withdrew his hand from his doublet, armed with a short dagger, and struck with all his force, aiming at Yaumi's heart.

"The *candle* was for me!" the lad said, as he fell heavily.

Master Luc made no reply, but the color came back into his cheeks and it was with a smile of perfect satisfaction that he crouched down to finish Yaumi off with a second thrust.

The next day, all was fear and desolation at the Château de Coquerel. Not only had everyone heard an infernal hullabaloo in the Devil's Tower, as usual, but a valet whose courage had returned with the daylight had gone to explore the haunted chamber and had found a corpse–poor Yaumi's corpse.

Monsieur Plougaz was the most desolate of all. He summoned Master Luc Morfil and said to him: "I want to sell the Château de Coquerel."

Master Luc felt a thrill of delight. "Milord," he replied, hypocritically, "you can still raise thousands of *écus* on the price of Coatvizillirouët."

"I want to sell Coquerel," Monsieur de Plougaz repeated.

"I am bound to obey your orders, but..."

"But what?"

"Nothing... I'll go draw up the contract of sale, and do my best to find a buyer."

"Go–and hurry!"

Master Luc went out and took a sheet of parchment, on which he inscribed, in his finest handwriting, a contract in good and due form. Then he straddled his mule and went to Bécherel, in order to have the banns published after mass on the following Sunday, to put the lovely Château de Coquerel up for sale.[31]

Having accomplished this duty, instead of returning to the manor right away, he went on to Dinan and passed through

143

its streets with a proud and triumphant air. Anyone who met him that day would have sworn that they had never seen Master Luc so red in the face and smiling so broadly. He rode on his mule with his legs jutting out and his fist on its haunch, neither more nor less than a worthy knight on his battle-charger, all the more so when he greeted his acquaintances with a lordly nod of the head.

These little people, he said to himself, *do not know who we are. There shall very soon be a serf in our shoes, thank God, and the steward will be a lord.*

From time to time, along his route, Master Luc dismounted to buy something: a child's plaything here, a velvet ribbon there, a polished silver casket containing quills and ink. He stuffed these purchases into the vast pockets of his doublet.

In the poorer part of Jerzual, which was then Dinan's only suburb, he tied his mule to an iron ring fastened in the wall of a house of wretched appearance, and lifted the knocker of a worm-eaten door, which served as entrance to the establishment of Master Roch Requin, attorney by profession and arrant thief by reputation.[32]

Master Roch resembled Master Luc as a prune resembles a plum. He was a little old man, wrinkled, wizened, desiccated and oven-baked. He did not laugh very often, for fear of showing people the cavernous void of his toothless mouth, but that did not prevent him from being a cheerful companion, and when he can drink for free, a Frenchman cannot keep his head. He was a widower, the father of a grown-up daughter for whom he had had difficulty providing a spouse; his family comprised, in addition, a multitude of children of both sexes.

As he came in, Master Luc kissed the hand of the eldest daughter in so gallant a fashion that Master Roch's nostrils scented a vague nuptial perfume. "Take this ribbon, my dear," the steward of Coquerel said. "I bought it for love of your beautiful black eyes."

The eldest daughter had grey eyes, but she took the ribbon anyway.

"And these are for you, my well-behaved brats," Master Luc continued, distributing his purchases. "Friend, your family becomes more delightful with every day that passes."

Master Roch Requin received this compliment warily. "It's nice of you to say so, friend," he replied. To himself, he added: *He has need of me, that's obvious. Let's be careful.*

Master Luc took up a chair and came to sit next to the aged attorney.

"Friend," he said, "the whim came upon me to dine with you. Isn't that a good idea?"

"Um!" said Master Roch.

"A simple family meal," the steward went on. "Nothing special."

"Nothing special," the attorney repeated.

"Pot luck... four little entrées, two roasts and a dozen bottles of French wine..."

"That's what you thought, did you?"

"I've ordered it all from an innkeeper I know. It'll be ready in a quarter of an hour. Don't worry—it's my treat."

Master Roch shut the ledger that he had been consulting with a bang, and extended his hand to his friend. The eldest daughter ground her long teeth, and the brats let out howls of jubilation. *He has need of me*, thought the attorney. *That's more and more obvious.*

When the two roasts, the four entrées and the basketful of wine arrived, ostentatiously carried by an adequate number of scullions, the Requin family hurried into the dining room. For a full half-hour, the only sounds to be heard were the muffled friction of energetic mastication and the scraping of knives on plates. Despite the absence of his teeth, the old lawyer worked marvels, but he was noticeably outdone by his eldest daughter, whose appetite seemed insatiable. Master Luc himself ate little and drank less, but he kept his friend's glass full.

The latter was on his guard and had a well-proven head; even so, he became expansive as the meal progressed, and displayed the concavity of his jaws more than once, in fits of cacophonous laughter. "Friend," he said, "your dinner is good. When you next have a whim to sit down at my table in this fashion, there's no need to hold back."

"I hope to treat you more generously before long," Master Luc replied, with a mysterious smile.

"You don't say! My family and I are always at your disposal."

Master Luc leaned closer to his ear. "Don't you think," he whispered, "that your daughter would be even more beautiful in the noble finery of a châtelaine?"

"What?" said the astonished attorney.

"Shh! I'd like to talk to you in private, my friend."

Master Roch remained dumbfounded for a moment. A swarm of bizarre ideas came into his head, which was slightly intoxicated by the French wine. Perhaps old Plougaz had set eyes on his eldest daughter. Perhaps... "Get out, children!" he cried, impatient to clear up his uncertainty.

The brats replied to this order with a concert of lamentations. Even the eldest daughter cast a distressed eye upon her plate, which was still half-full, and could not repress a groan. Nevertheless, everyone did as they were told, because Master Roch had an altogether Armorican way of teaching his heirs to be submissive.[33]

When the lawyer was left alone with the steward, the latter got up and locked the door. Then he scrupulously checked all the room's recesses.

"Why all the precautions, friend?" the attorney asked.

Instead of replying, Morfil filled his friend's glass to the brim and began speaking in a whisper. What he related, the reader already knows, or will discover in due course. He spoke for a long time–and with a certain eloquence, for Master Roch, with his eyes and mouth wide open, seemed to devour every word. "The Devil! The Devil!" he said, when the steward had finished. "This is an exceedingly funny business, my friend... I guessed that you had need of me."

"Will you do as I ask?"

146

"I'd have bet on it. I said to myself straight away: *he has need of me, that's obvious.*"

"Will you do it?"

"It's a funny business... Business that has the feel of the rope about it, my friend."

"I'll give you a thousand *écus.*"

"That's a pretty price, but, in conscience, it's quite a trick... You're a skillful rogue, my friend. I've half a mind to go tell it all to Plougaz. He'd give me more than a thousand *écus*... What do you say to that?"

Master Luc took from his doublet the same little dagger that had reduced poor Yaumi to silence and he stuck it into the table indifferently. "I don't say anything," he replied.

"The Devil! The Devil!" murmured Roch, scratching his ear. "You've an answer for everything, my excellent friend. You mentioned a thousand *écus*?"

"A thousand *écus*?"

"And my daughter?"

"I'll marry her."

"She's a treasure, friend. You'll be a happy husband. She's as good as she's beautiful..."

Master Luc, who had not lost his smile for a single instant during the conversation, made an equivocal grimace at this declaration, of which the attorney did not care to take heed.

"Let's do it!" the lawyer said. "Shake on it, son-in-law; I promise you my full cooperation." So saying, he got up and headed for the door.

Master Luc stopped him.

"*Verba volant!*" [34] he said. "I've put myself at your mercy. I need some safeguards."

"Safeguards!" the attorney repeated, with manifest repugnance. "In a project where it's a matter of the scaffold, one doesn't write anything down, my friend. I trust you implicitly, but I don't know anyone to whom I'd willingly give custody of my head."

"It must be put it writing, though, Master Roch," said Morfil firmly.

The old attorney looked around craftily. There was no way out.

"So be it!" he said, with feigned resignation. "I'll write whatever you please, son-in-law. Let's go find what we need to do that."

Once outside, Master Roch Requin might perhaps have changed his mind. Unfortunately for him, the Norman had anticipated every eventuality. He took a sheet of parchment from his pocket and the silver casket he had bought. "Don't go to any trouble, father-in-law," he said, putting on his best smile. "Here's a writing-set, which you may keep, if it pleases you, to remember me by."

The lawyer lowered his head. He was defeated.

Master Luc dictated an agreement by which he, Roch Requin, undertook, in consideration of the sum of a thousand *écus*, to buy in his own name, should the opportunity arise, the Château de Coquerel, and then to render the aforesaid château to Luc Morfil, the true purchaser. Roch Requin wrote it down, strongly contrary to his inclination, and signed it with ill grace.

"This way, my friend," Luc said, putting the contract in his pocket, "you won't be tempted to sell our secret, for we'd share the rope like the good friends we are. *Au revoir*, Master Roch Requin!"

"*Au revoir*, Master Luc Morfil," the attorney replied, dolefully.

In making his exit, the steward of Plougaz behaved far less gallantly than he had in the morning. He did not tell the eldest daughter that her grey eyes were black, and did not spare a glance for the numerous brats who awaited his fond farewell.

"I'd have bet that he had need of me!" grumbled the attorney. "The Devil! The Devil! Instead of having a hold on him, I let myself be taken in, and he's the one who has a hold on me. What a pity!"

When Master Luc mounted his mule, the Sun was sinking towards the horizon. From Dinan to Coquerel was three long leagues. The steward urged his mount to a trot and joyfully recapitulated the day's events. He had succeeded in everything. Plougaz had finally consented to sell his château, and the buyer had been found in advance. It was all for the best. Admittedly, Master Luc had made himself guilty of theft, imposture, murder and so on, but at least he was within reach of the price of his sins. He counted on imposing a strict silence on his memories once he was the master of the lovely château.

The Sun was hidden behind the green mountains fringing the river Rance before he had covered two leagues of his route. Dusk fell. Half the sky was veiled by a dark mourning-cloak, while the west remained lit by a somber fiery reflection, Master Luc whipped his mule with all his might and searched his memory for a Norman refrain to counter the anxiety whose approach he already felt. When the song finished, it was dark. Nothing but a red band marked the place where the Sun had vanished.

Master Luc whipped his mule for a second time, but the mule was old, lazy and obstinate. It continued its comfortable trot without taking any account whatsoever of its rider's impatience. The latter's heart was squeezed by a vague anguish. A bold rogue by day, by night he was a cowardly and superstitious rascal. Every tree along the road assumed a terrible form in his frightened imagination; his ears heard strange noises, and more than once, he thought he heard the sinister grating of the *barrow of the dead* in the distance.[35]

"I'm a good Christian!" he murmured, as if to deceive Heaven. "I'll have a mass said...ten masses. I have the means to pay..."

Then he tried to recite the forgotten verses of the *De profundis*, but soon interrupted himself and shuddered violently. A wild roe-deer had crossed the road. The wind brought him the funereal song of an owl hidden in the foliage.

All his limbs were trembling. A dull pallor had replaced the ruddy colors of his cheeks.

An hour went by. He was half a league from Coquerel. The Moon rose above the horizon, but its crescent, hidden by clouds, merely gave objects that uncertain glow which changes the appearance of dead nature and sows the country-side with strange phantoms. Master Luc, who was going along a sunken path bordered on either side with high slopes crowned with thick hedges, promised to light a candle to Notre-Dame de Gévezé for extending her powerful protection to him. The poor man bitterly repented of having prolonged his meal to such a late hour; he was so downcast that the thought of buying Coquerel no longer had the power to reanimate him.

He glued his eyes to the ground in order not to see any of the specters that were doubtless holding Sabbath in the air. He was in the process of congratulating himself on this simple stratagem when his mount suddenly came to a halt. Master Luc instinctively raised his eyes, and was petrified.

A black and gigantic form was standing in the middle of the road. Master Luc made the sign of the cross and asked God's pardon from the bottom of his heart, in order to prepare himself for death. His strength was failing; he felt that his last hour had come. Meanwhile, the mule did not budge, and nor did the black shape.

Master Luc mustered the courage to touch his mount's flank. It took a few paces forward and stopped again. He was now so close to the black shape that he could have reached out and touched it, but he had no intention of doing so.

The immobility of the frightful phantom reassured him somewhat, though. He looked up furtively and soon found the temerity to look the phantom in the face. The moonlight, momentarily freed from the vapors that surrounded it, fell directly upon the specter, in which Master Luc recognized the signpost marking the limit of the Coquerel domain.

"Cowardly mule!" he cried, striking the creature with all his might. "Afraid of a signpost! Go on, then, you idle beast!"

Master Luc's mule did not deserve this accusation of cowardice. It had stopped at the signpost, according to its custom, to await the orders of its rider, because the road forked at this point. The Norman was the one who was afraid— but now that he knew where he was, and felt that he was close to Coquerel, he forgot his apprehension and deceived himself. Another five minutes and he would see the windows of the château, lit up as befit the windows of a hospitable dwelling. How could he admit to himself that he had almost died of fright?

He sat up straight in his saddle then, and whistled the tune of a drinking song. The night held no more terrors for him. The oaks became oaks again, despite the fact that their long leafless branches, seen from a distance, resembled flesh-less arms. The signposts became signposts again. The barrow of the dead no longer screeched in the covert, and Master Luc was so brave that he replied to the hoot of an owl with a comical parody of the funereal plaint.

"Hoo-hoo! Hoo-hoo!" he called, laughing heartily. "Owl, my friend, I sing as well as you, and I've often repeated your scales by the bedhead of young Monsieur Arthur..."

His laughter stopped abruptly. At the moment when he pronounced the final word, a dull and prolonged howl made itself heard nearby, and Pluto crossed the road, dragging his broken chain.

Two men were following Pluto. When they passed in front of the steward, the Moon lit their pale faces, their hollow cheeks and the orbits where there were no eyes. They were dressed in long shrouds, as white as snow. The first, whose shroud had the form of a pilgrim's robe, displayed a breast pierced through by a Saracen arrow. The other, whose shroud resembled a peasant's smock, had a bloody wound above his heart.

Master Luc fell off his horse and fell heavily on his back in the dust of the road.

"Arthur de Plougaz! Yaumi!" he murmured, in a strangled voice. "Have pity! Have mercy!"

Pluto howled. The two white-clad men glided away like two wisps of mist impelled by the evening breeze. The mule pricked up its ears and sniffed loudly, although its flanks were shivering. Master Luc tried to get up, but his legs buckled, and he fell back unconscious.

IV. The Elixir

Monsieur Plougaz had spent that entire day sadly shut away in his apartment. The poor lord bitterly regretted his lovely Château de Coquerel. He thought about all the beautiful parties that he had given in his great hall, all the fine meals he had served on his vast dinging-room table. He thought about his magnificent stables, where 100 horses slept at their ease, of his kennels, renowned throughout the land, where 100 pairs of dogs of every size, color and breed frolicked and gave voice when the Sun rose. He thought about all of that–and, because sadness rends the heart of a good man, he thought too about his son Arthur, whom he had not seen for more than ten years.

"Alas, alas!" he said. "My Arthur and my Coquerel, my poor son and my poor château! Old Plougaz no longer has a manor or a family!"

And he reproached himself for having let the sole heir to his name depart so easily.

It was not the first time that Monsieur de Plougaz had remembered Arthur. On several occasions, he had instructed Master Luc to send fairly considerable sums to the Knights Hospitallers of Saint John to be forwarded to the young man. We know what use Master Luc had made of these sums.

While he gave his heart to these somber thoughts, the old lord walked incessantly back and forth across the floor of his room with a halting step. His brain was becoming feverish. He could not stay still, and every hour seemed as long as a week.

When evening came, he left his apartment to see if Master Luc had returned from his expedition. The Sun's disc, reddened by terrestrial vapors, was touching the line of the horizon. Its last rays flooded the rooms and galleries of Coquerel. The lovely château was resplendent. The stained-glass lights in the windows, decomposing that ardent radiance as it passed through, tinted the decorated panels of the wainscot purple or blue. The decorations of the vaulted ceilings, the polished steel of the military trophies and the crystal pendants of the chandeliers seemed to light up, as if with brilliant stars.

It seemed to Monsieur Plougaz that he was seeing these marvels for the first time, so wholeheartedly did he admire them. And the more he admired them, the more unsteady the unhappy old man became on his feet. Were not all these beautiful things soon to change masters? How many more times would he be able to see the Sun set through the stained glass of Coquerel's high windows?

It was a frightful sacrifice. But it was a necessary sacrifice, because, for a nobleman—or even a simple Christian—it is better to live in a hovel than share a dwelling with Satan.

While Monsieur de Plougaz walked in this way from room to room, from corridor to gallery, like a soul in pain, strange things were happening in his manor.

About an hour after noon, a man wearing the white robe of pilgrims from overseas, had lifted the knocker of the main door and asked for hospitality. There was no instance of such a request ever having been refused at Coquerel. The mendicant was introduced. He was a person of tall stature, whose emaciated and weary features testified to long years of suffering. His robe was dirty and ragged.

As he crossed the courtyard, Pluto, retained by his chain, was sleeping in the sunlight in front of the opening of his kennel. His sleep seemed to become suddenly agitated. His large nostrils dilated. He yapped softly and shook his tail as dogs do when they see someone they recognize. Then, as the stranger passed him by, he awoke with a start and leapt up.

"Down, Pluto!" said Francin, who had filled the office of introducer. "Don't be alarmed, master. The chain is strong,"

"I'm not afraid in the slightest," the stranger replied, gravely.

"Well, Sir Pilgrim, there's reason to be, I assure you. Pluto is a wicked beast, and you wouldn't be safe were it not for the chain... What are you doing? Stop!"

The stranger was advancing towards Pluto. Without taking any account of the vassal's warning, he put his hand on the redoubtable beast's head.

Francin held his hands up in terror. He thought that the pilgrim was about to be devoured–but Pluto lay down again. His great red eyes became soft and moist. His entire body began to quiver, and he opened his mouth to lick the stranger's dusty sandals.

"God preserve us!" muttered Francin, looking at the stranger now with respect mingled with suspicion. "We're living in evil times. The Devil by night, sorcerers by day..." He did not finish his sentence, but he crossed himself furtively.

The stranger came back to his guide, who ushered him into the kitchen. Old Anne Parker was alone beside the fire, which had almost gone out. She was plunged in her habitual somnolence, winding thread about her non-existent distaff.

"Warm yourself and rest your legs, master," Francin said. "Excuse me if I don't keep you company, but you've arrived at the Château de Coquerel at a sad time. We're holding a vigil over a dead man just now, in the chapel. My poor comrade Yaumi will cry at my bedhead for a long time, on winter nights, if I don't do what a good Christian can to shorten his time in Purgatory."

"Is there a priest to lead the vigil?" the stranger asked.

"No priest has crossed the threshold of Coquerel for some years, alas," Francin replied.

"Has the dead man received the help of a physician?"

"Physicians are rare, Sir Pilgrim–and besides, there are maladies that the arts of men cannot cure. A dagger-thrust in the heart..."

"Science can do anything!" the stranger put in, severely. "Go–I'll rejoin you presently." He added, in a low voice: "A man who has spent five years among the infidels and discovered their most marvelous secrets, has the right to call himself a master of the arts of healing. I shall fill the office of physician."

Francin shook his head.

"Go, I tell you," the pilgrim repeated. "If he's dead, I'll pray to God for his soul; if a spark of life remains within him, I'll cure him."

"So be it!" murmured Francin, incredulously. He went out.

The stranger sat down on a stool and poked the embers to reanimate the fire. "Lady," he said, addressing old Anne. "Is Luc Morfil still Plougaz's steward?"

The centenarian shuddered at that voice. Her fingers, moved by a sudden and mechanical ardor, pressed on with their imaginary work. She did not reply.

The stranger repeated his question in a curt and imperious tone.

Anne let go of her spinning-wheel then, moved her dry lips without producing any sound, and lifted her staring and dejected eyes towards the stranger. She looked at him thus for a long time. Her eyes, as dull as unpolished crystal, reflected nothing of what passed behind them, but the wrinkles of her cheeks moved and clashed; her extended fingers seemed to be trying to repel a vision.

"Will you not tell me, Lady" the pilgrim persisted, again, "the name of Plougaz's steward?"

"Simon Troarec," the centenarian's broken voice finally replied. "But he has another name... A name that must not be repeated, a name that no one knows. I know it, myself, because I spent a night in the Devil's Tower. His name is Satan."

The stranger got up and went to the door, believing that the poor madwoman could not tell him anything. Anne slowly turned around, completely, in order to follow him with her gaze. Then, with a smile, she repeated mysteriously: "His name is Satan. The château is his... and me, I'm his fiancée."

The pilgrim went through the corridors of the château unhesitatingly, as if he were perfectly familiar with the layout of the building, and arrived at the threshold of the chapel. It was an ancient edifice, whose style was in harmony with that of the château, but which, having been neglected by the recent lords of Plougaz, had a mournful and desolate appearance. The floor was covered by a thick layer of moist dirt. The altar was bare, long cobwebs hung down from the ceiling, and the wind penetrated from every direction through the broken lights in the Saxon windows.

Poor Yaumi had been laid out on a table covered with a linen cloth in the middle of the nave. Four resin candles fixed in the ground were burning at the four corners of the catafalque, substituting for church candles. The people of Coquerel were sitting on the surrounding benches. Some were praying, others were pretending to pray. Those inclined to gossip were chatting. Yaumi's fiancée was weeping.

The Sun, hidden behind opaque clouds, left the interior of the ruined chapel in a somber half-light, which made the ruddy and vacillating light of the resin candles seem even more melancholy.

The decoration of that mortuary scene was marvelous; its actors, like all Breton peasants, were more disposed than others by natural inclination to the sentiments of lugubrious poetry. The Breton, in fact, loves that which makes him sad and frightens him. When he sings, he sings mystical refrains of lamentation; when he tells stories, they are terrible. His tales have the Devil and Death for their principal characters, cemeteries or the bare demon-haunted summits of mountains for their settings. The whistling of the tempest is audible within them, and the distant vibrations of a tolling bell.

One final circumstance was heaped upon the disquiet experienced by the greater part of the assembly. Francin had not neglected to mention the pilgrim whose gaze had tamed Pluto and who boasted of possessing the secrets of pagan doctors.

156

Everyone felt moved by curiosity, mingled with dread. They were waiting impatiently for the arrival of this extraordinary person, and the thought of a possible miracle slipped into all their minds.

When the stranger finally appeared on the threshold, a tremor ran through the ranks of the Plougaz servants. Those who were praying were distracted. Those who were chatting shut up. Even Yaumi's fiancée wiped away her tears and looked at him.

The pilgrim came through the chapel at a slow and ponderous pace. He stopped in front of the table on which Yaumi had been laid and placed his hand on the cadaver's breast. For a minute, he remained in that position, immobile and profoundly attentive. Then he shook his head.

"I've come too late," he said. "This man is dead."

Yaumi's fiancée emitted a heart-rending sob. The stranger raised his eyes to look at her, and seemed to be touched by her sorrow. He took a metal flask from his bosom, which he opened with difficulty. A piercing acrid perfume immediately filled the chapel. The stranger let a drop of the flask's contents run on to Yaumi's lips, and he replaced his hand on the lad's heart.

This time, he waited longer. When a few minutes had passed, a satisfied smile lifted his thin black moustache. Yvonne, Yaumi's fiancée, felt a vague hope return to her heart. Plougaz's other servants opened their eyes and ears.

"His heart is beating," the pilgrim said, in a voice so faint that they could hardly hear it. "He's suspended between life and death. It will require a great deal to save him; to lose him would require but a breath. Leave, good people, and pray to God devotedly, for God alone can give a man the power to effect such a cure."

So saying, the stranger knelt down. Plougaz's people withdrew without a sound. Yvonne alone came towards the pilgrim and presented him with a little gold cross that she wore about her neck.

"I only have this," she said. "If I had a beautiful château like Coquerel, I would give it to you."

The stranger imposed silence upon her with an imperious gesture, and the poor girl went out in her turn.

Once he was alone, the pilgrim rolled up the trailing sleeves of his robe and went to work. He had neither an instrument-case nor a pharmacopoeia, but he had arms as white as ivory and eyes that shone like two flames. They served him so well that Yaumi came back to life and stirred on his bed of stone. His wounds, it must be said, had been slight. Master Luc's dagger had not touched any vital organ, but the cold of the night, combined with an enormous loss of blood, had made the crop-cutter so torpid that his comrades had been unable to see him as anything but a corpse.

When he had recovered his senses, Yaumi was greatly surprised by the funereal pomp that surrounded him. He tried to demand an explanation, but the stranger would have none of it. After making him drink a few drops of the cordial, whose recipe remained a secret between him and the pagans of Palestine, the pilgrim ordered him to remain still.

Four or five hours passed thus, during which Yaumi enjoyed a beneficial rest. Plougaz's people came to look at him from time to time through the half-open door, but the pilgrim's severe and haughty manner always kept them at a distance.

Night was falling when Yaumi woke up again. Sleep had restored his strength. He raised himself up without overmuch effort and sat on the table.

"Yaumi," the stranger said, "were you the foster-brother of the sole heir of Plougaz?" [36]

"May God have the soul of that poor young lord," the lad replied, crossing himself. "That's true."

"Would you recognize him?" the pilgrim continued.

"I've not set eyes on him for 12 years, but his features are here." He pointed to his heart. "I would recognize him."

The stranger threw back his long hair, and lifted up a resin candle to light his features. Yaumi looked at him doubtfully for a second. Then, putting his hand on a pillar, he attempted to bend his knee.

"Milord," he murmured, "I thank God that you have returned safe and sound to the lovely Château de Coquerel."

Arthur de Plougaz extended his hand, which his foster-brother kissed with respectful affection. A long conversation followed between master and servant. Arthur learned what he had asked old Anne Parker in vain, that Luc Morfil was still the steward of Coquerel. He heard, without overmuch surprise, the story of what had befallen Yaumi in the Devil's Tower. One detail that interested him greatly, though, was the existence of the hidden door and the secret stairway that led from the courtyard to the room that he had formerly occupied.

That's how he got in, the wretch! he thought. *Well, the route can serve two ends; that's the way he'll go, if it pleases God.* Aloud, he added: "I know all this, my man—or, at least, I've suspected it since yesterday. After encountering many obstacles, I arrived yesterday in Dinan. There I learned that my father's château was haunted by evil spirits. I remembered certain diabolical tricks that were the cause of my departure for the Holy Land long ago. But God willing, my man, this treacherous valet will never be lord of Coquerel!"

"I owe him something too," said Yaumi, in a somber voice.

"So much the better—you will help me all the more zealously. Can you walk?"

Yaumi took a few unsteady paces.

"One more drop of my elixir!" Arthur said.

Yaumi drank, and felt a new vigor circulating in all his limbs. "By my patron Saint Guillaume!" he cried, in amazement, "If you were not as noble as the Valois, I would think you a sorcerer, my lord."

Night had fallen. As was their habit, the inhabitants of Coquerel were gathered around the fireplace, watching two or three damp tree-trunks smoking in the grate. Old Anne Parker

159

was at her post, mumbling and spinning. Only Yaumi and Pluto were missing.

The session was even sadder than the previous evening. A dismal silence reigned over the hearth, interrupted only by Yvonne's stifled sobbing. The young men took turns to get up periodically and go to see what was happening in the chapel. The gooseherd, who had been the last to leave his corner, had come back to report that Yaumi was still lying on the table.

The boy had lied. Fear had taken hold of him in the dark corridors. He had not dared to go as far as the chapel.

"The poor young man is dead, my boys," said Marthe. "Completely dead. Didn't someone see the *candle* yesterday?"

"Yes, that's true," the assembly said, sadly.

"The best thing we can do is to recite a *De profundis* for the repose of his soul."

This proposition met with general agreement. The men took off their cloth caps, the young women took up their rosaries, and Dame Marthe began the first verse of the funereal hymn.

At that moment, though, Anne Parker sat up on her stool and let out a loud burst of laughter, which was followed by a stunned silence.

When Dame Marthe tried to continue her prayer, after the moment of stupefaction, old Anne started laughing again. "Hee hee," she said. "Simon Troarec has had it... Plougaz has come back... I've seen him."

"What's she saying?" several voices exclaimed.

"Peace, Dame Anne," said Marthe. "Let us pray for the dead."

"For the dead? You lie, my dear, you and Simon... He's alive, very much alive...hee hee hee!" Her dry and broken laugh extended for a few seconds, then died away.

Marthe resumed her *De profundis*.

"Shh!" said the centenarian. "You can't sing, my dear... Listen!" And she intoned, in a hoarse and quavering voice, a local ditty:

"In the forests of Brittany
"They make pretty shoes:
"Keep your little feet warm,
"Lovely brown-eyed girl.
"And you, lover boy,
"Seek your fortune!"

"Silence, Dame!" cried the indignant Marthe. "You'd have to be damned in advance to sing at a time like this!"

The old woman went on:

"The cliffs there are stone,
"Stone from top to toe;
"The sun cannot melt them
"Any more than the moon...
"And you, lover boy,
"Seek your fortune!"

This frivolous song, which interrupted the prayer for the dead so inappropriately, chilled the assembled servants of Plougaz with a kind of horror. They looked at one another anxiously and indecisively.

"Faggot have been wasted burning witches worth more than her," Dame Marthe complained, angrily.

The old woman looked at her in bewilderment, then went on, clapping her wrinkled hands:

"By night, they dance on the floor,
"Where the grain is threshed:
"Ah, they leap so well,
"When the twilight comes...
"And you, lover boy,
"Seek your fortune!" [37]

While she sang the last verse, her voice became more raucous and muffled. As she finished, she released a profound sigh and let her hands fall. "Ha ha!" she murmured. "I'm glad to have seen Plougaz before I die... But I don't know if I shall die, for I'm the fiancée of Simon Troarec...who is the Devil."

She leaned back against the chimney-breast and remained still.

161

It took some time for the assembly to shake off the impression caused by this bizarre incident. Finally, Francin got up and announced that he was going to see what was happening in the chapel.

In the meantime, Dame Marthe, who was a stubborn woman, set out to finish her *De profundis*–but her pious intention was fated to be frustrated that night. Indeed, scarcely had she pronounced the first Latin words when Francin came back, his expression distraught and his forehead pale.

"What is it?" The exclamation came from every side.

"There's nothing!" Francin stammered, fear cutting short his speech. "In the chapel... no more...!"

Yvonne threw herself towards him and gripped his arm. "What are you saying?" she murmured. "Is he healed?"

Francin looked at her in astonishment.

"Answer me, then," she cried, impatiently. "Has the pilgrim kept his promise?"

"What times we're living in, alas!" said the young man, "The accursed sorcerer was only wearing a pilgrim's habit. Poor Yaumi! The sorcerer has fled with his corpse."

Yvonne released a cry of horror, and all of Plougaz's people ran precipitately to the chapel to verify Francin's report. He had told the truth. By the light of the expiring resin candles, they saw the table on which there was no longer either a dead man or a winding-sheet.

The chapel's side-door was still open. That was the way the false pilgrim must have gone. Plougaz's people went out. When they arrived in the courtyard, they realized that Pluto was no longer in his kennel. There was nothing but a piece of broken chain hanging from the iron ring fixed to the kennel wall.

"May Our Lady have pity on us," they murmured, "and may God protect us against the assaults of the Evil One."

A distant howl from Pluto replied to this invocation, and the quavering voice of Anne Parker launched its merry refrain through the open windows of the kitchen:

"Ah, they leap so well,
"When the twilight comes...
"And you, lover boy,
"Seek your fortune!"

V. A Knight, a Squire and a Dog

Nothing extraordinary happened that night at the lovely Château de Coquerel. The northern tower remained dark and mute. No fantastic lights were seen moving from one loophole to another. Nothing was heard of chains, groans, screams or any of the other noises from the afterlife that had thrown so much fear into Plougaz's servants. Everyone slept peacefully, as if there were no Devil's Tower at Coquerel.

Our readers will not be astonished by this circumstance, if they care to recall that Master Luc had fallen unconscious in the middle of the road at about 10 p.m. When he awoke, it was past midnight; the hour of the Sabbath had passed, and the brave steward was too familiar with infernal etiquette to presume to set his resin lamps and scrap-iron swinging at 1 a.m. Besides, he was in no condition to go to work. The cold of the night had disabled his body and terror had paralyzed his mind. When he recovered his senses, his first thought was to look around anxiously.

The Moon, having reached the highest point of its elevation, was shining its white and limpid light over the countryside. Master Luc could no longer see the specter of young Monsieur Arthur, nor that of Yaumi, nor that of Pluto. There was nothing close by but his faithful mule, which was waiting for him, sleeping standing up.

Master Luc took a few steps along the road to restore some elasticity to his limbs. Then, mounting his beast, he hastened back to his lodgings.

"I must have been dreaming," he told himself. "Dead men don't come back, thank God, and Pluto's chain is solid iron. I must have been dreaming..."

As he crossed the courtyard, he whistled for Pluto, who made no response. He went to the kennel then, and saw that the dog really had disappeared.

"Is the Devil mixed up in this for good and all?" he muttered, anxiously.

Master Luc had great difficulty going to sleep.

The following morning, he learned of the theft of Yaumi's cadaver, which succeeded in convincing him that he had not been dreaming the previous night. Despite the new terrors that the series of extraordinary events inspired in him, he hardened his determination to complete his spoliatory project, and resolved to do battle with Hell, if necessary, rather than give up the lovely château.

Monsieur de Plougaz, by contrast, awoke refreshed. It was a long time since the worthy lord had slept so peacefully. On getting up, he demanded, for his breakfast, a hare, five quails, two partridges and a fat chicken from Guerche–a city almost as famous for capons as Le Mans. For his dessert, he ate three buckwheat pancakes, any one of which would have sated the appetite of a modern Auvergnian. In those heroic times, though, the human stomach was in its prime; its faculties cannot be compared with the feeble capacity of our degenerate organs.

When Monsieur de Plougaz had washed down his morning meal with a jug of claret, he lay back in his large armchair with the emblazoned back and, instead of cleaning his teeth, as a contemporary gourmand would, asked himself how he ought to spend his day.

He liked hunting a great deal, but his legs were no longer as strong as they had been, and gout was fighting frequent and successful duels with his toes. Fishing is an insipid pleasure at best, and Monsieur Plougaz thought it a pastime fit for serfs. He might have employed a few hours riffling through the half-dozen books that formed the Coquerel library, but he did not know how to read. What, then was he to do?

As he was asking himself this question, Master Luc Morfil came into the dining-room. The latter was pale, and the piteous traces of a bad night were evident in his face. "May the Lord protect you, my lord," he said, bowing deeply.

"Thank you. Luc, my friend," Monsieur de Plougaz replied. "You've come at exactly the right moment. I was in a very awkward situation."

"Milord knows that I am at his disposal."

"Doubtless, Luc. That's what I pay you for. Tell me—what should I do today to distract myself."

Master Luc could not restrain a grimace. This freedom of spirit on the part of his lord seemed to him not to augur well for his project. Had it only required one good night's sleep to restore all of Plougaz's serenity? Was he no longer thinking about the Devil's Tower and the terrible apparitions that had caused such a stir in the Château de Coquerel?

"Well?" said Monsieur de Plougaz.

"Would milord like me to give him an account of the steps I took yesterday?"

Monsieur de Plougaz shrugged his shoulders irritably. "To the Devil with your accounts and your steps!" he cried. "Do you think you can distract me by talking to me about such things? Go away, Master, and send in my huntsman."

The steward obeyed immediately—but the blow had been struck. It had only required one word to return the old gentleman to his somber thoughts. When the huntsman presented himself, Monsieur de Plougaz looked at him bleakly, and gave him a cool reception. "I don't require your services, knave," he said to him. "Go away, and send in my steward."

Master Luc Morfil soon appeared at the half-open door for the second time, red-faced and smiling slyly. He came forward hesitantly, making a slight bow, and stood in front of Plougaz.

"What did you do yesterday, Master Luc?" said the latter.

"I carried out your orders, my lord."

"What orders?"

"Milord ordered me to advertise the imminent sale of Coquerel."

"I ordered that?"

"Yes, my lord... and to search for buyers."

"Are you quite sure, Master Luc, that I ordered that?"

"Yes, my lord," the steward answered, again.

"Well, Master Luc," Plougaz went on, "I believe that you're right. I remember something of the sort... but I hope that it has not yet been possible to advertise the sale."

"It has, milord."

"At least you haven't found a buyer?"

"I have."

Plougaz got up and walked around the room twice, whistling an old march. Then he leaned on a windowsill and looked at the grey clouds that were racing across the sky.

Master Luc followed him with his gaze, like a cat watching its prey. *You're done for*, he thought. *You're caught by the neck. The more you struggle, the quicker you'll be strangled.*

"What time is it?" Monsieur de Plougaz suddenly asked.

"Eleven o'clock in the morning, milord."

"There's still time! Master Luc, my friend, mount your mule and go to Bécherel. Order the crier to proclaim that he was mistaken, and that his previous publication is to be considered null and void..."

"You think so!" the steward tried to say.

"Then," Monsieur de Plougaz continued, calmly, "you must go to the buyer you have found. Tell him not to bother taking his *écus* out of his strongbox. I shall keep my lovely Château de Coquerel."

The steward sighed deeply. "But what reason shall I give?" he asked, dispiritedly.

"My pleasure, Master Luc."

"That's not enough..."

"Master Luc, I give you permission to say that you were subject to a fit of madness, and that your madness took the form of wanting to sell Coquerel."

Wanting to buy it, more like! Luc thought. Aloud, he said: "Milord, I am eager to obey you... but who knows whether you might change your mind?"

"I detest *buts*, Master Luc."

"Alas, milord, this is the first time that I've ever disputed your orders."

"It's one too many."

"If the Evil One..."

Plougaz looked his steward in the face. The latter lost his newly-restored color; he did not have the strength to finish.

The old lord reflected for a few moments. "Do you mean, Master Luc," he resumed, after a pause, "that you know the intentions of the Malign Spirit?"

"God forbid!" Morfil murmured, making the sign of the cross.

"Go saddle your mount. Come back before you go to receive my final orders."

Master Luc did not rub his hands as he went down the great staircase of Coquerel. The day was not as good as the previous one. The lovely château was slipping through his fingers. Nevertheless, he did not lose heart, and resolved to fight until the end.

"Tomorrow," he said to himself, "the Devil's Tower will have done its work, and Plougaz will not be so intractable."

When he had put the halter and saddle on his mule, he went back to the dining-room. A new idea seemed to have come into the old châtelain's mind; he had struck a pose of joyous determination.

"There are brave gentlemen in the vicinity of Dinan, Master Luc," he said, on seeing the other come in. "By the blood of Yan Plugastel, [38] my benevolent ancestor, we'll find ten there who'll want to take on the adventure for every one who won't!"

"What adventure?" asked the anxious Norman.

"Milord Bertrand du Guesclin,[39] the redoubtable Constable, did not take all the good blood in his veins into his tomb," Monsieur de Plougaz continued, instead of answering. "We have hard heads and warm hearts... Ah, Master Luc, Satan will meet his match!"

Morfil felt gooseflesh forming.

"We shall fight him, Master Luc!" Plougaz added. "For the glory of God! We shall fight him with the pyx and the sword: the arms of Heaven and the arms of Earth. Ah! When Plougaz awakes, his enemies must beware!"

The pyx may come and go, Morfil thought, *but the sword...*

"And on that note, Master, seek out the buyer to whom you have promised the windfall. If I am vanquished in the struggle, then I shall be entirely ready to sell Coquerel. During your absence, all my people will mount horses and summon my noble friends. There's a feast this evening, Master Luc, at the lovely château. After supper, I shall propose that the most valiant among them should sleep in the Devil's Tower, in company with my noble cousin, the prior of Saint-Pierre-en-Plesguen. Oh, get on with it, Master Luc!"

Half an hour later, 30 of Plougaz's servants were carrying their lord's invitations at the gallop. The lovely château was known throughout the region for its splendid feasts; all those invited accepted.

Master Luc, for his part, urged his mule to a trot on the road to Dinan, and racked his brains for a means to conjure up a storm. If it had only been a matter of braving the exorcism of the venerable prior of Saint-Pierre-en-Plesguen, the Norman would not have been greatly distressed, but the sword of a gentleman–the most valiant, Monsieur de Plougaz had said– was not the sort of thing to be held in scorn.

Nevertheless, there was no going back. The crisis that was in preparation would be decisive. It was necessary to win, or to renounce the lovely château de Coquerel forever.

When he lifted the knocker at the establishment of his friend the attorney, the grown-up daughter with the grey eyes came to open it, and wished him welcome in an embarrassed manner.

"I'm in a hurry," the steward said. "Where's Master Roch, my girl?"

"My father's busy," replied the attorney's heir, darting a furtive glance at Master Luc's hands to see whether he might be carrying a velvet ribbon.

"That doesn't matter. Friends don't stand on ceremony." The steward pushed the girl aside unceremoniously and went in.

Master Roch Requin's retreat, possessed of a single window whose dusty panes did not allow much light to pass, enjoyed a half-light that would have been admirably suited to the boudoir of a famous coquette. In the middle of the room, objects could be made out fairly distinctly, but in the corners and in the shadow of the massive items of black oak furniture, nothing at all could be seen. This circumstance explained why Master Luc, on entering, did not see two men and a dog standing next to the wall, sheltered from the daylight by the edge of an ancient dresser.

"Down, Pluto!" one of these men murmured, softly.

The dog sank down on his paws, put his muzzle to the ground and remained motionless, quite inert.

"Oh! Good day, friend!" cried Master Roch Requin and Master Luc Morfil simultaneously.

They embraced one another with passionate satisfaction. as men do who cannot stand one another.

"Friend," Master Luc added, "you are invited to come to the Château de Coquerel this evening."

"Why?"

"To buy the manor, friend, if it pleases God, and with the aid of the benevolent evangelist, my patron saint."

"The Devil! The Devil!" said Master Roch.

Master Luc performed a pirouette, and made as if to begin a promenade around the room—which would doubtless have enabled him to discover the eyes hidden behind the dresser.

"Friend!" cried the attorney, grasping the steward's doublet in his hand and holding hard, "stay where you are if you want us to make plans. I have a delicate nervous system, and rapidly fall ill when people move around me too much."

Master Luc sat down on a chair.

"So you were saying," Requin continued, with evident relief, "that you had a pleasant journey home yesterday."

"I said nothing of the kind, friend. I said that it's necessary that you come to the château this evening."

"On due reflection, I can't see any reason why not, friend. You'll have the thousand *écus* ready?"

"Of course."

"And you'll marry my daughter?"

"With pleasure."

"I'm giving you a treasure there, friend."

"You've already told me that!" murmured the steward, ungraciously. "*Au revoir*, Master Roch, and let us not delay."

As the steward went to the door, Master Roch followed him with a mocking and superior gaze.

As soon as he had gone, Pluto shook his shaggy mane and stood up. The two men came out of hiding.

"You see, milord," Master Roch said to one of them, "that I have not deceived you. I hope that the frankness of my confession will protect my head."

"I'll need two good horses and the complete costume of a gentleman for this evening," the young lord said, seemingly lost in thought, "and a velvet mask."

"You shall have them."

"My companion will need a mask too, and a squire's costume."

"I shall be only too happy to provide them."

"You'll be paid later, Master. The horses must be thoroughbreds, and the clothes magnificent."

Master Roch went out to carry out these instructions. The two men waited in silence, with the dog stretched out at their feet.

When dusk fell, the lovely château was illuminated from bottom to top. Plougaz had not been wasting his time while his servants were on the road. A splendid table covered with fooodstuffs of every sort stood in the great hall. The chandeliers were all lit. There was a man-at-arms carrying a flaming torch on every step of the *perron*, lighting the courtyard.

The noise of a cavalcade was soon heard. The firm and brisk hoofbeats of noble horses sounded on the distant heath. The noise was briefly muffled by the grass in the avenue, then it resumed, crisper and clearer, on the paving-stones of the courtyard. It was Plougaz's guests, responding to his summons. Master Luc, lurking in an obscure corner, counted 30, and measured 30 swords with his eyes, the shortest of which seemed extraordinarily long.

They arrived one after another; their well-trained horses stopped at the foot of the perron. They threw their bridles to their squires and leapt to the ground, making the golden rowels of their spurs clink.

It was, in truth, a fine spectacle to see the proud bearing of all these noble men. Their faces, lit by the ruddy torchlight, seemed more haughty, their costumes more picturesque. The nocturnal breeze caused the plumes in their felt hats to undulate gently while they mounted the steps of the perron.

The prior of Saint-Pierre-en-Plesguen did not come.

The kitchen also had its festival atmosphere. A blazing fire was set in the hearth, and old Anne, in the midst of vessels of every sort and superimposed spits, could scarcely find enough room to burn her insensible toes at her ease and turn the handle of her spinning-wheel. She remained silent and dejected in the middle of the noise and movement. The odor of roasting meat did not seem to affect her sense of smell; the noise did not penetrate her ears. Perhaps her mind was wandering in the mysterious spaces that constitute the world of witches. Perhaps, while her feet still touched the Earth of the living, her soul was already testing the unknown footpaths of the domain of the dead.

The people of Coquerel had forgotten their terrors. The night of respite that Satan had granted the château might be the beginning of a permanent peace. The most cowardly recovered their courage. There was a general movement, a universal activity, a contagious and exciting joy. No one was insensible but old Anne and Yaumi's fiancée, Yvonne, who was hiding away to pour out her tears.

Monsieur de Plougaz, standing in the middle of his drawing-room, received his guests with respect, cordiality and condescension, according to whether they were his superiors, his equals or his inferiors–but he always maintained an irreproachable courtesy towards everyone, because, beyond accidental and natural distinctions, there was a fundamental equality between them all. He was surrounded by his peers.

When the last invited guest had come in, the outer door was closed and the feast began.

It is scarcely necessary to say that the guests gave themselves wholeheartedly to their joyous duty. The foodstuffs disappeared, the cups clinked together incessantly, and the Breton spirit–which is not very delicate by nature but susceptible nevertheless to the occasional production of a witty remark, a stunning argument or a renovated cock-and-bull story–wrought marvels that night. According to the chronicle from which our story is taken, Monsieur de Plougaz alone made 56 puns. He launched so many sarcasms at Sir Judicaël Trévesron, lord of Conantruiltz–a rich capitalist–that the aforementioned knight half-drew his six-foot sword three or four times. (It is necessary to observe at this point that the aforementioned capitalist had recently acquired the manor of Coatvizillirouët, which is why Monsieur de Plougaz bore him a legitimate grudge.)

During the second serving, at the moment when the general merriment was at its height, Plougaz summoned his steward. Morfil appeared immediately, in his formal costume, wearing his silver chain of office around his neck.

"Master Luc," said Monsieur de Plougaz, "go and fetch this buyer you have found for my Château de Coquerel."

All the guests opened their eyes wide in astonishment. Master Luc did as he was told.

"What, Plougaz!" said a Porhoët bastard. "You're going to sell your lovely château, my old friend!"

"Sell Coquerel!" the amazed assembly repeated.

"The Devil is forcing my hand, Messieurs," said Plougaz, calmly.

They mistook the meaning of these words.

"I'll give you ten thousand *livres*..."

"A thousand *ducats*..."

"Ten thousand *écus*..."

The bids came from every direction. This is what was said; we affirm it in all conscience. What would they have done the next day? That is a difficult question.

Master Luc came back in, leading Master Roch by the hand.

"The attorney!" they said, disgustedly. "Sell the nicest fief in the district to a parchment-scratcher...!" And they started to bid more warmly.

"Plougaz, I'll give you 20,000 *livres*..."

"Two thousand *ducats*..."

"Twenty thousand *écus*...."

The Chevalier de Conantruiltz was the only one who said nothing. For that reason, he told no lies.

"I don't want your money, my loyal companions," Plougaz relied, "but I have a favor to ask you."

"What must we do?"

"You've misunderstood me. Listen."

At this point, Monsieur Plougaz told them what happened every night in the Devil's Tower. While he told his tale, half a dozen of the guests slipped away discreetly. "What must we do?" he said, as he finished. "One of you must sleep in the Devil's Tower tonight."

Intrepidity is commonplace in Brittany, but Breton intrepidity only braves material dangers. Among all these warriors, the least valiant of whom would willingly have fought ten men

173

in an enclosed field, there was not one who did not shiver at Plougaz's proposition."

"You don't reply!" the latter went on, anxiously and reproachfully.

"Neighbor," said the Chevalier de Conantruiltz, "I offer you my kindest regards. Farewell, my friends!"

He went out. A few others followed his example. Twenty guests remained around the table.

"It will be necessary, then, to sell the lovely Château de Coquerel," Monsieur de Plougaz said, sadly,

Master Luc could scarcely contain his joy. Master Roch said nothing, and gave no thought to the matter.

Suddenly, the Porhoët bastard rapped on the table with his gauntlet, cheerfully. "By Saint Guignolé, Messieurs!" he cried. "The lovely château shall not be sold, and Plougaz will have satisfaction from his tenebrous enemy. Here we have, in this room, 20 honest lords, who fear God but nothing else. Can we not all sleep together in the haunted room?"

Master Luc bit his thin lip until it bled.

At the moment when the bastard had begun to speak, the door had opened quietly. A richly-dressed gentlemen, with his face covered by a velvet mask, appeared on the threshold and paused, unnoticed. Behind him was a squire, similarly masked. Behind the squire, in the shadows, one might have been able to perceive two round red luminous eyes–the eyes of the dog Pluto.

"Well, Messieurs, what do you think?" said the Porhoët bastard.

Plougaz's guests drained their cups and came to their feet. "So be it!" they replied. "We shall sleep in the haunted room."

The gentleman in the velvet mask crossed the room, followed by his squire, who was followed by Pluto. At the sight of him, a mocking smile formed on the lips of Master Roch, who glanced covertly at his friend, Master Luc.

"Fie, my lords!" said the newcomer, in a curt and haughty tone. "Twenty against one–that's 19 too many."

At the sound of that voice, Master Luc felt his heart leap in his breast. Monsieur Plougaz himself felt his emotions stir, without knowing why.

"Go make your beds, my valiant lords, in rooms where you may sleep in peace," the stranger went on. "For the honor of the land of Brittany, I will not suffer 20 blades to be unsheathed against one single weapon, even if that weapon is Satan's horn!"

"Who are you?" demanded ten angry voices at the same time. "Who are you to dare to speak thus?"

"My name is scarcely important, my lords; if it pleases you, I shall not tell you until tomorrow. Hold your peace. I, my squire and my dog will sleep in the Devil's Tower."

As he spoke these words, the stranger seized a lighted torch from the table and went to the door, unhesitatingly choosing the one that led to the northern tower. His squire marched in his wake, and Pluto followed the squire. In the general disquiet, no one was wary of the dog.

The guests remained where they were, stupefied. Plougaz had put his head in his hands. Master Luc regained his smile. Master Roch winked an eye in an expressive fashion. We must suppose that the attorney knew that it would not be necessary to keep up appearances for much longer.

VI. In Which the Devil Laughs

We know that the haunted room had once served as young Monsieur de Plougaz's private quarters, before his departure for Palestine. During the day, everything had been done to render it habitable. Two beds had been made up. On the bedside tables, two jugs full of wine, with silver cups, invited the guests of Coquerel to drink a nightcap before retiring.

Now, it was Master Luc who had placed these jugs there, and Master Luc did nothing without a good reason.

The stranger and his squire came in, still followed by Pluto. They took off their masks. The master was Arthur de Plougaz; the servant was Yaumi.

Arthur looked around the room, sadly and bleakly.

The last time I saw these paintings and tapestries, he thought, *they were bright and shining; my heart was young and warm. The years have taken care of all that. I have penetrated the mysteries of life. My heart has wilted as these paintings have faded.*

When Arthur and Yaumi had said their evening prayers, dutifully, they drank a cup of wine to give them strength in case of a nocturnal attack, and threw themselves on their beds fully dressed, holding their naked swords in their hands. Pluto slipped silently beneath Arthur's bed.

Scarcely had the master and the servant lain down than they fell into a leaden sleep. Master Luc had mixed the wine set on their tables with a narcotic liquor. From 10 p.m. to midnight, they tried to outdo one another with their snores.

At midnight, Master Luc, with his face blackened and his head crowned with frightful horns, came in by the hidden door. He was carrying all his apparatus: chains, resin lamps, pieces of iron, etc. We may suppose that he had not forgotten his little dagger.

He crept up to the bed.

"It's certainly them," he said, after having studied them momentarily.

He deposited his burden and took out his dagger.

"All things considered," he murmured, "my conscience will be neither more nor less heavy, since I thought I had killed them both already."

In consequence of this argument, Master Luc dispatched Yaumi to the other world with the aid of his little dagger. This time, he took care to strike as hard as necessary, in order not to have to do it yet again.

There remained Arthur de Plougaz. At the moment when Morfil turned to attend to him, a muffled groan was audible. Master Luc cocked an ear and paused.

Bah! he thought, after a moment's anxiety. *My ears are ringing.*

He lifted his hand and drew aside Plougaz's bedclothes. A second howl seemed to emanate from the floor.

Even so, Master Luc struck Arthur. The young man released a loud cry and yielded up his soul.

At that cry, Pluto leapt out of the refuge that he had found beneath his master's bed and put his forepaws on the coverlet. Morfil, at his appearance, had recoiled to the other end of the room. The dog licked the bloody wound and yapped plaintively.

Luc was afraid. He tried to slide along the wall to reach the secret door, but he had scarcely got half way when Pluto, suddenly leaving the bed, leapt into the middle of the room and barred his passage.

Man and dog looked at one another. Never had Pluto's red eyes displayed a scarlet so ardent. They were two globes of fire radiating beneath the bristly hair of his eyelids. He had gathered himself on his muscular legs; his belly touched the floor.

Master Luc began trembling like a leaf. His teeth chattered. The dagger slipped out of his hand.

"Mercy, Pluto, mercy!" he cried, mad with terror.

Pluto growled deeply, opened his mouth wide, and stood up on his extended limbs. Then he seized the steward by the neck, and brought his powerful jaws into play.

Master Luc became livid, then red, then violet. When Pluto let go, he fell backwards heavily.

When the count was complete, there were three dead men in the room. For which of them had the *candle* come down?

Here the tradition bifurcates into two versions, of which one is marvelous and the other natural. As one might expect, the former is more widely credited. This is it:

Only one cadaver was found in the Devil's Tower: that of Master Luc Morfil. Nothing was ever heard of the knight who had gone to bed in the haunted chamber, nor of his squire.

A few months afterwards, Monsieur de Plougaz received a missive from the Holy Land, which told him of the death of his son. That death had taken place on the day when the people of Coquerel saw a *candle* floating above the chimneys of the lovely château.

Clever men inferred from this that the knight and his squire were the specters of young Plougaz and poor Yaumi. The steward's two victims had emerged from the tomb in order to avenge themselves. Pluto was nothing but a subaltern demon awaiting the death of Master Luc to carry his soul away to Hell.

This is the second version:

Monsieur Plougaz buried his sole heir with great ceremony. Yaumi had a humble cross in the cemetery, and Yvonne was often seen kneeling at the foot of that cross. Master Luc's corpse was thrown to the crows, but the crows did not want it.

Since that day, no diabolical apparition has troubled the lovely Château de Coquerel.

Pluto, the faithful animal, lived for a long time and was honorably stuffed.

As the name of Plougaz did not become extinct until three or four centuries later, one must presume that the old lord took a wife, as is the duty of a noble man who has seen his heir die. In Master Luc's strongbox, he found the means to pay for the wedding.

When the costs of the wedding had been paid, enough *écus* remained in the chest for Plougaz to repair the lovely château's chapel and retrieve the manor of Coatvizillirouët–whose name he suddenly ceased to find ridiculous–from the hands of Conantruiltz.

As for old Anne Parker, she attained an age so implausible that we do not dare say what it was. The great-grandchildren of the characters in the story saw her moving her lips without speaking, wriggling her toes in the ashes of the fire, and spinning with neither thread nor distaff. From time to time, every ten or 15 years, she recovered the power of speech to ask for news of Simon Troarec, the handsome steward of Plougaz.

One day, at the hour of vespers, she stopped turning her spinning-wheel and began singing:

"By night, they dance on the floor,
"Where the grain is threshed:
"Ah, they leap so well,
"When the twilight comes...
"And you, lover boy,
"Seek your fortune!"

While she sang thus, the flame of the fire chanced to touch the hem of her skirt. The old woman burst into flames immediately, and was consumed in the blink of an eye like a bundle of dry straw.

Between Bécherel and Dinan, the general opinion is that, had it not been for that fortuitous occurrence, old Anne Parker would be living still.

The Belles-de-Nuit

I. The Legend

The Château de Penhoël was a very old house of melancholy appearance, which had a row of 21 windows on each floor of its façade. Its plaintive weather-vanes stood up above the great oaks of the Forêt du Theil, between the Lande-Triste and the marshes of Saint-Vincent on the borders of Morbihan and the Île de Vilaine.

The long straight avenue extended its six rows of chestnut trees as far as the road between Redon and Gacilly, and two curtains of fir trees, projecting from the château like two unfurled wings, gave its physiognomy a strangely sepulchral expression–for houses too have their physiognomy. I know austere ones that have the grey beards and large wrinkles of gentlemen weighed down by age and anxiety. I know vain ones that proudly dominate the vassal countryside as if they were loudly proclaiming the haughty devices inscribed on the brand new coats-of-arms above their gateways. I know stupidly puffed-up ones, whose modern rotundity swells like a turkey's crop. I know innocent ones, which display their white façades with all the naïve self-satisfaction that shines on the florid cheeks of an upstart dealer in ladies' clothing.

There are houses all over Paris that reproduce the pretensions of their bourgeois châtelains. They are exactly the kinds of shells required by the snails of the boutiques and salons–which are, for the most part, exceedingly pretty little animals–that are known as Parisiennes. Such houses owe their form to architects who have designed them like items of confectionery, behind little gates that are the owner's pride and joy, in the middle of little parks that are masterpieces of bad taste. They have fountains, lakes, woods and lawns, but have fountains, lakes, woods and lawns, but they have to be closed whenever there is a thaw, for fear that they might be carried away, stuck to the soles of someone's shoes.

It is not like that in Brittany. The hard granite that is everywhere in that poor land, like the bones beneath the muscles of an athlete's body, makes solid and heavy houses that are black in the dusk and whose stony faces cannot be unwrinkled even by the Sun. You see them along the roads, in the depths of water-filled vales or on shaggy mountain-crests. The forest always accompanies them, extending backwards like the mane on a lion's neck. They are large, often solitary; their pride is never puerile or talkative. One might think that they were gazing sadly at the large estates surrounding them; they invariably seem regretful of something, or of someone. The Château de Penhoël was one of these vast dwellings, built as circumstances demanded to fit the family's needs. That was perhaps fortunate, since utilitarian architecture is often the most beautiful.

Penhoël, sprawling across the summit of a mountain with its massive main section and its two unequal wings, was the pride of the district and would have intrigued the eye of a painter. It seemed—and this is the highest possible compliment—to be a necessary part of the scene that the hand of God had designed. It could not have been taken away without destroying the harmony of the view, and it was impossible to imagine that it might be replaced by another dwelling.

There was nothing about it that was monumental in itself, save for its very simplicity. One saw at first glance that it had belonged to Bretons of the old sort: landed gentlemen living and dying on the soil. The domestic accommodations, in fact, only occupied one side of the courtyard; the other was the farm, which thus formed an integral part of the building, while the smallholders, to all appearances, qualified as part of the family.

The farm had an enormous ground-floor room surrounded by items of rustic furniture, among which it was possible to distinguish two-story beds, flanked by block-mounted dressers and enclosed by curtains of coarse green serge. The floor was compacted earth. The light entered by the door, which had no other auxiliary than a tiny glazed window that could not be opened. In the hearth, a few half-consumed firebrands covered with white ash sent lazy spirals of smoke along the pot-hook, which resembled a gigantic saw. The rays of the setting Sun added a purplish blue tint to the vague transparency of the smoke as they passed through it.

Turk was asleep, his sticky eyes closed and his paws lost in the cinders. Turk was a sturdy dog of good pedigree, forced by lean times to accept the work of a guard-dog. Families were in decline in Brittany—the families of dogs as well as those of men.

In the fireplace itself, on two square blocks of wood polished by the friction of pantaloons and canvas trousers, two old peasants were smoking their little short-stemmed pipes. Marthe was operating her spinning-wheel. Jacqueline was cutting up resolidified buckwheat porridge to make soup in the huge tin-plated cauldron. Around the table, three or four youths were sipping cider from bowls.

Marthe was the smallholder's mother. She was nearly 80 years old. Jacqueline, the lady of the house, was in the prime of life. The two old men were neighbors. The youths gathered around the table had been bringing in the harvest. It was mid-August in the year 1846.

"The grain's thick and heavy this year, and that's no lie," said Josille, one of the harvesters.

"Good straw too, then," added Joson, his friend.

"Tall and free, as true as I'm sitting here!" agreed José, the third grain-cutter.

The old mother spat on her hemp. "Cut grain isn't threshed," she pronounced, in a dull and sententious tone.

"Threshed grain isn't gathered," old Vincent added.

"Gathered grain isn't eaten," the mother concluded, making her spinning-wheel turn more rapidly.

In Brittany, village conversations proceed thus, in sets of axioms–but these axioms nearly always contain allusions to present matters and imply much more than they say.

"Is there some news, mother?" asked Jacqueline, the lady of the house.

"There is," replied the smallholder as he came in. "It's that *our master* wants to put *our monsieur* in prison to finish him off."

The smallholder was named Jean-Marie Dolet. He was a handsome peasant of about 40, of Herculean build, brazened by the mists of the marshes. He threw his large hat on the table and sat down gloomily.

Ordinarily, the two expressions *our master* and *our monsieur* are identical in their significance. When the Breton peasant separates them, it is because his farm has recently changed its ownership. *Our master* is then the man who collects the rent; *our monsieur* is the one who previously collected it. In general, *our master* does not purchase the farmer's affection along with the farm. People are very slow to adapt, out there, to new things and new people. If he has been a good landlord, *our monsieur* takes all the tenderness of those good hearts, obstinate in their affection, away with him.

This was the case here. Monsieur le Marquis de Pontalès, *our master*, who was not yet beloved, had bought the property of the Vicomte Hoël de Penhoël, *our monsieur*, who was still beloved.

"A lot of water will have passed under the bridge at Gacilly before this is finished, Jean-Marie my son," said the other, "you mark my words."

"Why do you say that, old woman?"

"Because the Belles-de-Nuit are haunting the river, boy."

"Will the Belles-de-Nuit bring money to Penhoël?"

"Perhaps."

Old Marthe's spinning-wheel groaned again and the spindle turned. Jacqueline had put the cauldron on the pot-hook and reanimated the half-extinct firebrands. Large bubbles emerged from the murmurous water.

"Put the buckwheat flour in the stewpot, daughter," the old woman ordered, abruptly. "The Belles-de-Nuit will come for their share this evening."

"Who told you that, mother?"

"My little finger."

A slight shiver ran through the assembly.

"Pontalès," Mother Marthe went on, "has forbidden the taking of bread, vegetables or animal flesh to the Maison Gaillot, where *our monsieur* and is wife are in distress. But Monsieur le Recteur [40] says from the pulpit: 'Feed those who are hungry.' Pontalès wanted to put old Turk down, because he had belonged to Penhoël. There are good men and wicked men. Should we obey the good who can do nothing for us? Should we obey the wicked who can turn us out, as naked as earthworms, when the lease rums out?"

Jean-Marie seized a handful of his long tawny hair and drew it across his brow, which was bathed with sweat.

"The Recteur speaks in the name of the crucified Lord," old Vincent said, shaking the ash from his pipe.

"Jean-Marie Dolet has four children," the other old man replied. "What concerns him is whether he wants to see them begging for bread by the roadside."

"What concerns him concerns you, too, Pierre Dolet," the mother retorted, emphatically, "spying on your parents and your friends for Pontalès, to whom you've sold your soul." She resumed her work, saying: "Put a portion aside for the Belles-de-Nuit anyway, lady of the house."

The Belles-de-Nuit may not be well-known elsewhere, so I shall tell you the pleasing legend inspired in our Breton poets by the sight of wisps of mist floating on the marsh between the Earth and the sky. Stars, flowers and transparent vapors reminiscent of long veils floating about invisible phantoms are all "Belles-de-Nuit" to them—but there is a story.

The first Belles-de-Nuit were three young women, the nieces of King Grallon, whose heiress, Ahès, committed enough crimes to bring down on the city of Is the divine wrath that annihilated Sodom and Gomorrah. The three nieces were as pure as Princess Ahès was wicked, and–as is often the case–their saintliness was regarded as a crime by Ahès' favorites. Good King Grallon was too weak to defend his nieces against his daughter. Apart from his weakness, he was a very worthy King.

It is necessary to say that the city of Is, of which you might never have heard mention, was, at the time of King Grallon, Saint Guénolé and Saint Corentin,[41] the finest city in the world. It is from her that Paris took her name. Paris, being the most beautiful capital after the city of Is, was called Par-Is–which is to say, similar to the city of Is. The fact is absolutely certain, although the majority of historians have omitted to mention it.

The city of Is was build on the edge of the sea and occupied an immense area. Its bell-towers were so numerous that no one was able to count them. Its palaces dazzled the eyes, as much by their multitudinousness as their magnificence.

In one of these palaces, which was devoted to the fine arts, a thousand young people were brought up at the state's expense, receiving lessons from 100 professors, every one a man of genius. The French came to see the city of Is as the people of southern Brittany now throng to Paris; the city of Is laughed heartily at their accent and their manners. When people encountered some badly-dressed dimwit at a chariot-race, a concert or on the promenade, mooning over the marvels of the splendid capital, everyone thought: *that must be a bumpkin from Paris.*

In addition to all the miracles of her grandeur, the city of Is had one item of ornamentation that Paris will always lack. She had the sea: the vast sea, beloved by God and men alike; the mirror in which the sky contemplates, by turns, the starry azure of its firmament and the gold of its radiant Sun.

The world desired that its metropolis should have its feet in the sea that was her wealth and her power. Some day, the sea will come to Paris, or Paris will go to the sea.

The entire city of Is was within sight of the sea. The windows of her palaces looked out upon the bed of purple and gold in which the evening Sun lays its dazzling fatigue to rest. A forest of masts, longer and broader than the forest of Broceliande, set the flags of all the countries in the universe swaying around its quays. It is the city of London, sullen and gloomy but unmatchably opulent, that has gathered that part of the heritage of King Grallon. Thus, each of the two races has its share according to its genius: to the French, the artistic glory; to the English, the wealth generated by navigation and trade.

An excess of prosperity leads to evil. The saints, who were then abundant in the hermitages of Brittany, came together once, and the city of Is was astonished by the sight of that army of soldiers of Christ, which bore no weapons: all those long white beards, all those humble faces crowned with halos. It is said that the saints had come to tell King Grallon the story of the fall of Babylon.

King Grallon was afraid. He would have been quite prepared to cast corruption out of his city, but corruption was named Ahès, and King Grallon had a father's foolish tenderness.

Besides which, who ever listens to saints?

The city of Is was protected from the sea by a marble rampart, which had a dozen gates in order that the tide could fill its docks. The King kept the keys of these 12 gates under the pillow on his bed, for a treacherous or imprudent hand might use them to introduce death.

One morning, Princess Ahès arrived while the King was getting up. She offered to his kisses a forehead overhung by the curls of her black hair, steeped in exotic unctions. She summoned a smile to her lips, which intoxicated like strong liquor, and said: "Lord, your three nieces, Princesses Ysol, Ellé and Milla, have insulted your daughter."

"And how, beloved," the King asked her, "have the three saintly recluses been able to insult the queen of my heart?"

Ahès could only reply that it was their very saintliness that censured her debauchery. She summoned tears to her aid.

When Grallon saw her weep, he gave her his nieces Ellé, Ysol and Milla.

He would have given her his soul.

Ahès found her smile again to thank her father. Before leaving, though, she stole the keys to the floodgates that were beneath his pillow.

There was an Oriental vessel at anchor, carrying a powerful Prince who had promised Princess Ahès the three most beautiful diamonds in Golconda if she would let him into the city.[42] She loved diamonds; evil had no cost to her damned soul. It was to let the foreign Prince in that she had stolen the keys from her father's bedhead.

A great feast was prepared in her palace to welcome the Oriental Prince. During dessert, Ahès intended to summon her three cousins and give them to the Orientals as slaves, so that they might be taken away to the infidel lands.

Now, that same morning, a tonsured man passed through the city streets, riding on a grey donkey marked with a white cross. The tonsured man did not speak to anyone, but he sang the Latin verses of the *Dies irae* in a strong deep voice as he went on his way.[43] As he passed by, he blessed the churches, which opened all the high windows in their Gothic arches in response to his voice, to give passage to the statues of saints and the characters in pious paintings, which flew up into the sky.

It was an extraordinary thing, and one that had never been seen before.

The people of the city of Is asked one another: *What does it mean? What can it mean?* But none of them knew the answer.

Princess Ahès, informed of the fact, gave the order to seize the tonsured man and his donkey. Laughing–for she was cheerful by nature–she said: "Since the stone saints are yielding their places to us, we shall use the churches to accommodate our horses."

Others have said, and even done, similar things since those times, for man without God descends to a level below four-legged brutes.

The tonsured man was thrown off his donkey. Even so, he arrived at the King's palace and called out three times: "Grallon! Grallon! Grallon!" Then he added: "Famed Grallon, your city is lost; save your soul!"

He stopped in front of the prison in which the three young sisters, Milla, Ellé and Ysol, were being held. He made the sign of the cross on the door, saying "Soul of the Earth, Soul of the Sea, Soul of the Air!" As Princess Ahès' guards ran forward to seize him, he vanished like a mist, pronouncing the name of Saint Guénolé.

The donkey escaped from those who had stolen it and took refuge in King Grallon's palace. It was there when night fell.

Princess Ahès' palace stood out amid of the darkness, as resplendent as a great crystal chandelier. The feast commenced, and the Oriental Prince himself placed the three diamonds, as big as eggs and sparkling from a thousand facets, in the beautiful Ahès' black tresses.

Outside, a storm was raging. The sea boomed and the ships groaned as they were thrown about on their anchors. Ahès heard the storm. She lifted her glass and challenged the Ocean, crying: "To your health, tempest!"

The dam was as high, thick and solid as a mountain. One could make merry in the city of Is, despite the sea's threats; the rampart had long been proof against the most powerful storms and the highest tides.

Good King Grallon, however, had gone to bed at 9 p.m., as was his custom, for he led an orderly life.

At midnight, he was woken up by a voice, which said to him: "Get up, famed Grallon!"

He looked around, rubbing his eyes, and saw the donkey, which fixed its fiery eyes upon him. The sea was howling so loudly that he thought the English were in the city.

"Who spoke?" he asked. "Donkey, was that you?"

It must have been the donkey, for the donkey replied: "Your city is lost; save your soul."

King Grallon was not yet fully awake. He set himself astride the donkey's back anyway, and the donkey went down the stairs four at a time. When they were in the street, the King said: "If there really is danger, we must go warn my daughter Ahès."

"Save your soul," his mount retorted.

The King saw that the donkey was obviously prejudiced against Princess Ahès. To get around it, he brought up the three saints.

"We must go look for my three nieces, Ysol, Ellé and Milla," he said.

"Save your soul!"

Good King Grallon held tight to the bridle; the donkey was going faster than the wind. It went towards the east, where the mountains were. It was unstoppable.

Behind him, the King heard a strange noise, which no longer resembled the distant clamor of the tempest.

"What's that?" he asked.

The donkey replied, for the fourth time: "Save your soul."

That was more than sufficient, for a donkey; few men speak as well as that.

Meanwhile, Ahès, in her palace, cried: "Hey! Bring me my three dear cousins, Ellé, Ysol and Milla!" The French wine had put fire into her cheeks. The Oriental Prince paid her the compliments of Golconda, as sparkling as its diamonds.

The three young saints were brought in–three angels of the Lord! Their soft blue eyes fixed themselves on Ahès, and all three of them murmured at the same time: "Repent, Daughter of the King!"

Ahès burst out laughing.

At that moment, the strange noise that Grallon had heard reached the hall where the feast was being held, and the Princess likewise asked; "What's that?"

"It's the wrath of the Lord," the three virgins replied.

"It's the Ocean, which is also having a party," said the Oriental Prince, whose eyes were bright with terrible laughter.

"So much the better!" cried the Princess. "If the Ocean comes, we'll drink it!"

One should not judge the Princesses of that era by the beautiful Ahès. It is because of her that certain young ladies of today are still called "Princesses"–meaning that they have got shamefully drunk and thrown their hats to the wind. The fact is that other Princesses were not in the habit of behaving like Ahès, who drank a lot, and had drunk even more than usual that night.

In her gaiety, she ordered her officers to lock the three princesses in a dungeon. On hearing that order, Ysol, Ellé and Milla joined hands and asked God to pardon their persecutrix.

But the Ocean had heard Princess Ahès' foolish challenge. A heart-rending voice like the cry of a storm, which came from who knows where, pronounced these words: "Daughter of the King, drink me!" And an enormous wave swept in through the shattered windows.

There was but one cry in that feasting-hall, compounded of a thousand blasphemies. Above that cry, the voices of the three virgins rose, saying: "Hosanna to the Highest of the Heavens!"

The Oriental Prince had seized Ahès in his knotty arms. His eyes shone like two fiery coals. Smoke was coming out of his mouth. The sea rose within the room as on a beach. The sea, as it rose, could not drown his eyes. It requires something more than sea-water to extinguish the stare of a demon.

But where had the sea come from? Had it broken the dam, as high and strong as a mountain?

The sea was coming through the gates that Ahès herself had opened with the keys stolen from King Grallon's bedhead. The Princess had found the diamonds so beautiful that she had forgotten to close the floodgate through which, at low tide, she had let in the Oriental Prince. And the Ocean had entered at high tide–and Princess Ahès, as she had said by way of bravado, *drank the Ocean.*

All the guests were under the water, which was already stifling their last breaths. The three virgins were floating above the waves, and praising God.

Meanwhile, good King Grallon, mounted on his donkey, had reached the top of a mountain. He turned round to look at his capital city–the largest, the most beautiful, the most noble city lit by the Sun. Good King Grallon could no longer see anything: neither towers, nor belfries, nor balconies, nor gilded domes, nor ramparts serrated like scallops. Instead of all that, there was the sea, for the tempest had suddenly abated, and the Ocean had unfolded an immense shroud upon the dead city.

There was nothing left–nothing, you understand, but three floating white forms.

King Grallon fell to his knees and beat his breast. The donkey had vanished, but when King Grallon got up again, he found Saint Guénolé standing next to him, with a halo around his bald head and a long grey beard that hung down to his breast.

They both went down to the strand to look at the white objects floating above the disaster. There was one star of the sky, one flower of the Earth and one wisp of vapor.

The little star is one that appears in the morning, perceived by the diligent as a sign of hope. The simple flower engarlands our hedges, suspending its silvery bells from the verdure of wild plums; they are the Virgin's bells.[44] The vapor, finally, is the pretty little cloud that rises over a moist, recently-closed grave, and shows us once more–vaguely, as in dream–the terrestrial form of the angel who has gone to Heaven.

The Belles-de-Nuit, the three Belles-de-Nuit: the star, the flower, the errant spirit; the soul of the water, the soul of the Earth, the soul of the air; Ysol, Ellé, Milla.

In Brittany, there are thousands of them. All the stars in its skies are souls; all the flowers in its fields are souls; all the vapors of its fields and lakes are souls! The nocturnal traveler is never alone on his path. He has the star that watches over him; if the star is hidden by a cloud, the cloud watches out instead of the star and refreshes the sleeping flower by letting a crystal tear fall into the white chalice of its corolla.

They are there, beneath the willows and the oaks, along the water and on the heath: a mysterious trinity whose three individuals bring the Earth and the sky together in taking one another by the hand. They are there, all of them: the virgins of Brittany; all those that God withdraws from the world before the hour of marriage; all the dear little souls as white as stars. And the tenderness that our poor peasants have for them is slightly mingled with fear. The Belles-de-Nuit are sometimes severe with evildoers, and with those who do not give bread to the needy.

A custom arises therefrom, which is touching even though it has a pagan taint, as so many old Breton customs do. When a young woman dies in a village, her parents, her friends and all those who loved her continue for a long time to make her share of a meal. They set that portion outside the threshold, at night. It is always taken away, without fail, for the Belle-de-Nuit takes it to *the poorest of the poor*, when the poorest of the poor cannot come in search of it themselves.

II. The Belles' Portion

The Sun had set behind the old wall bristling with ivy. Jacqueline came to light the candle held by a stick of hazelwood fixed between the stones under he mantelpiece. There was a perceptible odor produced by the little piece of lard that greased the saucepan, and gourmand nostrils were beginning to open up around the table.

The children had come back in after their games or labors. Simonne, the eldest, had been attending to the three cows. Annaïc, the younger daughter, had made the calf's bed of straw. Yvon, the elder son, had taken good care of the harness used on the grey horse and the two oxen. Little Pelo, I must confess, was still cording a whip for his spinning-top from three strands of carefully-plaited eelskin.

It was supper time; the household was gathered around the table and everyone was waiting impatiently for the lady of the house to pronounce the sacramental words: "To the soup, if you please, everyone," before saying a rustic grace.

Pelo, a plump child with hair more tangled than the ivy on the wall, took something out of his pocket. It was not a handkerchief–holy savior, handkerchiefs are for Monsieur le Recteur!–but a fourth piece of the eelskin that he was using to make his whip. The eelskin pulled another object out along with it, which fell, making a ringing noise as it collided with a ploughshare that Vincent was in the process of cleaning.

"What do you have there, boy?" the lady of the house asked. "It clinks like silver."

"As true as God is great," affirmed Monique, the servant, "it clinks like silver all right."

Joson, José and Josille did not disagree that it sounded like silver, for sure, and Jean-Marie, the father, affirmed in a grave tone: "No lie, that sounds like silver."

Pelo was red and rather sheepish. He scratched his head and made a show of looking under the table. When everyone bent down, they could see a 40-*sou* coin next to the ploughshare.

The lady of the house said: "Yes, it's silver."

"It certainly is!" confirmed the father. "That's silver, wife."

"True as I tell you, and no less, silver, for sure and for true! Forty *sous* marked on a little coin," said Josille.

"Yes it is!" added José.

As you can imagine, this conversation could have gone on for weeks without exhausting the intelligence of the participants. I can assure you that they put a very lively animation into it, which occasionally became passionate. The language they spoke is composed of a very small number of words; what its users think is not in the words but in their accompaniment. In this instance, astonishment was heaped up and curiosity vividly excited, but it was not until several minutes had lapsed, when the soup was already on the table, that the lady of the house finally asked: "Who gave it to you, boy?"

The old mother pushed her spinning-wheel away and put her spindle in its place. "Someone that has silver, for sure," she muttered, in a mocking tone that was not typical of her.

Then she sang, in a quavering voice:

Close to where we live there's
A seaport from whose dirty water:
Come shellfish,
Sea kale,
Sweet milk,
Trimmed cod!
Hoo-hoo!
That's the owl!

Aboard a boat there's
A naval admiral
And his sailors
Braggarts;
The cider's warm,
Grill the sardine!
Ho Ho!
That's the crow!

He says: I've forgotten
The way to my father's house;
Show it to me,
My lads,
Who smoke:
Where's my lady-friend?
Ha ha!
That's the cat!

Having sung thus, the old lady sat down in the middle of the bench and crossed her wrinkled hands on the table. If she had not been a good God-fearing woman with a rosary dangling from the belt of her skirt, many people might have taken her for a witch. She always knew much more than she said, but God alone knew how she knew it. She had not crossed the threshold of the farm to go out for a very long time.

"You've got something on your mind, mother, that's for sure," murmured the farmer, not without a certain anxiety.

"Tell us what it is," added his wife.

Everyone listened. The old woman made the sign of the cross and recited her grace, as everyone else had done, as best she could. It isn't always the best Latin that pleases the good Lord the most.

"Yes, yes," she murmured, wiping her wooden plate with her apron. "It must be a long time since he left, to have forgotten the way to his father's house!"

"Who are you talking about, mother?"

Instead of answering, the old woman called little Pelo and stroked his hair.

"Who gave you the coin, little beggar?" she asked, in a tone that mixed prayer and threat in such precise doses that the unruly child was felled by the first stroke.

"I don't know," he replied, in a sulky tone. "It was a bourgeois who's not from around here. I was catching elvers in the mud for my top. They're swarming like earthworms just now. Boy, were there a lot of elvers! *Hey, Poulot!* he said. I thought he'd said, Pelo, which is my name, so I looked up. He was well-to-do and shiny right as *our monsieur* used to be, and he said to me, *Poulot*, and I said *You mean Pelo*. He went on: *Poulot, is there somewhere around here, not far, the place where Monsieur le Vicomte de Penhoël lives?* Me, I said *What's that to you?* He'd just made me miss the fattest elver, you see. He said: *I'd like to know*. I laughed, because he put his hand in his waistcoat pocket. He laughed too, and I laughed louder. Oh, I laughed. I thought it'd be a *sou*. I saw the silver and I turned a cartwheel. But I didn't know it was worth 40 *sous*, grandma–give them to me!"

"We'll keep them for when you're older, Pelo," said the lady of the house.

Pelo took his place at the table, glumly.

The old woman leaned her grizzled head on her hand. "Who lives shall live," she murmured. "Pontalès is rich, but the good Lord sees clearly. Since the little demoiselles died, there are two more Belles-de-Nuit under the Moon, and when the uncle in clogs passes our doorway to go pray in the cemetery, I can hear what the wind says."

"What does the wind say, mother?" the lady of the house asked, in a low voice.

"The wind says: *We're here, we're here, we're here...* And the wind sings their names in the branches of the big fig-tree, my lads and lasses. The wind sings like this: *Louise! Marie! Louise! Louise! Marie! Marie!*"

"Good evening, everyone," said a soft and serious voice from outside the doorway. "Don't forget my two girls, Louise and Marie de Penhoël, in your prayers."

There was not one of them who remained seated. The ancestress herself got to her tottering feet, while the old dog stretched his neck towards the doorway. By the last gleam of twilight, they could see the tall figure of an old man, dressed in the costume of a gentleman, which was tailored in the traditional fashion, but very old and well-worn. A large peasant's hat covered his white hair.

It required only one voice to say, with profound respect: "Good evening to you, Monsieur le Chevalier de Penhoël!"

It was the uncle in clogs, the good Chevalier Jean de Penhoël, returning from the cemetery where his two daughters were sleeping. He did not pause. When he had passed by, the old woman said, as if giving an order: "Make up a portion for the Belles-de-Nuit, lady of the house!"

She was immediately obeyed.

Before anyone had lifted a spoon to their lips, two full bowls of soup were removed, with two pieces of lard and two crusts of bread. Little Simonne was told to open the half-door and place the two offerings on the slate step outside the threshold.

Simonne, trembling slightly, did as she was told and returned very pale, making the sign of the cross as she came.

Then the lady of the house filled the bowls in turn, and everyone set about eating avidly, their hearty appetite chasing away the sad thoughts that were in the air.

"The soup's good," said Vincent.

"Good and tasty, that's no lie," opined Monique.

Jean-Marie Dolet, the master of the house, drank the last drop of his soup, not without sensual satisfaction, and concluded with authority, as if everyone in the world had been against him: "As true as I'm telling you, lads and lasses, the soup's well-cooked, very smooth and beautifully thickened."

"No mistake!" José, Joson and Josille cried, resolutely. "It's good, the soup. Yes, my lady, it certainly is."

The lady of the house thanked them with a nod of the head all round, for the compliment was for her, and added from the bottom of her good heart: "I only wish that *our monsieur*, Madame and the poor angel had its like every evening at the Maison Galliot."

"Listen!" said the old woman, suddenly.

Turk stood up on all fours and stretched the long arch of his back.

The wind began to shake the leaves of the large fig-trees, which rustled like pieces of parchment.

The old lady's desiccated and wrinkled finger pointed to the door. Those who dared to look saw two white forms pass by outside.

Turk howled hoarsely.

The old woman got up and walked to the door, without the aid of her stick. She opened it. She took the two bowls from the slate step that served as a threshold and came back to place them solemnly in the middle of the table.

The two bowls were empty.

"The Belles have taken their portion," she said.

III. The Clogmaker's Song

Eighteen years before, the Château de Penhoël had been an opulent and hospitable house; in all the country for ten leagues round, none swore by any but Penhoël.

Vicomte Hoël de Penhoël had one of the most beautiful estates in Brittany. His domain contained 20 farms, watermills along the river Oust and windmills on the hills, in the midst of vast heaths, thickets, forests and expanses of gorse that one could not walk around in a day. There was no hunting to compare with his from la Roche-Bernard to Paimpont, where the Cyclops were. When he collected the farm-rents for Saint-Jean and Saint-Michel, he did not know what to do with his money—but the poor certainly knew what he did.

He was old. He was the father of the man we have heard referred to as *our monsieur* in Jean-Marie Dolet's farm. He had two sons, Philippe and Pierre—two brave young men who loved one another. His family comprised, in addition, a poor younger brother, Jean, Chevalier de Penhoël, who received hospitality from his elders, and Juliette, a young orphan, who was the niece of the late Vicomtesse de Penhoël.

In those days, they dubbed Jean de Penhoël the *uncle in clogs*, because he kept an eye on the domain, in recognition of how much he owed his rich relative.

Philippe and Pierre loved one another, as we have said, but they were very different from one another. Philippe was sturdy, headstrong, brilliant, bold, as honest as gold, generous and scatter-brained. Pierre was sickly, also good and brave at times, but weak in body and mind. They were both handsome. There was only one year's difference in their ages.

When Philippe turned 21, he went to his father and said to him: "Papa, my cousin Juliette suits me, and I suit my cousin Juliette. Give us your consent, if you will, so that we may be husband and wife."

"I will, boy," Penhoël replied. "The late Vicomtesse, my dear wife, your mother, loved Juliette like a daughter. It is good that she sees from on high that I have done as she would have wished, for she often said: *The children are suited to one another, and will make a household.*"

Philippe fell into his father's arms; he was beside himself with joy. They began arranging the wedding immediately. The entire district rejoiced, from the poorest farmer to the richest gentleman, for Philippe, the bold young man, and Juliette, the gentle young woman, were beloved by everyone.

The only one who did not rejoice was Pierre, the younger brother. Pierre fell ill, shut himself up in his room and put himself to bed to die.

Everyone loved Pierre too, for he had no wickedness in his heart. The best physicians were summoned from Redon; even those from Vannes and Rennes were summoned, at great expense. They all came to take Pierre's pulse. There were ten of them, and there were ten different opinions–eleven, if one counts the general opinion that each of the doctors believed his nine colleagues to be donkeys. One after another, they uttered a few insults in Latin, but poor Pierre was still dying.

One evening, when the last doctor had been sent away, the entire family was assembled in the invalid's room. The old Vicomte was talking about sending for the demigods of the Faculty of Paris, when the *uncle in clogs* said–in a quiet voice, for he was timid–"Monsieur my cousin, physicians can do nothing in this case."

"What are you saying, Jean?" cried Penhoël. "Is it really you who brings a bad omen into my house?"

"God forbid, Penhoël! I'm only saying that physicians have no drugs to cure love-sickness."

At these words, the Vicomte threw himself on his son's bed. "Is that true, Pierre?" he asked. "Is it true! Are you letting yourself die because you don't trust your old father? Do you, too, desire to marry? Name whoever you please. Be she a Princess, you shall have her–and you shall have her if she is a poor girl from the farmyard."

Two tears rolled down the cheeks of the invalid's blanched cheeks. He drew his father's head towards his mouth and murmured in his ear. "I'm dying for the one who cannot be mine."

"Is she higher than a Princess, then, or lower than a farm-girl?"

"She's my brother Philippe's fiancée," Pierre stammered, falling back unconscious on his pillow.

There was great astonishment and mourning. The *uncle in clogs* was obliged to support the tottering Penhoël in his arms.

A few minutes later, Juliette and Philippe were alone together. They were weeping. Philippe had the most generous of hearts and was his brother's best friend. Juliette loved Pierre as if she had been his sister.

"It's necessary that he live!" Philippe said.

"It's necessary that he live!" Juliette repeated, sobbing bitterly.

They fell into one another's arms, their broken hearts beating in unison.

"Juliette," Philippe went on, "my mother called you her dear daughter. Would you like to be the salvation of my mother's son?"

"It mortifies me, but I wish it," the young woman replied.

"For myself, I shall go away to be mortified," Philippe said, in a choked voice. "I shall carry your image away in my heart, Juliette. Disappointment will kill me—that is my hope."

Then they came to the feet of old Penhoël, and said to him: "Father, we were mistaken; we don't want to marry one another."

Penhoël hugged them both to his bosom, because he understood.

The following day, Pierre was smiling in his bed, and the color was coming back to his cheeks. The preparations for the wedding continued; henceforth, he was to be the groom.

Philippe left several days before the wedding. The first letter that they received from him bore the postmark of an American port. It contained a full and entire donation of all his patrimonial property to Pierre, Juliette and their future children. Philippe announced in addition that he would never return to Brittany. From the bottom of his heart, he wished the young spouses all the happiness that he had lost.

There are sacrifices that God will not accept, heroic acts that surpass the limits of the possible and bring misfortune, because they transgress a law. Ask one who knows the code of generosities and delicacies how the devotion of Philippe and Juliette exceeded that which is permitted to human beings; he will explain the sacred mysteries of the family, and you will know that it is forbidden even to heroism to tamper with that social ark we call marriage. One does not marry for devotion. One can give away one's fortune, one's blood, everything, except the family that is in embryo in the free accord of those engaged to be married. That base, which religion and the law prepare as the seat for the honor and happiness of children, must be solid and in no way unsound.

There was unprecedented rejoicing at the wedding of Pierre and Juliette. There was a sort of encampment around the château—which, vast as it was, could not accommodate a tenth of the guests. Old Penhoël was sad, though; he regretted the absentee. Juliette had the appearance of a dead woman. Pierre was gloomy; he knew perfectly well that he had received an exorbitant gift. He was jealous of a memory.

It was like those Judean fruits which ripen their appearance deceptively on the shores of Lake Asphaltite.[45] On the outside, they are brilliantly colored; on the inside, they enclose nothing but ashes. Here, the excited joy of the guests enveloped a bleak unhappiness.

Juliette had a pious and noble heart. She accepted her duty, but she could not recover her smile.

Old Penhoël went to the cemetery in the first year of the marriage. He blessed his children and died with the name of the absentee on his lips.

Pierre heard that name remorsefully. He was good and gentle; he held suffering at bay for a long time, and the birth of a daughter, a dear angel with a heavenly smile, brought a semblance of happiness into the house for several months. One day, though, when Pierre was leaning over Blanche de Penhoël's cradle, he went pale and said: "She is already sad! Everyone here is sad!"

From that moment on, a darker cloud descended upon the manor.

The *uncle in clogs* had married a noble but poor woman from the neighborhood, rather late in life. His wife had borne him two daughters before dying. Marie and Louise were like the smiles of that house in mourning. They cared for Blanche, whom they named the *angel of Penhoël*, and Juliette, a gentle woman who had no other joy, had their faithful love to add to the consolations of her piety. Pierre cherished them too; with respect to him, they very often played the role of the infant David soothing the anguish of Saul. Without them, despair and death would have entered into the house, whose wealth was the envy of the surrounding countryside.

Pierre Hoël, Vicomte de Penhoël, had indeed inherited his father's title and domain, without division. Philippe's donation was in due form; since he had sent it, no further news of him had been received. Many people began to say that grief had killed him far from his native land. Pierre was one of the richest landowners in Brittany.

Years passed while this state of affairs persisted. Blanche grew up, alternately idolized and pushed away by her father.

The two daughters of the *uncle in clogs* became the two most delightful children that one could hope to see. At that château, there was, if not happiness, a sort of numbness that resembled repose.

In Breton comedies, Parisians are mistrusted as Normans are feared. One day, in 1840, or thereabouts, a stranger of fine appearance arrived in the parish, who made a great show of his purse and talked about purchasing what was not for sale.

He was from the lovely city of Paris, or so it was said. His name sounded Breton; he called himself Monsieur de Pontalès.

He was a middle-aged man, possessed of a witty tongue and a cheerful manner–and, in consequence, every appearance of a man who enjoyed life. He loved the neighborhood from the first moment he wandered through the Penhoël domain. He bought a little manor nearby, and declared to anyone who would listen that he would be a benefactor of the common people. Everyone, except for the *uncle in clogs*, thought that Monsieur de Pontalès was a charming Marquis.

In almost every parish out there, there is race of rogues whose members take the name of "men of law." Bretons love litigation almost as much as people from Vire or Saint-Lô. Men of law are advocates without diplomas, unlicensed attorneys who do as much harm as the marsh fever, dysentery and pretended witches put together.

There was a man of law in the town, who handled the details of Penhoël's business affairs, Monsieur le Marquis de Pontalès sought him out and said, out of the blue: "Monsieur le Hivain, you have the face of a man jaundiced by the desire to make his fortune."

Monsieur le Hivain had heard many other such observations in his lifetime. His philosophy was to hate everyone and not to take exception to anyone. He fixed his suspicious eyes on Monsieur le Marquis, scratched his large red ears, and opened his toothless mouth in an equivocal smile. "Monsieur le Marquis," he said, "is too kind."

Pontalès clapped him on the shoulder heartily and put 20 louis in his hand.

The man of law nearly got down on all fours as he bowed in acknowledgement of such a magnificent lord. "How can I help Monsieur le Marquis?" he asked, in bewilderment.

"A trivial matter," Pontalès replied. "I wouldn't be sorry to buy the Penhoël domain."

"I shall have to inform Monsieur le Marquis that the Penhoël domain is not for sale."

"All the same, I wouldn't be sorry to buy it."

"Has Monsieur de Marquis a price in mind?"

"About 1,200,000 francs?"

"No small amount."

"A mere trifle!"

Pontalès pronounced the last word with such disdain that the man of law put his hands together as if to make the shape of a church. "Does Monsieur le Marquis possess the necessary funds?" he stammered.

"Of course!"

Le Hivain conceived a desire to kiss the tips of his feet.

"My good man," Pontalès went on, "I would not be far distant from giving you 3,000 or 4,000 *livres* a year on completion of this transaction."

"Oh, Monsieur le Marquis!" cried le Hivain, rapturously. "Just tell me what I need to do."

Pontalès had come for precisely that reason. The conversation lasted for a long time. Monsieur le Hivain and Pontalès parted quite content with one another. It was agreed in principle that Monsieur le Marquis would obtain the Penhoël lands and that Monsieur le Hivain would have a commission of 60,000 francs on completion of the deal.

All was well–except that, of the 1,200,000 francs, Monsieur de Pontalès only possessed 1,000 *écus*, in addition to his title–which we shall not evaluate too highly, since he had picked it up in his travels, from the corner of a hedge. But he had industry and was devoid of prejudices. He was the stuff of which conquerors are made. Paris was not built in a day. It takes time to bring such a business to completion. He worked hard for two years, imperceptibly. The 1,000 *écus* were sufficient, because Monsieur le Marquis de Pontalès had instilled a taste for gambling in his neighborhood, and he was a very good-humored gambler.

When the two years were up, Monsieur de Hivain had confused Penhoël's financial situation quite nicely. He had been put to unaccustomed expense in following the current fashion, for the local people lived much better since Monsieur de Pontales' arrival. Penhoël was embarrassed; as he did not want to put pressure on his farmers, who owed him a good deal of money, he borrowed. The first mortgage was celebrated in the le Hivain household as one celebrates the appearance of the first tooth in a beloved child's mouth.

The borrowed money flowed away like an avalanche. More was needed. Is it necessary to go on? Disorder easily takes hold of those who cannot be happy in their home. Penhoël was not happy. He appealed to God. His wife Juliette, poor saintly creature, had loved him well, and proved it to him every day, but there was a shadow between the two spouses: the memory of a sacrifice. Someone had been too generous to Penhoël. Penhoël could not forgive that.

To distract himself from the dolorous ideas that possessed him, Penhoël gambled, surrendering to the pleasures of the table. Thanks to the new mores imported by the Parisian Marquis, there were now half a dozen houses within a three-league radius in which one could divert oneself as one wished. A number of worthy gentlemen threw their affairs into disorder to follow the trend, and a few brainless ladies followed suit. Monsieur de Larouelh de Voz de Kercravatalapoil said that the canton had become a little Paris, thank God! Madame Larouelh, who had been born Le Pesquehennec de Treffichidon, applauded him while rolling her rs like a cartload of rubble unloaded on to a drum.

Whenever Penhoël went home to the manor, he found Juliette very sad. She was miserable because of her husband's conduct, but Penhoël attributed Juliette's sadness to regrets inflicted by him. If she tried to smile, he accused her of hypocrisy. The time came when his household horrified him, because he read a merited reproach on every face.

Two more years passed, and–thank God–the breaches made in his fortune were soon filled in. For him, Pontalès was no more and no less than a providence. To begin with, he had obligingly purchased pieces of the domain's lands to put some ready money into Penhoël's pocket. He had won the money back from him gambling, but did that matter? In the second place, to avoid embarrassing his friend, he had paid off the loan and kept the security. Finally, in the third and most important place, he had plunged Penhoël up to the neck in commerce. Penhoël was a ship-owner; he was making enormous profits from long-haul and coastal trade. Two years more and Penhoël would be crowning his pawns in all the houses of Le Havre and Nantes. May God protect your ships, at least until you get your sea-legs!

Thus it came about that, at the end of the two years, Penhoël no longer knew where to put his head. An honest and clever man would still have been able to extricate himself from his predicament, but his business manager was le Hivain–who had become, little by little, a man of importance. He had bought meadows, this le Hivain; he washed his hands on Sundays and offered tobacco to the farmers in a silver box.

At the beginning of 1846, Penhoël was in such trouble that someone had to talk to him about selling the château. Until then, he had spent without reflection or regret. Every noble quality was against him; disinterest often has carelessness for a companion and Penhoël was more careless than disinterested. The thought had never crossed his mind that he might have to sell his father's house.

He resisted, for the first time–and, as every good action brings a benefit, he drew those who loved him closer for a while. Poor Juliette, the *uncle in clogs* and his two daughters did not know much about business, but they had an instinct that knew no deception. Since Pontalès and le Hivain were pestering him to sell, selling would be ruination. Such was the unanimous opinion of the naïve family council. Penhoël was entirely revived. He dined at home that day and took veritable pleasure in spending the evening among those warm hearts, which overwhelmed him with affection and caresses.

Unfortunately, the two wolves were still prowling around the manor.

Pontalès and le Hivain found a means to encounter Penhoël the following morning, while he was out hunting. Pontalès told him about a business deal in which once could make a million with 50,000 francs. It is not just in Paris that these marvelous speculations ran through the streets. At the same time, he let him know that in a few days there would be a no-limit lansquenet game at the home of Monsieur Larouelh de Voz de Keretcoeterac, one of Monsieur de Kercravatapoil's brothers. The table would be heaped with gold!

Penhoël tried to go on his way. Le Hivain attacked then, like a reserve corps. He mentioned a buyer who had consented to buy the château with an option of repurchase. That is not a Greek term; it is Latin for chicanery. Repurchase means... but you will understand better by means of an example.

Suppose that your doll has sustained terrible losses in the wake of floods or some such. She no longer has anything left but her diamonds. She is invited to a ball. She does not want to be dispossessed of her diamonds, but she wants to go to the ball. It's very simple. There is always a good man who will take your 1,000-louis diamonds and give you 2,000 or 3,000-franc banknotes, with the provision that he will return your pledge if you reimburse him within a month. It sometimes happens that one can reimburse him, but it happens far more often, alas, that the good soul keeps the diamonds.

Substitute immovable property for the diamonds; in the place of your doll, put a landowner with his back to the wall, and you have an option to repurchase–an infernal lure, a diabolical snare, invented by usurers in the expectation that it will be possible to slip châteaux into a pawnbroker's chests of drawers.

One always thinks that it will be easy to pay; one even goes so far, on occasion, so thick a blindfold does distress wear, as to count on the mercy of the two-legged jackal!

Penhoël was dazzled by that word *repurchase*. With the benefit of the golden opportunity proposed by Pontalès and what he might win at cards with the younger brother of Larouelh de Voz, he would have what was necessary to buy back his manor.

He promised almost immediately.

The conversation took place in the thickest part of the forest, not far from the vale of Theil, a little lake surrounded by wooded slopes, whose trees dipped their branches in the water like tresses. It is said in the region that the lake is bottomless and that its shores are hollowed out in the raw granite, like the walls of a cistern, as if by a pickaxe.

Penhoël and his two tempters separated at the edge of the vale.

As soon as Penhoël had gone, the two rogues burst out laughing and continued talking together frankly.

"He's ours!" cried le Hivain.

"What if he's able to pay it back?" Pontalès objected.

"I'll draw up the contract myself," the man of law replied, "and I'll keep it safe."

As he spoke the last word, he made a significant grimace. They both shivered, because a voice came out of the thicket, saying: "You shall not draw up the contract, Monsieur le Hivain, and you shall not keep it. My uncle will finally see through you."

Two light footfalls brushed the moss in the forest. Pontalès launched himself after them, heedless of all risk. Le Hivain remained motionless, as if thunderstruck.

Pontalès soon saw two dresses floating among the trees; he recognized Marie and Louise, the two daughters of the *uncle in clogs*. They were running like deer, and he would never have caught up with them if Louise, the younger, had not tripped over a dead root. She fell. Marie stopped to help her up, and Pontalès seized her by the hair.

At that moment, he was no longer the corrupt but elegant gentleman who had introduced good Breton country-folk to the gilded vices of Paris. Circumstances had suddenly torn the mask from the wretch's face.

He saw that he was discovered; it was necessary, at any price, to annihilate the two witnesses who might divulge his rascality. There were a few more arrangements to be made.

The two girls released a cry of terror on seeing the hideous ferocity that was now painted on Pontalès' face. They had gone through the vale in order to reach a hunting-path that snaked hereabouts. Louise had fallen 20 paces from the water.

Pontalès whistled. Le Hivain's approach was audible. He brushed the branches as he came like a wild boar. The man of law was pale with fright, but he seized the other sister in response to a mute signal from the Marquis.

Marie was already breathless. The man of law's head-scarf gagged Louise's lips. Then the two of them–le Hivain and Pontalès–consulted one another by means of a momentary glance, because they could hear a voice singing in the distance, in the woods.

"We have time," said Pontalès.

That was the death-sentence. Each of them seized his prey, and the water of the little lake splashed twice in response to the fall of the bodies of the two unfortunate children.

The singing voice came closer.

"It's Haligan the clog-maker," murmured the man of law, more dead than alive.

"He's come too late," replied the Marquis.

Le Hivain wanted to flee immediately, but Pontalès stopped him. This could not have been his first crime; he had the cold-bloodedness of a hardened assassin. "It's necessary to be sure that they won't come back to the surface," he said.

The seething surface of the pool had found its level. The two poor girls had not come back up. Haligan was very close, singing:

> *'Tis in the lovely land of Brittany*
> *That they make such pretty shoes;*
> *Hold out your pretty warm feet*
> *Halloo Hallay!*
> *My lovely brunette.*
> *Those who whittle clogs*
> *Don't make a fortune.*

There was no longer a single ripple on the surface of the little lake. Pontalès said, mockingly: "We've made two more Belles-de-Nuit, Monsieur le Hivain."

Le Hivain tried to laugh, but his teeth were chattering.[46]

They both fled, cutting through the thicket.

As Haligan passed by, he sang at the top of his voice:

The rocks are made of stone
Of stone from bottom to top;
The sun cannot melt them
Halloo, hallay!
Nor can the moon.
Those who dig the ground,
Don't make a fortune...

IV. The Maison Gaillot

While everyone was eating soup at Jean-Marie Dolet's house, a meager resin candle was lit in a little house with cracked and crumbling walls, which seemed to be lost in the lonely depths of the forest. There was no fire in the hearth and no food awaited those in attendance at the worm-eaten table. The dwelling presented an appearance of misery and abandonment that rent the heart.

Three people were gathered there, one of whom was a man still young, wearing the worn and dirty costume of a gentleman; this man sat to one side, on a stool, with his head between his hands, Next to the table stood a beautiful woman, whose features had been ravaged by suffering, with her arms around a child of 14, as pretty as an angel but very pale and seemingly in distress.

They were the former masters of the château: Pierre Hoël, Vicomte de Penhoël, his wife Juliette and their daughter Blanche.

A bleak silence reigned, which was broken by the child's voice, saying: "Mother, I'm hungry."

A rattling cough escaped the Vicomte's throat, while two large tears rolled down Juliette's blanched cheek.

Stout clogs sounded on the stony path. The husband and wife lifted their heads at the same time.

"It's Jean de Penhoël!" said Juliette in a hopeful voice.

And little Blanche added: "I'll wager that he's bringing us some bread."

The door opened. The *uncle in clogs* showed his face, which was an old man's, but still broad and handsome. It was framed by long white hair, which fell in the Breton fashion upon his ancient frock-coat.

"Good evening, everyone," he said, sadly. "May the good Lord be with you." And he sat down on a bench, seemingly very tired.

"Haven't you brought us anything to eat, Uncle Jean?" asked Blanche.

The old man's eyelids fluttered, as if in response to interior tears. "Nothing, my poor little angel," he replied. Then, putting his large hat between his knees, he continued: "Vicomte, my nephew, and you, Madame de Penhoël, my niece, I have done what I could. This morning, I got up at dawn; it is harvest-time. I set off for the fields. I offered my services at every farm I entered, saying: 'Here I am; I need to earn my living now; I am old but I am strong and willing. I've come to you to ask for work that you don't refuse to anyone–not even the vagabonds who come from France at harvest-time. Give me a sickle and you shall see how I will work!'

"Some did not reply, because they are ingrates. The others said to me: 'Listen uncle–we cannot do as we wish. Pontalès is the master. He has put about the rumor that you have insulted him by leaving the château. He has forbidden all his tenant farmers to give you any aid.'

"If God had left me my two dear little daughters, they would have been in Redon working as seamstresses, for they sew like the fairies! But God has taken them from me, as you know. They found Marie's scarf and Louise's belt on the shore of the pool in the vale of Theis, which is bottomless. They are dead, both of them, without their dear bodies having the shelter of a tomb.

"May the crime be punished, if crime there was!

"I tied my scarf around my waist and took the road to Redon. At Redon, I wanted to buy all the bread in the shops. It was not for me; I no longer get hungry, while you are in want here. I am hungry for you. There is only one thing I know how to do: I know how to fight. I looked for the sign of a fencing-master and I went in. I said: 'Here I am; I am a former soldier; have you need of an assistant?'

"The master looked at me, laughing, and said: 'Yes, old man, I do indeed need an assistant.'

" 'Hire me, then.'

"He laughed louder, asking: 'Did they already know how to fence before the Flood?'

" 'I am old, but I am strong,' I said, for the second time. 'Let's try.'

"I unhooked a foil and put myself *en garde*. 'Positively Gothic!' he cried, taking a foil in his turn. And he called all his pupils to see how one fights a poor old man.

" 'Ancient,' he said, 'If you touch me once out of 12, I'll make you assistant in my hall.'

"We only played seven bouts; I struck him seven times. He sent me away angrily, saying that I did not fight fair.

"As I went out of his establishment, I ran into the Comte de Kerbris, who once spent six winter months and six summer months in our home. He is rich. I said to him: 'Good day to you, Comte de Kerbris. I am Jean de Penhoël, and I would like to speak to you in private.' He turned his back on me and I heard him say: 'I have my own poor...'

"Then I pulled my hat down over my eyes, because I was weeping copiously, and I came back as far as the cemetery to kneel at the foot of the two little crosses. I thought about stealing, but my medallion of the Virgin burned my beast; I have nothing to give you but my flesh and my blood..."

There was a deep silence. Then a sob racked the mother's breast as she saw the child's head sink like a wilting flower.

Pierre de Penhoël groaned.

"Marie! Louise!" cried the *uncle in clogs*, seized by a kind of delirium. "If you are now children of God, help us!"

There was a slight noise outside, which drew all eyes towards the door. Each of them, involuntarily, thought of the helpful Belles-de-Nuit, who brought offerings to *the poorest of the poor*.

It was as if two white clouds were drifting past on the other side of the threshold. The *uncle in clogs* cried out, and ran forward. The two white clouds were already disappearing into the shadows of a nearby copse.

On the threshold, there were two large bowls, full to the brim, with two fine crusts of bread.

Thank you, poor Belles! The angel of Penhoël shall have bread! Thank you, Belles-de-Nuit, gentle spirits that the mercy of God allows to wander in the poor by-ways of Brittany!

V. The Hut

It was shaped like a beehive. In the middle, there was a woodchip fire whose smoke escaped as it might through a hole pierced in the roof. Its only furnishings were blocks of wood, axes, paring-knives and the various tools of a clog-maker's trade. In one corner, two heaps of dry leaves served as beds.

Haligan, an old man with honest and masculine features, was heating a new pair of clogs by the fire. A stranger was sitting on a stool. Standing next to him were two adorably pretty girls, who were breathless. They were wiping their foreheads, crowned with damp curls, for they had been running through the twilight that evening, and fatigue was still making their hearts beat rapidly beneath the white pleats of their dresses.

The stranger called himself Montalt. He was tall, and his eyes shone with a proud intelligence. "Speak, children," he said. "I want to know everything. You've told me about Penhoël's ruin. Why have you, who seem generous and good, abandoned Penhoël in his distress?"

"To help him," said Marie, the elder and more beautiful of the two girls. "Pontalès believes us to be dead, and that is what keeps us safe. We have hidden ourselves, even from the eyes of those who love us the most. Even Roger believes that Louise is no longer of this world."

"Roger?" Montalt repeated. "Who is Roger?"

"The man who is to marry Louise."

"And you, Marie? What is the name of the man who is to marry you?"

"No one is to marry me," the girl replied, blushing. "I know the story of my uncle Philippe. I don't want to get married."

"Why?"

"Because," Haligan retorted, "as she says herself, she'll never find a fiancé as great, as noble or as generous as her uncle Philippe."

"Is that true?" asked the stranger, smiling.

"That's true," said Marie.

"But how did you die?" the stranger asked, then.

"Murdered," Marie replied. "We had to die, because we discovered Pontalès' secret."

She described the scene at the vale of Theil. The two villains, as we know, had fled at the sound of Haligan's voice. As he went on his way, singing the third verse of his song, he heard a feeble cry, which seemed to come from under the water. He looked and saw nothing—but the cry was repeated, and the pronunciation of his name forced him to continue searching.

We have said that the vale of Theil was surrounded on every side by forest trees. The branches descended as far as the surface of the lake, hiding the banks beneath a ceiling of foliage. Two human bodies thrown into water inevitably return to the surface, if only momentarily; that is a law of physics. Marie and Louise had come up, but instead of returning to the place where they had disappeared, the impetus of their fall had carried them under the branches. With her dying hand, Marie had grabbed a bough, while her other hand clung to the dress of the unconscious Louise. It was thus that the brave clog-maker found them.

Haligan detested Pontalès as much as he loved Penhoël. He welcomed the two sisters into his hut; thanks to him, they were able to play the role of Belles-de-Nuit, which they adopted in order to help the abandoned family.

In the meantime, however, the crime had profited the murderers to a considerable extent. Marie and Louise had remained ill for several days, and had not been able to warn Penhoël, whose ruination had been completed. He had lost his last louis–the last louis provided by the sale of his château–in the lansquenet game hosted by Larouelh de Voz de Keter-coeterac, the younger brother of Monsieur de Kercravatapoil.

"I still don't know," the lovely Marie added, when she had finished her story, "why you're so interested in our family. You're a stranger to us, but from the very first I trusted you as I trust my father... more than that, as I would trust my beloved uncle Philippe de Penhoël. I read the generosity of your heart in your eyes. Hurry, I beg of you, if you want to save us, for the term of the right of repurchase expires tomorrow..."

"Tomorrow," repeated Moltalt, who was lost in thought. Then, changing the quality of his smile, he added: "Tomorrow is a long way off."

"Have you enough money to enable Penhoël to buy back his château?" Louise asked.

"It's not money that we need," Montalt replied. "The wretches have had enough Penhoël money. I'd like to have the contract of sale, though..."

"Monsieur le Hivain has it!" cried the two sisters, simultaneously.

Haligan had finished burnishing his new clogs. "If you wish," he said, "I'll get my axe and go with you to look for it."

Montalt shook his head. "That's work for our Belles-de-Nuit," he replied, looking at the two children.

"We're ready!" they replied.

Before letting them go, Montalt asked: "Is old Penhoël's furniture still at the château?"

"All of it," Marie replied. "Pontalès kept everything."

"You're sure that the late Vicomte's writing-desk is still in its place?"

"I'm sure of it."

"Go, then–bring me the contract of sale, and we'll begin the battle."

VI. The Nightmare

Monsieur le Hivain now had a very nice house in the town. He had a lot of money in the bank, and had it in mind to take a wife. In the meantime, he lived alone and dined almost every day at the château, for he and his friend Pontalès were becoming inseparable.

That evening, he returned home at about 10 p.m., after an excellent meal. Pontalès had a Parisian cook who could have restored the appetite of a dead man, and Penhoël's long-established wine-cellar was far from being emptied of all its bottles. Our two rogues had enjoyed themselves to their hearts' content.

As he passed through the town, Monsieur le Hivain wandered in his course, singing *Mère Godichon* or some similar bucolic refrain, like a man of law conscious of being full of venison and Médoc. It amused him to see two cocks atop the bell-tower, two Moons in the sky and 36 candles at the end of his nose.

His house was not far away; habit ensured that he would not mistake its door.

He had some difficulty extracting his key from his pocket, but bid himself be patient, for he would soon be snoring in his fine bedclothes.

Was he seeing things? He thought he saw two white shadows in the darkness of the courtyard, and exclaimed: "Who's there? If you're Belles-de-Nuit go away, vagabonds!"

Monsieur le Hivain was not the kind of man to put bowls of soup on his doorstep for passers-by. Since reaching the age of reason, he had never given a single *sou* to a poor man. But there were no Belles-de-Nuit! They were superstitious lies! Philosophers did not believe in that sort of thing.

Monsieur le Hivain went to bed singing "Tomorrow morning, the term of the option to repurchase expires," to the tune of *If I should die, bury me in a cellar where's there's wine*. "Or tomorrow evening," he went on. "Not that it matters. In consequence, it's tomorrow that my friend Pontalès will set me up with an annual income of 4,000 francs. It's not enough! I ought to get five. If I asked for six... no, seven... oh, he can afford to give me eight, or even nine... why not ten?"

By the time he fell asleep, he had 30,000 a year, guaranteed by a first mortgage and a peaceful mind. He slept like an honest men. Proverbs notwithstanding, honest men do not snore half as loudly as rogues.

What was he dreaming about? His marriage. There was a demoiselle of mature years, with red hair, a squint, bandy legs and a crooked back, but a pleasant personality, whose fingers were hooked like a grappling-iron, whom he would obtain as a housekeeper. He saw the dowry...

Ah, a lovely dream!

Suddenly, however, the dream became a nightmare. Venison can play tricks when one has eaten more than the regulation amount, and Monsieur le Hivain had eaten enough for three men of law, equivalent to the daily quota of six wolves!

The red-haired woman was still in the dream. but, instead of putting her dowry on the table in a reasonable manner, she had put it, all in coin, on Monsieur le Hivain's puny chest and it was choking him.

"Hey, redhead, let your husband breathe!"

Not at all! The red-haired woman was in a mischievous mood. In addition to her dowry, she had her ten hooked fingers, which seized the unfortunate man by the throat and gaily set about strangling him.

"Redhead! Redhead! No nasty tricks!"

Monsieur le Hivain opened his eyes and nearly died of fright. There was, indeed, someone perched on his breathless torso, but it was neither the redhead nor her dowry; it was one of the two dead girls of the vale of Theil. It was Marie de Penhoël, the elder daughter of the *uncle in clogs*.

He tried to make the sign of the cross–for all the damned have recourse to God when they tremble–but his hands were trapped by his bedclothes.

"Who are you?" he stammered.

"Belle-de-Nuit, Belle-de-Nuit," the nightmare replied.

And another voice repeated from the shadows in the middle of the room: "Belle-de-Nuit! Belle-de-Nuit!"

Cold sweat soaked the man of law's cotton nightcap.

"And what do you want, in the name of my patron saint?"

"Your soul, your soul, which your patron saint has abandoned."

The invisible echo added: "Abandoned, your soul, your soul!"

"What do you want with my soul?"

"To bear it away. To bear it far away, far below."

The echo: "Far below, far away, to bear it away, to bear it away."

"Where will you take it?"

"To Hell."

The echo: "To Hell."

And in unison, the voice and the echo: "Your soul! Your soul! To Hell! To Hell!"

Monsieur le Hivain did not have a dry spot on his entire body. Sweat streamed down his soiled cheeks and his tongue hung out like that of a panting dog. "Pardon, my good imps!" he cried. "Have pity, my dear demoiselles. Let me at least have time to repent!"

"One buys time," said the voice. "It's dear."

"Time costs," repeated the echo. "Dear, very dear!"

"I'm a very poor man, and I have no money."

"Buy! Buy! Buy!"

"Or die, die, die!"

His breast was still crushed, his hands were still trapped, and his throat was still being choked.

"Name your price!" he cried, from the depths of his anguish. "How much do you want?"

"Give us the contract of sale and repurchase."

"I don't have it, on my word of honor!"

"It's honor that you don't have."

"Nor word."

"Nor word, nor word!"

"Nor honor, nor honor!"

Mocking laughter grated in duplicate within the room, piercing the unfortunate's ears like the sound of a scythe. He was utterly terrified–but if he gave up the contract, what would become of his income?

The nightmare weighed down upon him more heavily, and squeezed harder.

"Mercy, mercy!" he cried.

"Did you have mercy on the edge of the lake?" was the answer he received.

"There were two of us. Why am I the only one being punished?"

"Patience, patience, patience!"

He felt as if he could not breathe.

"In the chest of drawers next to the door," he said, in the end, "under my dirty shirts. Villainesses! You're ruining an honest man!"

The echo opened the drawer and took the contract of sale, saying: "Here it is! Here it is! Here it is!"

The nightmare let go of Monsieur le Hivain's throat, and gave him three sharp slaps, alternating her hands.

"Thank you! Thank you! Thank you!"

As they disappeared through the pen window like shadows, the two Belles-de-Nuit murmured in unison: "*Au revoir, au revoir, au revoir!*"

VII. The Adventurer

As the château clock sounded 11 p.m., the inhabitants of the farm were awoken with a start by the old mother's voice, crying: "The will of God shall be done!"

She was sitting upright in her bed and her staring eyes were facing across the courtyard, where the darkness between the farm and the château was black.

Turk howled and tugged at his chain like a mad dog.

"What's the matter, mother? Why are you waking those who toil by day and need to rest by night?" demanded Jacqueline, in an annoyed tone.

"Did I say that aloud?" murmured the old woman, lowering her eyes. "I was dreaming about one who is unfortunately absent, and would not have let down the name of Penhoël."

She fell silent.

But Turk, the huge old dog, did not fall silent, and his howls were reminiscent of a song of victory.

The boys awoke one after another.

"That's odd, that is," said Joson.

"As odd goes, that's odd," added José.

"Odd, to be sure, that's no lie," Josille concluded.

Jean-Marie Dolet lifted the bar from the door to see what was happening in the courtyard. There was nothing there, but lights were burning on the first floor of the château, where Monsieur Pontalès now had his rooms.

Pontalès was accustomed to going to bed late. He sat up alone until midnight or thereabouts, between his pipe and his bottle. His valet was in the process of telling him that a stranger was asking to see him.

"A stranger!" cried the Marquis. "At this hour!"

"Here is his card," the valet added. "He has the appearance of a gentleman."

Pontalès took the card and read: *P.-P. Montalt of New Orleans.*

He frowned deeply, but he said: "Show him in!"

Montalt was introduced, and bowed very politely–but in mid-bow his face changed and he drew himself up to his full height. "This is not Monsieur de Marquis to whom I have the honor of speaking?"

"It certainly is," replied the master of the château, dryly.

Montalt put his hat back on his head and said, coldly: "I have a better memory than you think, Monsieur Charles Boulanger. Why this name Pontalès and this title of Marquis? This is an unexpected encounter; it was not you that I was looking for."

He sat down as he spoke, and gestured to a seat with his hand, as though their roles had been reversed and Pontalès had become the visitor. The latter remained standing. He could scarcely conceal his anxiety.

"Trust me, and do as I do," Montalt continued. "The conversation might be a long one–why tire yourself?"

"The conversation will not be a long one, Monsieur," replied Pontalès, who had recovered his self-possession. "We are not in New Orleans, where your position as a jurist made you all-powerful. Here, advocates are exceedingly petty noblemen. I tell you very frankly, my dear Monsieur Montalt, that your presence is unwanted, and I am impatient to get you out of my house."

Montalt crossed his legs. "Are you perfectly sure that this is your house?" he asked.

"Unless Monsieur le Vicomte de Penhoël buys his château back from me..."

"I have come for the precise purpose of buying back Monsieur de Penhoël's château."

The Marquis went pale, but did not lose his smile.

"You've taken charge of Monsieur de Penhoël's business affairs?" he said, interrogatively. "That's your job?"

"Yes, Monsieur Charles Boulanger, that is my job. I have taken charge of Monsieur de Penhoël's business affairs."

"Do you have the contract of sale?"

"What does that matter? We'll consult your copy."

"It matters a great deal, my dear Monsieur," Pontalès put in, interrupting him triumphantly. "I may have lost my copy."

"Then nothing can be done," said Montalt, still armored by American self-confidence.

"With your permission! The clause relating to repurchase is a private matter. The sale–the true sale, with neither term nor condition–has been completed and notarized, and the original document is in a safe place."

Montalt smiled in his turn. "We have the contract, Monsieur Charles Boulanger," he said.

Pontalès could not suppress a start of surprise. "And the money?" he stammered.

"We also have the money."

As if this unexpected declaration had thrown him into confusion, Pontalès turned round and strode hastily across the room.

"When you get tired," Montalt said, imperturbably, "I'll invite you to sit down again,"

Pontalès came back abruptly. His excursion had not been wasted; he held a pistol in each hand. For his own part, Montalt only had one, but it was an American revolver of the latest model, which could fire six shots in three seconds.

The two adversaries looked one another in the face for a moment; then Montalt said for the third time: "Monsieur Charles Boulanger, I suggest that you sit down."

The Marquis obeyed. "Now, what is this comedy?" he said. "You know very well that I am the Marquis de Pontalès."

"I know that you have been convicted of a crime in New Orleans under the name of Charles Boulanger. It was me who pleaded your case, and you said then that you owed me your life. The district court did, indeed, content itself with dishonoring you; I have the warrant in my briefcase. I only know you under the name of Charles Boulanger."

"And what do you want of me?"

"That you leave the Château de Penhoël at this very instant."

"We'll talk about that again tomorrow."

"Tomorrow, you'll be far away, whether you're traveling in a post-chaise or between two policemen–that's your choice."

There was a pause, after which Pontalès, plucking up his courage, went on in a more confident tone: "Monsieur, things don't work here as they do in your country. In France, one does not speak that way to a man in his own home."

"I have already asked you," Montalt replied, "whether this house is yours."

"It will be, as soon as Penhoël, my vendor..."

"I ask you now," Montalt put in, "if you are quite sure that this house belongs to Penhoël, your vendor."

"The evidence..." the Marquis began.

"We are both businessmen. Evidence is only a word. Proof is necessary in a court of law."

"The best title is the law of heredity, it seems. Do you contest the fact that Pierre de Penhoël is his father's son?"

"I contest nothing. I am in the process of acquainting you with facts of which you appear to be ignorant, that's all, I beg you to do me the favor of opening that item of furniture." He pointed at an antique writing-desk placed beside the head of Pontalès' bed.

The latter shrugged his shoulders, and opened the writing-desk.

"As chance would have it," Montalt went on, "you have chosen the room in which the late Vicomte de Penhoël used to sleep. It was in that desk that he filed his family papers. Would you open the fourth drawer on the left... yes, that one, the one that you're holding... pull it out it all the way. Pull hard; it's necessary that it comes out."

The drawer came out in response to Pontalès' efforts.

"Do you see a silver button in the interior of the slot?" Montalt asked, retaining his perfect tranquillity.

"Yes, there is one," Pontalès replied.

"Press the silver button, if you please."

The Marquis obeyed, for he sensed a mystery and curiosity took hold of him. Old items of furniture often have their hidey-holes. He only regretted not having thought to sound out the writing-desk before.

As soon as he pressed the silver button, the solid piece separating the two neighboring drawers came towards him like the leaf of a table. The shelf was itself a shallow drawer, which contained a single sheet of paper, on the back of which was written: *The duplicate of this testament is in the hands of my elder son, Vicomte Philippe Hoël de Penhoël.*

"Oh!" said Pontalès, attempting to hide his distress. "Might we be disinherited, by any chance?"

"I give you permission," Montalt said, gravely, "to acquaint yourself with the contents of that document."

The Marquis unfolded the sheet of paper. While he read it, Montalt continued placidly: "In days of old, my poor Monsieur Charles Boulanger, men of my kind, who have good feet, good eyes, and never recoil before anything, save for God, took the trouble to fight gentlemen of your sort with fire and iron. Times have changed. The pen has replaced the sword. It is advocates who are now knights errant. One no longer slays traitors and felons with thrusts of the lance; one sends them to prison, when they have not done enough to be put to hard labor, and that's all."

Many objections might have been raised against this pompous eulogy to advocates, particularly from a political point of view, but Montalt came from America, where all lawyers might perhaps be paladins.

"This appears to me to be a properly formulated will," Pontalès relied, having read the document rapidly and recovered some of his self-possession, "in favor of Philippe, Penhoël's elder son, which deprives us of our strict legitimacy—but I am a lawyer, as you are, my dear colleague, and felonious knights have just as many rights now as any others. I must point out to you that this precious testament is invalid, by virtue of the renunciation signed by the elder Penhoël."

"I have it in my pocket," said Montalt. "Monsieur le Hivain was good enough to entrust it to me, along with the option to repurchase."

Pontalès stifled a blasphemy. "Violence must have been employed," he muttered, "to procure those documents."

"There's no need, when it's so easy to use trickery."

"In any case, this Philippe de Penhoël has disappeared. He must be dead."

"Not at all. You have had the honor, Monsieur le Marquis de Pontalès, of meeting him face to face, very much alive."

"Where?"

"The first time was in New Orleans, where he prevented a certain Monsieur Charles Boulanger from being hanged."

"You mean..." cried the nonplussed Marquis.

"Exactly," Montalt interrupted him, almost gaily. "And the second time, here, in his father's château, from which that same Philippe de Penhoël is in the process of evicting you, so that you might be hanged elsewhere!"

"But the money that I've paid!" the Parisian said, without offering any further resistance.

"Money is a weapon," Montalt replied, his extended finger pointing to the door. "I don't want to leave you any weapons. It will be some recompense to the one to whom you really owe it, and an equal sum will be deposited in the hands of the Bishop of Vannes for distribution to the poor. You might witness the accomplishment of that promise.

"Now, Monsieur Charles Boulanger, it's getting late, and it's necessary that Monsieur and Madame de Penhoël sleep in their beds tonight. That's what I want. Move out, without any fuss—and, believe me, you do not want to cross my path for a third time; it would be dangerous for you. I am your humble servant."

VIII. *The Feast at Penhoël*

It appeared that Monsieur le Marquis de Pontalès, or Monsieur Charles Boulanger, whichever you want to call him, had serious reasons for not prolonging the discussion any further, for he decamped without asking to stay the night.

As he passed through the town, he went to the house of Monsieur le Hivain, who was asleep, perhaps still dreaming of the redhead's dowry. He gave himself the consolation of beating him to a pulp. Let us pity Monsieur le Hivain, who was an ugly rogue and had nothing but that volley of blows, paid in full, to take the place of his 3,000 *livres* a year.

America is an odd place—I mean that new-born Republic the United States, which is already dying of old age and which might, within ten or 12 years, fall into dissolution like a living corpse. It's said, however, that there are many good things out there. They preach with dagger-thrusts in that new and energetic country; the eloquence of the bar and the tribune is supported there by an entirely American engine that enraged France did not invent: the revolver. It follows that, in order to exercise the profession of lawyer in the United States, it is not only necessary to be a man of words, but also a man of action.

That is particularly true nowadays in the slave states, where entirely original mores alternate Republican brutalities with fancies apparently borrowed from Oriental despotism. Among all these states, New Orleans, where the old Spanish and French civilizations are now patched in harlequin fashion with the pretended austerities of liberal conquest—in which

227

dollars successfully take the place of cannon–is the one that offers the strangest and most variegated physiognomy. As rich as Babylon, but plague-ridden for half the year, the capital of the South, bathed in the soapy waves of the great Mississippi, offers visiting foreigners opulence or death. It is always full of adventurers, as in the time when Louisiana brought so much gold to the mud of the Rue Quincampoix. Some make their fortune there in a few months; others die there in a matter of days; others still succumb to fatal attacks of apoplexy caused by the rope that swings from the beam of the gibbet: the English malady.

Philippe de Penhoël, on leaving France after sacrificing his happiness, had nothing in his heart but an immense sorrow. His hope in this world was dead. He was not in search of a fatherland but a tomb. And notwithstanding the solid faith that was the legacy of his Breton mother, he had heeded the evil advice of despair.

He was then a bold, noble and somewhat wild child. He would not have become an advocate in Paris, to plead in a black robe before judges who have the right to say to eloquence itself: *You shall go no further*. He became an advocate in New Orleans because the bar, out there, is a battlefield, and he was a born warrior. In a short time, he had made a fortune, twice or three times as great as the one he had left in France.

Charles Boulanger would have made a fortune too, had it not been for the rope that was knotted around his neck one day. Philippe, who had changed his name on leaving his native land, took pity on the poor Parisian buccaneer, whom he deemed to be even more imprudent than culpable, pleaded on his behalf and saved him. Advocates are not responsible, in any country, for the sins they commit in saving rogues in this fashion. That was how Montalt and Monsieur le Marquis de Pontalès had first met.

There is a cruel and dear affliction whose name alone makes the heart grow tender, like the distant echo of the songs of the fatherland: homesickness–which I beg you on bended knee never to call nostalgia. Pedantry is the art of creating ridiculous words that give a moldy taste to poetry itself.

One day, Philippe de Penhoël became homesick. He, who had the vegetal plumage of tamarinds, the spangled grapes of catalpas and the colossal flowers of waxen-leaved magnolias beneath his window, wanted to see great oaks and fir-trees again. One may die if one does not give way to that blessed fever; Philippe departed. He had remained single. His heart had kept intact the memories of his childhood tenderness. He crossed the sea again. He came to Penhoël.

What did he want?

Nothing.

To see the humble lake whose waters stretched away from the hills of Saint-Vincent; to spend a day running through the Forêt du Theil; to kneel on the cracked flagstones of the little parish church; to lean his joined hands upon the balustrade where he had taken his first communion; perhaps to sit by the fireside of some old peasant friend; to kiss the threshold of the house of his ancestors; and–again perhaps–to look from afar upon the blonde child who must have the features of Juliette.

He was determined not to show himself, for he knew his brother and divined his mistrustful weaknesses.

We know what he found on his return: the stranger in the château, his brother, Juliette and their daughter in the wretched hut where none of them had bread. Marie and Louise, his Belles-de-Nuit, had told him the lamentable story of recent years.

He had enough in his pocket-book to buy back the Penhoël domain twice over, but he had said it himself: he was that modern knight errant, a lawyer. He had come from America. He fought with the weapons at his disposal. His forefathers would have acted differently; other times, other mores. Pray to God that our modern weapons will always be in such loyal hands! At least, he was still French, in the petulance of his bounty, and a gentleman, in his generous delicacy. In the blink of an eye, the entire château was placed at his disposal.

Midnight as it was, the coachman had to hitch four horses to the old family carriage. The domestic servants were ordered to light torches. The farm laborers, awakened by cries of joy, were commissioned to assemble the tenants. Old mother Marthe took up her walking-stick and left the farm for the first time in 15 years. You should have seen Joson, Josille and José bounding barefoot along the stony paths! "Come to the feast! Come to the feast, people of the parish! Come to the great feast, lads and lasses! Jesus, Mary, Joseph and all the saints! Our Messieurs have returned. The Parisian has gone for good!"

I do not know who pulled the rope, but the church bell rang out its full peal, as if for Christmas mass.

"Come to the feast! Come to the feast! Get up, everyone! There's a great feast at the Château de Penhoël! The Parisian is out and the Messieurs are coming home."

On the heath and in the sunken paths, beneath the tall chestnut-trees bordering the marsh and along the main road, lanterns were on the march. The dogs were baying for three leagues around. The roe deer took fright in the woods. And the wandering Belles-de-Nuit, who dislike noise and crowds, climbed above the foliage to watch all these joys go past from their celestial balcony. There were two among them, however, who did not hide at all, for the *uncle in clogs* was weeping as he pressed them to his heart. Oh, how happy that poor old father was!

"Marie! Louise! Blessed children! So it was you who brought manna to the abandoned poor."

Vicomte Pierre de Penhoël thought he was dreaming. Tomorrow would be, for him, complete and certain ruin. It was tomorrow that the chateau would pass into the hands of the despoilers. What am I saying, tomorrow? Midnight had sounded. It was today, this very day! And here was the first hour of that terrible day, begun like a joyful dream!

"Get up, *our master*! Come, our good lady! And you, our dear little demoiselle! Come home! Come on! Come on!"

The carriage was at the door of the Maison Gaillot: the carriage pulled by four horses, surrounded by smoking torches, which were burning red in the humid night, displaying the arms of old Hoël, which Pontalès had not had time to efface.

Pierre de Penhoël was much changed. The excess of misfortune had weighed upon his body and mind alike. He allowed himself to be carried into the carriage, where Madame la Vicomtesse and Mademoiselle Blanche, the gentle angel of Penhoël, took their places beside him.

The *uncle in clogs* followed on foot with his two Belles-de-Nuit. The people who carried the torches shivered more than a little at the sight of Marie and Louise brought back to life–but they were so pretty that everyone ended up smiling by virtue of looking at them.

The old carriage got under way. With every step, the four horses took the procession grew larger. When they arrived, the whole parish was in front or behind. To the feast! To the feast! Let joy be unconfined!

Montalt was standing at the foot of the steps, his handsome face fully illuminated by the torchlight.

The *uncle in clogs* felt Marie's delicate arms tremble. "What's the matter, little beauty?" he asked.

"Nothing," she replied.

"Philippe!" cried Vicomte Pierre, recognizing his older brother.

The two brothers embraced for a long time, but everyone could see that the Vicomte was very pale.

He regained his color, however, when the elder Penhoël said: "Here I am, returned–but not to remain a youth. Where's Uncle Jean; I want to ask for the hand of his daughter Marie."

Whoever wanted joy, here it is! Two casks of cider are opened in the courtyard! The fiddler is on the barrel! Dance the litra,[47] boys and girls! And the clog-dance too! Dance, Jacqueline! Dance, little Simonne! Dance, José, Josille and Joson! Dance, Monique! Dance, brave Haligan! Dance! The old dog Turk crouches down, howling with joy. The old

231

mother sheds her last tear. To the feast! To the feast! It's the great feast. The masters want to sleep in their own beds–and we shall dance again at the wedding!

IX. Three Months Later

There were two marriages, therefore, on the same day–Louise and Roger; Marie and Philippe–once the time required for publishing the banns in the parish had elapsed.

What a feast! They talked about it for a long time afterwards, from Ploërmel to Rome.

"Beautiful weddings, that's no lie. Oh, definitely."

"Beautiful, oh yes. As true as I'm telling you. That's a fact, all right."

"Too true! Good cider, right taste! And soup so thick that you could stand your spoon in it, for sure and true. Beautiful weddings! So much to eat and drink you could make yourself ill if you wanted, my dear!"

"Beautiful weddings, no need to lie–it's a sin!"

Jacqueline was there, and brave Haligan, who sang his song, and Josille and Joson and José, and the old mother and Turk. And little Pelo, who had had the first silver coin from the good man who had come home!

It was said that Monsieur le Hivain found a means to worm his way in, with his smooth hair and his long ears. As for Monsieur de Pontalès, he went somewhere else and was hanged there, when the occasion arose.

If you ever hear people mocking the old legends of the region, say that these naïve beliefs do not hurt anyone and can be useful to some. What harm is there in personifying the stars in the sky, the little flowers in the hedgerow and the little clouds that dance above the moist grass, if that sweet fable emits charity like a perfume? May the custom remain for a long time–a very long time–in Mother Brittany of putting the Belles-de-Nuits' portion on the doorstep, so that the Belles-de-

Nuit might carry it to *the poorest of the poor*. God does not worry about that, for God has said, in speaking of those who are hungry: "That which you give to them shall be given to me."

Notes

Introduction

[1] Féval's own stage play adaptation of *Les mystères de Londres* was translated by Frank J. Morlock and released by Black Coat Press as *Gentlemen of the Night* (978-1-932983-81-4).

[2] The result, *La fille du juif errant*, is available in a Black Coat Press translation as *The Wandering Jew's Daughter* (ISBN 978-1-932983-30-2).

[3] Translated as *The Black Coats: 'Salem Street* in a Black Coat Press edition (ISBN 978-1-932983-46-3).

[4] Also known as *La soeur des fantômes, Les revenants, Une histoire de revenants* and *Nuits de terreur*; translated in a Black Coat Press edition as *Revenants* (ISBN 978-1-932983-70-8).

[5] See, for instance, the last paragraph of the Black Coat Press edition of *The Black Coats: The Invisible Weapon* (ISBN 978-1-932983-80-7).

[6] *Vampire City* is available in a Black Coat Press translation (ISBN 978-0-9740711-6-9) along with Féval's other two forays in the vampire genre: *The Vampire Countess* (ISBN 978-0-9740711-5-2) and *Knightshade* (978-0-9740711-4-5).

Anne of the Isles

[7] Féval adds a footnote to this subtitle, which translates as follows: "This tradition, which is still popular in Morbihan, but which the inhabitants of the Yroise coast have, by contrast, forgotten, was doubtless brought to Sourdéac (in Morbihan) by the vassals of the Marquis d'Ouessant, the lord of Sourdéac. The anachronisms that the rustic tellers have introduced into the story are obvious to everyone, and we felt that they should be retained in order to conserve the story's color. We have written, so far as is possible, that which we have often heard recounted in Brittany, in the neighborhood of the ruined manor of the ancient lords of Rieux, who were masters of Ouessant for a long time."

[8] *Baie des Trépassés* translates as "Bay of the Dead." The bay in question–so called because of the number of shipwreck victims whose bodies washed ashore there–although it was also rumored to be the site of the drowned city of Ys–is some 30 kilometers west of the port of Douardenez, within walking distance of both the Pointe du Raz (the westernmost point of the Brittany peninsula) and the much smaller port of Audierne, which is in Baie d'Audierne on the southern side of the point. The Île de Sein–which Féval renders as Sen–is visible from the point, a few kilometers out to sea.

[9] Féval adds a footnote to explain that the reference is to Jean de Rieux, Marquis d'Ouessant.

[10] Féval adds a footnote here to say that the Yroise is a gulf lying between Ouessant and the Pointe du Raz, some way to the south of the island. The more usual modern spelling is Iroise–the word is has the same etymology as of "Irish." The channel passing between Ouessant and the Île de Sein/Sen retains its dangerous reputation–occasioned by its numerous sandbanks and submerged rocks–to the present day. Féval supplements his own footnote with the observation that the causeway of Sen (which he casually mistranslates as "the Saints") is at the southwestern edge of the Yroise. It is, however, doubtful that he had ever visited the island, which does not rise more than six meters above sea level and certainly does not possess the cliffs he describes.

[11] Féval inserts a footnote here, which translates as follows: "Several writers have described this phenomenon, and everyone knows about that barbarous practice which consists of hanging lanterns on the horns of hobbled cattle–which is to say, animals rendered lame by cords hindering their limbs. The limping of these animals as they walk along the edges of cliffs, imitates the swaying movement of a ship under sail, deceiving mariners who have entered the bay."

[12] Had Féval not inserted a footnote here, his contemporary readers, as well as many modern ones, would certainly have inferred that the unvoiced term was *druides* (druids). The

word he actually uses in his terse footnote is, however, *bardes* (bards).

[13] I have used the exact English equivalent of Féval's *anfranctuosité*, although it is a rather esoteric term, because "cave" would not do it justice. More usually encountered in the plural, it refers to a particular type of deep and irregular hollow produced in conglomerate cliffs by the differential weathering of their constituent rocks.

The White Lady of the Marshes

[14] The Rohan family, whose estates were in Morbihan in Brittany, were among of the most prominent French converts to Calvinism in the 16th century, and prospered as a result while the Protestant King Henri III was on the throne. René de Rohan became Commander of the Calvinist army in 1570, while Cardinal de Rohan distinguished himself in the defense of Lusignan against a Catholic army in 1754-55. The latter's son, Henry, became the first Duc de Rohan. The term by which Calvinist converts were known in France (*Huguenots*) was derived by the corruption of a German term signifying a party bound together by an oath.

[15] Philippe-Emanuel de Mercoeur, Duc de Lorraine (1558-1602) succeeded the Guises as head of the confederation known as *la Ligue* or *la Sainte-Ligue*: an organization founded in 1576, ostensibly for the defense of the Catholic faith against the threat of Calvinism, although its true purpose was to depose the King, Henri III, and place the Duc de Guise on the throne. The cause foundered when Henri IV renounced Calvinism in 1593, four years after the ill-fated siege of Paris, although it had already fallen into discredit by making an alliance with Philip II of Spain in order to withstand that siege. Féval's story is set against the background of *la Ligue*'s last ill-fated military expedition in southern Brittany.

[16] Vannes is a département of Morbihan, which comprises the major part of the southern part of the Brittany peninsula; the city of Vannes is its most important port. The Oust runs to the

north-east of the region, more-or-less parallel to the coast for the greater part of its course. The Châteaux de Guer, de Malestroit and de la Roche-Bernard were all located within the département of Vannes; the Château de Guéméné-sur-Scorf was in the neighboring département of Pontivy. None survived into modern times.

[17] The captain is construing the "pie" in his prisoner's nickname as synonymous with "magpie"–a bird whose cawing is, of course, singularly unmusical. The other meaning of *pie* in French is "pious," so "Chantepie" also suggests something akin to "hymn." Given that Chantepie's real name is Noël, the nickname is obviously intended to signify "[Christmas] carol." The portmanteau term Chantepie had no formal existence in 19th-century French, but it must have been common in *argot*; it is nowadays proudly borne by a chain of hotels and campsites.

[18] Féval adds a footnote of his own at this point to explain that a *macre*–which I have translated as "water-chestnut"–is an aquatic fruit in the shape of a tricorn hat (although it actually only has two spines) which is found in some abundance in the Oust marshes. He also states that the river-dwellers dry them and then boil them like chestnuts, whose taste is vaguely similar. Their usual English name is derived from the same similarity, although they are also known as "water-caltrops" because of the spines, which also determine the Latin name of the genus, *Trapa*.

Another reference in the paragraph that might require annotation here is "*Nantais écus*." At the time in which the story is set, different regions of France produced their own coins, whose value was determined by their weight. References to *écus* (gold coins) were, therefore often qualified by reference to their region of origin. At one later point in the text, Guy de Plélan also makes reference to Tournois *écus*, produced in Tours, and sometimes refers to *écus* minted in Nantes simply as "Nantais."

[19] Brittany lost the last vestiges of its effective independence in the 15th century, when Duc François II was forced to accept the Treaty of Sablé in 1488. He had no son, and the treaty bound him not to marry off his two daughters without the permission of the King of France. His heir, Anne, married Charles VIII of France, and then Louis XII. To all intents and purposes, the feudal era–mythologized in countless verse and prose romances as the Age of Chivalry–was already long dead, but Anne's marriages brought Brittany firmly under the dominion of the emergent nation-state into which France was being transformed. Féval, relentlessly nostalgic for the mythical Age of Chivalry, considered the event a tragedy akin to the Reformation or the Revolution of 1789, both of which brought far worse plagues of bloody violence to the Breton lands.

[20] Féval adds a footnote at this point to explain that his *percher*, which I have translated as "punt," is the word used in the marshes to signify the action of steering a *chaland*–a flat-bottomed boat–by means of a long pole.

[21] What the robber actually says where I have substituted "I'm a Calvinist" is "*je suis de la vache à Colas*"–*La vache à Colas* evokes an incident which allegedly took place in 1605 in Chécy: a cow which had wandered inside a protestant temple during the sermon was slaughtered and eaten by the congregation. The term then became a synonym for *Huguenots*.

[22] Féval inserts a footnote of his own to explain that his *éterpeur*, which I have translated as "field-digger," is a Breton dialect term, and that an *éterpe* is a kind of sharp-bladed mattock used by local peasants to break up the earth–presumably for want of ploughs and horses able to draw them. When the latter word recurs, I have translated it as "mattock."

[23] The French version of All Saints–more usually known in England as All Hallows, for which reason the previous day is known as Hallowe'en–is, of course, *Toussaint*, just as Christmas is *Noël*; the resultant wordplay brings the quasi-allegorical significance of the story to the surface in this

chapter, which presumably appeared in the issue published immediately before the Christmas holiday.

[24] A *mascle*, in heraldry, is a "voided lozenge"–a diamond-shaped device with a diamond-shaped hole in the middle. The term is derived from the Latin word from which the English "mesh" is derived; an ensemble of seven mascles could be seen as a symbolic fishing-net.

[25] A *halbran* is a young wild duck.

[26] Tinténiac, like Malestroit, is the name of one of the oldest noble families of Brittany; the château of that name was founded in 1036. Although de Torrec is not uncommon as a Breton surname, there does not appear to be a château of that name.

The Lovely Château

[27] Féval inserts two long footnotes beneath this paragraph in order to explain the terms *chats courtauds* and *laveuses de nuit*.

Of the former he says: "These are cats of enormous size, which hold councils at midnight on the stiles of northern Brittany. They are very spiteful and do not like to be disturbed. When an intruder interrupts their grave conversation, they surround him and subject him to a thousand humiliations. Afterwards, the president of the council arms himself with a long needle and sinks it into the heart of the victim, who becomes a hypochondriac and slowly wastes away." This is a slight, but by no means inappropriate, embellishment of actual folkloristic notions of *chats courtauds* (whose name means "cats with docked tails").

Féval defines the *laveuses de nuit*–whose name translates as "nocturnal washerwomen"–as "female demons who bleach the shrouds of the dead by moonlight." He goes on to say: "When a delayed traveler passes within their range, they seize him and force him to wring their linen with them. This is not an easy thing to do; indeed, the washerwomen have a way of working that prolongs the task indefinitely. As the unfortunate exhausts himself, twisting in one direction or another, they apply a counter-twist with marvelous alacrity, and without becoming in the least tired. The traveler, meanwhile, sweats blood and water, all in vain. To console him, those washerwomen not engaged in the work begin to sing a wild and bizarre song in Breton dialect. Two verses of this strange song are retained in our memory, which we shall translate:

Wring the rags, wring
The shrouds
That snugly fit the dead.
Wring forever! The charnel-house
Has stained with dust
Our mourning-dress.
Now Satan desires his daughters
To be proper and genteel
On their coffin-boards.

Wring the rags, wring
The shrouds
That snugly fit the dead!
Wring! The spring is clear,
And runs, solitary,
Over the shining pebbles.
Wring! Let's go! Wring faster!
The night is passing and we must leave.
Wring, or we shall wring your neck!

"After this flattering promise, the demons take one another by the hand and begin an infernal dance, singing all the while. The unfortunate man continues wringing. Around him, the diabolical dance turns with an amazing rapidity. Eventually, he collapses, exhausted; his dazzled eyes close; his windpipe can scarcely form a word to recommend his soul to God!

"If he has the strength to make the sign of the cross, the demons vanish. If he is not afraid, the washerwomen suddenly cease their dancing and set about lashing him with their twisted linen. The noise of those damp scourges striking flesh is audible some distance away. The frightened peasants listen, and slip beneath their bedclothes.

"On the following day, beside the pond, the poor unfortunate is found, crippled and beaten black and blue. The washerwomen have returned to the tomb, resuming their funereal work on the following night if the Moon shines. May God keep you from encountering them when you go out at night on the lonely roads of Brittany!"

A more elaborate account of the *laveuses de nuit*, or *lavandières*, was offered at a later date by George Sand as a "*légende rustique.*" Sand included the additional detail that the washerwomen had been condemned to their particular purgatory for being bad mothers–a point to which she was inevitably more sensitive than Féval.

[28] The post-Revolutionary French government introduced a tax on doors and windows in 1798, whose burden fell most heavily on large aristocratic houses but also deterred the poor from letting light into their houses. It was in force throughout Féval's career, and was not abolished until 1926.

[29] In heraldry, *gules* signifies a red base-color. An *orle* is an inner frame within the body of the shield, reproducing its shape. A lion *passant* (walking) is depicted standing up with its right forepaw raised.

[30] Féval adds a footnote to explain this particular usage of the word *cierge*, which I have translated as "candle." His footnote translates as: "In every village of the Côtes-du-Nord, one can find more than a score of people who have seen–with their own eyes–the *candle of death*. It is one of the most widespread items of superstition in Brittany. When a man is about to die, a long lighted candle is seen to descend from the firmament towards his dwelling. This funereal meteor sinks slowly down; then it comes closer, so that its conical form is more easily distinguishable. It is certainly a true candle, except that it is turned upside down, and its flame, contrary to all the laws of physics, burns from the lower extremity. The dogs of the

household sense its coming from afar, and begin to howl deplorably. It enters the house of the moribund by means of the chimney. The majority claim that its mysterious course ends there, but others affirm that it penetrates as far as the room where the dying person lies and snuffs itself out on the curtains of the bed."

[31] Féval inserts a footnote in this sentence to explain the meaning of his *faire bannir*, explaining that this is a local term meaning to publish *bans* by means of a town crier. Although the equivalent English term nowadays refers only to announcements of forthcoming marriages posted on noticeboards, it remains more familiar here than in France.

[32] A *requin* is a shark; because *roche* is the French for "rock" the whole name has the phonetic implication of "land shark." This manner of describing a lawyer was probably less commonplace in the 1840s than it is today.

[33] *Armorique* [Armorica] was an old name for the region that eventually became *Bretagne* [Brittany]. The implication is that Master Roch's imposition of family discipline was trifle barbaric.

[34] This is the first half of a Latin proverb, *Verba volant, scripta manent* [words fly away, writing remains], which normally counsels caution regarding the possibility of leaving material proof of a conspiracy–the equivalent of "don't put anything in writing"–but the steward is using it in an almost opposite sense, as an approximate equivalent of "talk is cheap."

[35] Féval adds a footnote to explain *brouette de la mort* [barrow of the dead]. It reads: "On nights when there is no Moon in the sky, the Breton peasant walking alone along a deserted road hears and sees many things that the eyes and ears of a city-dweller cannot perceive at all, He hears, among other things, the baleful sound produced by the axle of the *barrow of the dead* scraping the wheel that the Devil has forgotten to grease. No one has ever seen that barrow, but it is heard approaching the doors of the dying, with its axle screeching. To encounter

it is a direly evil omen. Prudent people, when they hear it pass by, will have a mass said or recite a *De profundis*, according to their means. A few rare strong-minded individuals deny its existence and mock the notion, but they always die sooner or later, thus offering more than adequate proof that it does not do to speak lightly of the *barrow of the dead*." The *De profundis* is the 126th psalm, ordinarily employed as a prayer for the dead.

[36] Yaumi qualifies as Arthur's foster-brother–as the French term *frère de lait* makes clear–by virtue of the fact that aristocratic mothers almost invariably handed their children over to wet-nurses recruited from among their servants; most aristocratic scions had therefore been suckled at the same breast as at least one of their vassals.

[37] Féval adds a footnote here, which reads: "A Morbihanian song that has more than 100 verses. The words are generally lively and bizarre, like those of all such hotchpotches, but the tune is slow and remarkably melancholy."

[38] Plougastel-Daoulas is a commune in Finistère, not far from the commune of Plougasnou; the name Plougaz is presumably derived from one or the other. Several other communes in the region have names beginning with "Plou-" or "Plo-" in much the same way that many villages in Cornwall have names beginning with "Pol-." The prefixes "Pen-" and "Tre-" are common to both regions.

[39] Bertrand du Guesclin (c1320-1380) was Constable of France from 1370-80; he was reputed to be the greatest soldier of his era. His residences included the Château de Combourg, near St Malo.

The Belles-de-Nuit

[40] Féval adds a footnote here to explain that this is the title usually given in Brittany to a *curé*, the equivalent of an English parish priest.

[41] St Corentin was a Celtic hermit of unknown antiquity, Cornish by birth, who became a bishop in Brittany. A Breton cult

in his honor was "revived" in the 17th century following an alleged revelation, which resulted in various shrines being set up (or "restored"); Féval would have been familiar with them. St Guénolé's name is preserved by a small seaport in Finistère overlooking one of the sites where the city of Is was rumored to have been; he founded an abbey nearby in the early 6th century before dying in 532. Féval's remark about Brittany being replete with saints at the time of his story is borne out by the fact that both of Guénolé's parents and all of his siblings were canonized; he remains virtually unknown in Britain, so I have not Anglicized his name to Gwenole.

[42] *Golconde* [Golconda] was an ancient Indian kingdom in the region of modern Hyderabad, which was destroyed in 1687. Its sultans had accumulated a fabulous hoard of precious stones, which gave rise to many awe-stricken literary allusions to "the treasures of Golconda."

[43] *Dies irae* [Day of Wrath] are the first words of one of the prose pieces sung in Roman Catholic Masses for the dead.

[44] There seems to be some botanical confusion here. Although the name *belle-de-nuit* is popularly applied to several kinds of night-blooming plants, its primary reference is to the genus *Mirabilis* (an import from the Americas that would have been unknown in Europe before the 16th century, thus being an unlikely candidate for the inspiration of an ancient folktale). Féval appears to have confused this name with that of the *mirabelle*, a small yellow plum. The reference to *clochettes* [bells] is also odd; none of the plants usually referred to by that name in French parlance (the equivalents of the English bluebell, harebell, etc) is a night-bloomer, although the *clochette d'hiver* [snowdrop] has white flowers, as all night-blooming plants do.

[45] Lake Asphaltite is an alternative name for the Dead Sea.

[46] The teeth in question are presumably metaphorical, as le Hivain had none left earlier in the chapter.

[47] I have transcribed Féval's *litra* without modification, although it does not appear in any English dictionary I have

been able to consult. It does not appear in any French dictionary I have been able to consult either, so I cannot offer any suggestion as to what kind of dance it might be.